DEAD IN THE WATER

Also by Meredith Cole

Posed for Murder

DEAD IN THE WATER

Meredith Cole

Minotaur Books
A Thomas Dunne Book ✠ New York

This is a work of fiction. All of the characters, organizations, and events portrayed in this novel are either products of the author's imagination or are used fictitiously.

A THOMAS DUNNE BOOK FOR MINOTAUR BOOKS.
An imprint of St. Martin's Publishing Group.

DEAD IN THE WATER. Copyright © 2010 by Meredith Cole. All rights reserved. Printed in the United States of America. For information, address St. Martin's Press, 175 Fifth Avenue, New York, N.Y. 10010.

www.thomasdunnebooks.com
www.minotaurbooks.com

Library of Congress Cataloging-in-Publication Data

Cole, Meredith.
   Dead in the water / Meredith Cole. — 1st ed.
       p. cm.
   ISBN 978-0-312-62504-7
   1. Women photographers—Fiction.   2. Prostitutes—Crimes against—
Fiction.   3. Adultery—Fiction.   4. Williamsburg (Va.)—Fiction.   I. Title.
   PS3603.04295D43 2010
   813'.6—dc22
                                                          2009046144

First Edition: May 2010

10 9 8 7 6 5 4 3 2 1

In memory of Louise Holt, my childhood librarian, who never said I was too young to read anything or could only check out a limited number of books. And many thanks to librarians everywhere for doing more with less, and connecting readers with great books.

ACKNOWLEDGMENTS

To all the people worldwide who dedicate their lives to giving assistance and aid to sex workers—you are true heroes.

Many thanks to my agent, Faith Hamlin, for always steering me in the right direction. And all my gratitude to my "team" at Minotaur Books, for their support and wisdom: Ruth Cavin, Toni Plummer, Hector DeJean, and Anne Gardner.

To my writing group, Triss Stein, Jane Olson, and Mary Darby, some of the coolest women in Brooklyn. Occasionally we do remember to talk about writing at our meetings, but we always have fun.

And, as always, thank you to my family for their love and encouragement. I couldn't do it without you.

DEAD IN THE WATER

Chapter 1

Glenda's eyes appeared first, just below the surface. Dark and accusing, she looked as if she did not enjoy being submerged or photographed. As she floated up in the shimmering liquid bath, Lydia ruthlessly pushed her back down with her tongs. Thirty more seconds in the developer, and then she could move the black-and-white photograph to the stop bath.

Lydia felt she managed to capture both Glenda's identity and her profession in her world-weary face, her sassy pose, and her cheap clothes. But Lydia wished she didn't feel so guilty about missing Glenda's phone call that afternoon. She had ducked the call deliberately, assuming Glenda was trying to hit her up for cash again to buy drugs. When Lydia checked her messages several hours later, she was shocked by the fear in Glenda's voice.

"Lydia, you've got to help me. I don't know who else to ask. Call me, okay?" Fanning herself in the stuffy, overheated darkroom, Lydia called Glenda's cell phone as soon as she had listened to the message, but Glenda didn't pick up. She told herself it could be yet another false alarm. Drug addicts were notorious for taking everyone around them on emotional roller-coaster rides. But still Lydia felt uneasy. She called Glenda again several times, but received no response to any of her calls.

She lifted Glenda's image out of the developer and gave it a quick shake before she dropped it into the stop bath. The chemicals would halt the development process and prevent the developer from darkening the entire page. Ten seconds later, she moved the paper to the fixer to sear Glenda's image permanently onto the paper. She watched as thirty seconds ticked slowly by, then dropped the photo into the wash bath. The chemicals would have to rinse off completely before she could examine it in the light.

Lydia had first met Glenda on Wythe Avenue, on the waterfront of Williamsburg, Brooklyn. She had been leaving a party and waiting for a car service that took far longer than the promised five minutes. Glenda had been all bristling attitude as she swaggered over to prospective customers in the warm summer evening. She looked to be over forty, and Lydia had been shocked to learn later that she was twenty-three, five years younger than Lydia herself.

Glenda, seeing Lydia's interest, had propositioned her. Apparently, she charged fifty bucks for women and a hundred for threesomes. Lydia was speechless only for a moment, then she made a proposition of her own. She was looking for a portrait subject. Glenda was a little flattered, but always the good businesswoman, she wanted to be paid for her time. Since Lydia hoped to sell the photographs, she decided the request was fair. They negotiated a slightly lower rate than Glenda charged for blow jobs, and set their first photo shoot for a week later.

The first session with Glenda on a nearby street had been a disaster. Glenda was high, and Lydia was rattled by the vacant look in her eyes. She shot quickly and was careless with her focus, f-stops, and lighting. When she examined her proofs from the shoot she realized everything she had taken was useless. She decided to search for another subject and cut her losses. But Glenda was short on cash and customers and called her again.

"I can't do this when you're on drugs, okay?"

"I'll stay away from anything. I promise." Glenda sounded desperate. She probably couldn't afford to buy crack and that's why she wanted the portrait done, Lydia thought cynically. But she was itching to try again. She hated to fail, especially when she knew she could do better. Glenda had a certain inexplicable something about her that the camera loved.

Their second photo shoot went better. The two women relaxed a little and started to talk. Glenda's life of poverty and abuse was so far removed from Lydia's middle-class upbringing in Dayton, Ohio, with eccentric but loving parents, that it was hard for the two women to connect at first. Glenda had three kids by three different guys and her mother, Susa, was raising them in Bushwick. Glenda spoke of them fondly, but Lydia wondered how often she saw little Roberto, Brittany, and Carlos. But Glenda also hinted that a boyfriend of her mother's had raped her years ago and started her on the path to her current profession, and Lydia's heart went out to the young innocent girl Glenda once had been. Lydia doubted that anyone set out to become a hooker, and for all her tough talk, Glenda was full of regrets.

The photograph that rinsed in the wash bath now was from their third session together. Lydia had happened to have her equipment when she ran into Glenda waiting in line at a church soup kitchen. She had grown impatient waiting, so Lydia took her to a neighborhood café and bought her lunch. Their bellies full, they went to a nearby abandoned warehouse to try again. While Glenda stood defiantly, lit by only the meager natural light seeping through the dirty broken windows, Lydia experimented with using a long exposure time. The result looked eerie and almost haunted. Lydia had captured, for better or for worse, both the desperation and attitude that was Glenda.

More than a week had passed before Lydia could get into the darkroom to develop the film from the session and print it, but in the interim she thought about nothing else. Luckily, her job as an administrative assistant for the D'Angelos was mindless enough most of the time to allow her to obsess over her art. The D'Angelo brothers were two private eyes who had never been very busy, which never seemed to bother them much. But Lydia hated to be bored, so she had placed an ad in the yellow pages and built a Web site for the business. Since then business had doubled, and the D'Angelos weren't exactly over the moon. Her job still consisted of paying the bills, writing expense reports, and answering the phones; now she just had to do all of it more often.

The two minutes required for the wash bath were finally up, and Lydia lifted out the picture. The print would need to dry for several hours before she could take it home. With no one else working in the darkroom with her, Lydia could safely turn on the overhead light to take a look at the print. She examined the corners, and the light and dark spots of the photograph, anxiously looking for flaws. But the print looked fantastic, and her gaze was drawn again and again to Glenda's eyes. What had she wanted when she called? What kind of trouble was she in?

Lydia hung up the print to dry on the clothesline strung up above the sink and turned the lights back off. She pushed through the revolving black door that connected the darkroom to the locker room. Lydia rented the darkroom communally with a group of photographers, but she was the only one using the space that day. She fished her cell phone out of her locker and examined the screen. She had no messages. She tried calling Glenda again but hung up when she got her voice mail. Maybe she was overreacting. She didn't want to leave ten messages only to find that Glenda just needed a loan.

Lydia dialed another familiar number and couldn't resist a small smile as she listened to the phone ring on the other side. Having a boyfriend was a very recent phenomenon. She had met Jack Walsh at a gallery opening, after becoming convinced that all single men in New York were either gay or psychotic or both. Jack miraculously appeared to be neither. They had been seeing each other for a month, and the relationship only seemed to be getting better. She loved the way he scrunched up his face when he was thinking, and she found his sophisticated fashion sense inspiring. The sex was good and the conversations were even better. He was a painter, but had a good job at a brokerage firm to pay the bills. He was neither dull nor broke, and Lydia let herself hope that she might not spend the rest of her life single.

Jack picked up the phone after four rings. He had probably been in the middle of something, but he didn't sound annoyed. "Hey, gorgeous. How's the printing going?"

"Good. Are you done stretching canvases?"

"Yup. I even moved on to treating them and sketching out my next idea." Sunday was his studio day, too, and they were meeting later for a date after they'd both been productive and creative. Lydia got all tingly thinking about how compatible they were in every way.

She couldn't resist telling Jack about Glenda's call. "Am I crazy to worry?"

Jack was silent for a moment. "She's called you in a panic before, right? She isn't exactly reliable."

"But she was never like this." Lydia stopped. She couldn't explain why it felt different this time. Maybe it was because she had gotten to known Glenda a little better. Maybe it was because she thought Glenda had stopped giving her bullshit. Maybe it was because she saw something in Glenda's eyes that had stopped Lydia from seeing her as a whore and enabled her to start seeing Glenda as an individual.

"Don't worry about it. Get back to work and I'll see you at seven. We're still on for pizza and a movie?"

"Sure." Lydia let herself purr into the phone. She couldn't wait to snuggle up with Jack on the couch in front of a recent DVD. During the past week, she had been debating whether she was delusional or whether he was the real deal. She wasn't quite ready to introduce him to her parents yet, although doing so at this moment was impossible. Right now her parents were traveling around America in an RV, enjoying their retirement and mailing her postcards from the oddest places they had visited. The last card was from the SPAM Museum, and from the picture it appeared to be the canned meat variety, as opposed to unwanted e-mail. But Lydia did allow herself to imagine a rosy future with Jack that also included a house, a friendly dog, and a couple of kids.

Instead of feeling reassured by Jack's advice, Lydia felt more restless than ever. She decided to go over to Wythe, where Glenda usually trolled for customers, and see if she could find her. She'd take her camera, and if everything was okay, she would at least get a few photographs. She had so few hours during the week to work on her art, so if she wasn't going to be in the darkroom, she would do whatever she could to make the most of her studio day.

Glenda was nowhere to be found on Wythe Avenue. A few other women were standing around looking bored, but Lydia felt shy about asking if they'd seen Glenda. She was probably worrying unnecessarily. Glenda could have taken the day to visit her kids, Lydia tried to tell herself, or perhaps she was sleeping off a binge. Hopefully she would call the next day full of excuses.

At the end of Grand Street was the one small park Williamsburg had on the waterfront. To anyone outside of New York, it would not have qualified as scenic. The park was a small patch of green grass and along the river were large rocks. A glimpse of Manhattan's famous buildings could be seen from behind the power plants, ugly apartment buildings, and an elevated highway that made up Manhattan's waterfront. From the park you could also see the Williamsburg Bridge in all its rusting glory, usually the site of one big traffic jam. A slow-moving elevated train passed overhead from time to time, and occasionally a fast ferry kicked up large waves that crashed against the rocks. Sometimes a large industrial barge filled with garbage steamed past fragile-looking sailboats, creating a marked study in contrasts.

The park was quiet for a Sunday afternoon. The weather had been hot, steamy, and still all week, and Lydia imagined everyone who could was staying in, enjoying their air-conditioning. A Hasidic family, including three kids in matching navy blue outfits and a baby in a pram, sat on a park bench. A lone trumpeter played a bluesy number, apparently for the sheer joy of hearing it echo off the walls of the nearby Domino Sugar factory. A tan pit bull sniffed around a tree while his hipster owner chatted on a cell phone. Despite the available trash cans, the visitors to the park had managed to drop a lot of garbage that weekend. Lydia was still amazed at how lazy people could be, sometimes dropping trash right in front of a garbage can.

She set out for the rocks that lined the water. There was always a slight breeze off the river, and it lifted up her shoulder-length bright red hair and cooled off her neck. Her purple gladiator sandals weren't the best for climbing and neither was her multicolored polka-dotted sundress, but she pulled it up and kept going. She needed to see the water. The river always soothed her. Many restaurants in the neighborhood had installed fountains and pools to tap into that essential human need for running water, and their popularity was astounding.

She was annoyed to see more garbage floating in the water. There had been a statewide campaign to clean up the river, but when people couldn't even put their trash in cans, total cleanliness was impossible to hope for. The current was rushing by at top speed, but the rocks made an eddy that trapped the trash by the shore. Lydia climbed closer, wondering if it was something she could remove with a stick. A wave from a passing motorboat lifted it up and a pale hand floated to the surface.

Lydia froze. She wondered briefly if she was seeing things. What had looked like a large piece of trash was actually a body. She scrambled closer, hoping briefly that it was someone who could be saved and revived, someone who might have just fallen in. But the hand floated to the surface again, lifeless.

She stepped back slowly, fighting to breathe. Her stomach's contents were threatening to resurface, and she had to sit down on one of the boulders and put her head down to stop herself from losing it. The world had suddenly tilted on its axis. Someone who had once been a living, breathing, and loving individual was dead and floating in the river. But no one else in the park appeared to notice anything amiss.

Lydia fumbled in her bag for her cell phone. She had heard of the Coast Guard fishing people out of the water who had jumped or fallen from the bridge, but there wasn't any sort of search going on that she could see. With trembling fingers she began to dial 911, but stopped before hitting the final digit.

She opened up her phone book and scrolled down to a number she hadn't dialed in months. Detective Daniel Romero, New York Police Department, Homicide. She hesitated again, wondering if she was making a mistake. Romero and she had come into conflict in the past, and she wasn't sure she really wanted to see him again. But this was not about her. Someone had died and answers needed to be found. Romero was a good detective, and he would make sure that the body was treated respectfully, no matter how ambivalent his relationship with Lydia was.

Romero's phone rang just once before he answered it. "Romero here." His voice still made her skin tingle

"It's Lydia," she said. Lydia wondered belatedly if he knew it was her. Before he could utter some banal phrase about how he was wondering how she was doing, she got right to the point. "I'm at the waterfront park on Grand and Wythe and there's a body floating in the river."

Romero let out a soft curse in Spanish. "A floater. Did you call it in?"

"No. Not yet."

"Okay. I'll do it and be right over." And he hung up without saying good-bye.

Lydia kept an eye on the body while she waited. If it drifted, she wanted to be able to point to where it had gone. She had no desire to look like a delusional fool when Romero finally showed up.

Chapter 2

Lydia leaned back against Jack's broad chest, inhaling the faint scent of turpentine that infused his T-shirt. She was glad she had called him right after Romero, and Jack had rushed over in record time when he heard about her grisly discovery. Romero glanced over at him with curiosity but apparent indifference. He was occupied with the photographer and the forensic team who were working to preserve as much evidence as possible before the body was removed.

"Don't you want to get out of here?" Jack got points for sounding more concerned about her mental health than his lost studio time. She was fascinated by the proceedings, but she could understand that others might not enjoy watching this kind of investigation. The river had a sulfuric sort of stench, and the evening was hot and sticky.

Lydia shook her head. "Romero is going to want to ask me some questions."

"How do you know him?"

"Through work," Lydia said vaguely. It wasn't precisely true, but she had no desire to take Jack step by step through her past history with Romero. Her feelings for Romero were complex and too murky for even her to understand. He was prickly and occasionally abrasive, but he was very good at his job. Being a cop was not about power but about justice. His parents were in education, just like hers, and she had once caught him reading the new translation of *War and Peace*. Despite her best intentions, she found herself drawn to him.

Jack looked so young compared to Romero. He had none of the deep grooves around his mouth and eyes that scarred Romero's face or the worry lines in his forehead. His race was uncomplicatedly white, and although he dressed like a messy artist on the weekend, his clothes were all expensively made. She had liked his sense of style when they first met. But now, compared to Romero's uncomplicated khakis and polo shirts, Jack's clothes seemed too stuffy, too private school. He seemed too much of a dandy, with his manicured nails and his face clearly smoothed by manly scented beauty creams. Romero had neither the time nor patience for primping. Lydia found something tremendously attractive about a man who thought as little as possible about what he wore and still managed to look sexy.

She felt disloyal thinking about Jack that way, so she turned and gave him a kiss on his cheek. "Thanks for coming over when I called."

Jack kissed her back. "Anytime. But let's not make a habit of crime scenes, hmm?"

The scene at the water's edge reminded Lydia of a grisly highway accident. When she drove past one, she had two competing desires—to see nothing and to see everything. Usually the desire to look won out, and she'd catch a glimpse of twisted wreckage or someone bloodied and injured. And then she'd feel horrible for having looked.

There was a shout, and she could see Romero in the midst of the cops and forensic guys and uniformed cops lifting out the body.

She didn't want to see the bloated body, but she couldn't look away. She caught a glimpse of the soggy red material and a flash of dancing beads around the hem and knew the body was a woman. Not only that, Lydia knew who the woman was.

"Let's get out of here," Jack hissed in her ear with his arm around her shoulders.

Lydia shook her head with her eyes never leaving the team examining the body. Lydia wondered if they were about to have their first couple fight. So far it had been smooth sailing, but she knew it was only a matter of time before they found something they disagreed about. She just hoped it would be much later than this. She had such a good time when they were in total harmony with one another.

"I'm a witness."

"You were just the one who saw the body. What could you tell them?"

Lydia couldn't explain exactly why she felt a responsibility to the body. But she knew her name and her face, and the woman's family had not yet arrived to mourn. Only professionals surrounded the body, concerned with doing their jobs. Lydia felt that she had to stay and represent the dead woman's family until she was identified.

Romero, appearing to finally remember her, walked toward Lydia and Jack. Lydia stepped away from Jack and tried pinning a welcoming smile on her face. Her smile was not very convincing, because she saw Romero's step falter for a moment when he looked directly at her. He wiped his brow with an old-fashioned white handkerchief and took out a notebook.

"Tell me again how you found the body," Romero began, never one to stand on ceremony. "Was it right by the rocks, or did you move it?"

"Romero," Lydia began. Jack squeezed her arm. She knew he wanted her to back away and stay out of the investigation. But she couldn't.

There was a woman involved who had been discounted, dismissed, and perhaps even murdered. She deserved to be given a name.

Lydia took a deep breath. "Did she have a small tattoo on her right wrist?"

Romero went still, his eyes going carefully blank. "How did you know?"

"It's a small horseshoe, isn't it?"

"Did you find the body, or did you see it go in? If you're holding out on me again, Lydia—"

Jack stepped forward, testosterone bubbling up. "Hey, listen. She doesn't have to say a thing without a lawyer."

"And who are you?" Romero asked, his right eyebrow shooting up. Jack might have money, but Romero had about twenty cops ready to back him up. Lydia wondered if they were going to have a pissing contest soon.

"It's okay, Jack," she soothed him. "I can answer the detective's questions." Lydia turned back to Romero, biting her lip. "I recognized her clothing when you pulled her out. Does she have a tattoo of a horseshoe or not?"

Romero clenched his teeth. He had not been happy to have her involved in one of his cases before. "She does. Now tell me right now how you know and who she is."

Those dark and accusing eyes coming out of the whiteness, and now only preserved on paper. "Her name is Glenda. She's a prostitute I've been photographing. She called and asked me for help this morning. She sounded so afraid, but I let it go to voice mail. Later I called her back, but there was no answer. I guess you could say I killed her," Lydia said. And then she surprised even herself by bursting into tears.

Romero looked away and waited for her to compose herself. Jack gave her an awkward hug. But Lydia knew they both really wished she would just stop crying. She didn't want Glenda to be dead. She didn't want to feel so guilty about it. She sobbed harder.

Jack patted her shoulder. "You didn't kill her. You're not responsible for her."

Lydia took a deep breath. Her nose was running and she knew she probably looked like a disaster. She began to root around for a tissue in her bag. "She knew I worked for the D'Angelos. She might have been afraid to ask the police for help and wanted to know if a private eye could help her."

Lydia found an old butterscotch candy in her bag, a roll of un-marked film, and someone's phone number scrawled on a piece of paper, but she could not find a tissue. Jack sighed and took the bag from her. He found the packet of tissues and handed one to her. Lydia blew her nose noisily.

The crime scene crew had lifted Glenda's body onto a gurney and covered it with a sheet. Glenda hadn't been very large, and the sheet looked as if it could have been covering a small child. Lydia thought about Glenda's kids, and tears welled up in her eyes again. Those kids had started out with almost nothing. Now there was no hope that Glenda would become a real mother to them. They were orphans.

"Do you know who Glenda was afraid of?" Romero asked.

Lydia shook her head. "She got into cars with strangers every single night. She might have run into someone truly psycho. I don't know. The last time I spoke with her she was more concerned with her next fix than her personal safety."

"Did she have any close family?"

"A mother. Susa. She lived off Bushwick in the projects. I have her address somewhere."

"We'll check out whether or not it's Glenda and let you know. If it is, we'll want to talk to you further about your photographs."

"You don't believe me? I recognize her clothes and everything." If there was anyone who could make an ID based on clothing, it was Lydia. She was a vintage junkie who had converted her living room into a walk-in closet. She could spot fabric and design from blocks away and always remembered what people were wearing. She couldn't always remember what they said or did, but that was another matter.

"We'll have to make an official ID," Romero said "Do me a favor in the meantime, okay? Stay out of my case."

Lydia didn't like to be told what to do. But the main problem with looking for a killer was that killers kill. And if a killer thought you might catch them, they tried to kill you. Lydia had no desire to look down the barrel of a gun again and fight for her life. But being told to stay away from something made her dig in her heels.

Jack must have sensed that Lydia was going to lose her temper because he leaned over and put his arm around her in what looked like a protective gesture but felt like a vise. Irritated, Lydia shrugged his arm away. She stepped away from him to blow her nose again on the old tissue she had clutched in her hand.

"If you guys start acting like a prostitute killer isn't worth your while or you let the case go cold, don't get angry if I get involved. She was a human being, and she didn't deserve this."

Romero looked as if he wanted to say something else, but he and Jack exchanged a look and Romero just shook his head.

"Hey, Romero. Take a look at this." The doctor, a young Asian woman, waved to Romero and he hurried back to the scene of the crime without saying good-bye. Lydia craned her neck, anxious to see the new evidence. Instead of letting her catch a glimpse, Jack steadily steered her away from the river with his heavy arm around her shoulders.

"Let's get out of here, okay? Let the cops do their job."

"What a jerk! He acts like I'm planning to jump all over his case and make his life harder, not simpler."

"He probably doesn't want to be sued if you get hurt or something. It's no big deal, because you're going to let the cops do their job and stay out of the way."

Lydia bit back a sharp retort. Romero didn't worry about lawsuits. He just wanted her out of his business. Jack didn't understand Romero, but why should he? They'd just met and they were two very different men. Probably Jack's only interaction with the police was over a parking ticket. But she had no desire to fight with Jack. He was her perfect boyfriend. And she certainly didn't want to fight with him about Romero.

"Glenda was a person. I want to make sure they remember that and don't just file the case away."

"Glenda had a lot of problems, and anyone could have killed her. A customer. Her dealer. A crazy person on the street. Don't put yourself in harm's way just to find out who."

Jack had a point. Glenda had lived her life on the edge, and it would be healthier for Lydia to stay away. But she felt haunted by the woman. Not only had she cooperated with Lydia to create an amazing portrait, she had asked Lydia for help that morning. Lydia was the one who had found her body. She felt responsible for her. She was determined to at least visit Glenda's family and pay her respects. Maybe they would know why Glenda had called to ask for help. At least that would set Lydia's mind to rest on one question.

Chapter 3

Monday mornings were always difficult for Lydia. There had been a time when she had done odd jobs, or had been unemployed, and had slept until noon when she wanted to. Getting up and going to work by nine was a lot tougher. She always needed a lot of coffee to get her going, and a unique outfit to reflect her mind-set for the day. Today she had on high-heeled open-toed black boots, a pink mini-skirt, and a tight white shirt tied at the waist. She looked as if she had dressed in honor of the world's oldest profession.

The D'Angelos had inherited their private detective business from their dad, and they acted like changing the furnishings would somehow be disrespectful to his memory. Their office, therefore, was stuck circa 1954. The file cabinets were dented, the desks scratched and gouged, and the gray rug was hideous and stained. When Lydia first started working for them six months ago, she had gone through the office like a whirlwind, throwing out dead plants, sifting through all the piles to throw away useless paperwork, and hanging some of her own photographs on the walls to liven up the place. At first the D'Angelos resented everything she did. But they grudgingly began to accept the changes when they found out how much easier it was to find the information they needed without the clutter.

Frankie D'Angelo, the younger brother, was in his customary place at his desk, hidden behind a newspaper when Lydia came in. He loved to read headlines to people, but Lydia wasn't in the mood to listen. Luckily, Frankie had been trained by his brother Leo to shut up whenever anyone growled at him.

The office was stuffy and the air conditioner worked only intermittently. Lydia went to the coffee machine, filled her cup anew, and sat down at her desk.

Frankie was a good-natured, not too smart guy who would have been happy at any job. He wasn't a good strategist or businessman, but he excelled at soothing clients and assuring them of the company's discretion. He was also a decent private eye, since he methodically followed through and presented the evidence to their clients. He was always cheerful and kind, and Lydia couldn't help but like him.

Leo D'Angelo was skinny, tall, and dour. The two men would have looked completely unalike if they didn't dress the same, in oxford shirts, khaki pants, and loafers. Lydia sometimes wondered if their mother still picked out their clothes and dressed them the same to minimize arguments. Leo was smart but exacting. He always found Lydia's addition and spelling errors, then called her on the carpet as if she had done something malicious. She found him difficult to work for, but she always learned a lot when she watched what he did.

Lydia had originally taken the job with the D'Angelos because she thought the idea of being a private eye was exciting. She was brought down to earth her first week. She was head filer, writer of reports, and tracker of money and receipts. She occasionally did a small research job for them, which usually involved the phone or computer. Lydia still itched to get out into the field, if only to escape the gross furniture and the dull tasks, and she would love to do anything that would give her a chance to use her camera.

Lydia had decided she would make it her job to drag them kicking and screaming into the new century. She'd created a Web site for them, made sure they were listed online, and put an ad in the yellow pages. They needed more business if she was ever going to get her butt out of the office chair and not die of boredom.

Leo strolled in an hour later, carrying a gym bag. His normally slicked-down hair was wet and disheveled.

"Been to the gym again?" Frankie inquired. Lydia had never known the brothers to do anything more athletic than stroll over to their mother's restaurant for a pasta dinner. Even stranger, Leo blushed. Lydia couldn't help but stare.

"Just for a brief workout," Leo said quickly, recovering enough to glare at Lydia. Lydia ducked behind her computer to hide her smile. When a middle-aged guy suddenly started working out, it could mean only one of two things, as far as she knew: either his doctor told him do it or else, or he had his eye on a certain lady and wanted to impress her. Lydia wouldn't have been shocked to hear that one of the D'Angelos was having trouble with his ticker; eating too much of Mama's pastries could be deadly. But she got the feeling from the blush that Leo had found a new romance.

Leo sat down at the computer to track down someone's ex-husband who owed child support, and the office returned to its usual hush. Frankie put aside his paper and made a few phone calls to clients. And Lydia worked her way steadily through an expense report, adding up tiny bodega receipts for water and batteries until she thought her eyes were going to cross. They all looked up in relief when the door banged open around eleven o'clock.

"*Buon giorno!* I have brought you all something *delizioso*." Mama D'Angelo swept into the room wearing a pink tracksuit, and she brought with her the unmistakable scents of garlic and Chanel No. 5. Gold and diamond rings adorned every finger, and her usual black beehive hairdo was sprayed into place. She carried a steaming tray of food with several bags balanced on top. Leo and Frankie both leaped up and lifted the food out of her hands. Lydia couldn't tell if they were just being gentlemen or if they were really hungry.

"Mama, you didn't have to walk all the way over here in this heat. We were going to come for lunch in a few minutes."

Mama waved her hand dismissively at Leo. "I thought it would be better to speak here. I have some business to discuss."

Lydia wondered if she should leave, but she hated to miss the fun. Leo had a pained expression on his face, as if he was expecting the worst. Mama usually came over with food when she wanted them to do something for her. None of her favors were ever easy, and they usually involved one of their many ne'er-do-well family members.

"Business? Is it something at the restaurant?" Frankie asked cheerfully.

"No. It's *la famiglia*." Mama lowered her voice suggestively.

Leo shook his head. "You know we can't take on cases for free, Mama. The overhead here is too high. We have to pay the bills, and Lydia's salary."

Lydia straightened up, irritated. She earned every penny of her salary, and she resented being used as a part of their argument. Mama fed the brothers every day, and if you added up the cost of all the food it probably came to a lot of free PI help.

Mama's nostrils flared in a dangerous way. Lydia realized she'd seen Leo do the same thing right before he really lost it. "I don't expect anything for free. But it is your cousin Patricia we need to think about." Mama sounded just the right mixture of offended and noble. Lydia knew the brothers were going to fall like dominoes.

"You mean Cousin Rose's daughter Patricia?" Frankie asked. "What's the matter with her?"

Mama leaned toward Lydia. "Our cousin has had a hard life. Her father left the family when she was a baby. She struggled to go to college but dropped out. Then she finally met and married a man her family liked." She turned back to the boys. "You remember Al Savarese, right?"

Leo nodded, drumming his fingers on his desk impatiently. "I remember him."

"Rose came to me yesterday sobbing her heart out. Patricia's no good husband Al is cheating on her, and she thinks it's with *puttane*." Mama sat back and let the news sink in for a moment. Frankie and Leo looked shocked, although in their line of business they saw more bad marriages than good ones. No one in a happy marriage ever called up a private eye.

"Isn't he a lawyer or something?" Frankie asked.

"He's an insurance executive. Makes good money. And she thought he was a good Catholic, too." Lydia wondered if Mama was going to cross herself, but instead she twisted her rings like a rosary. "Patricia must get rid of this man before he gives her some horrible disease. So Rose asks if you could take photographs of Al." Pictures of Al *in flagrante delicto* Mama meant, but was too ladylike to say.

"Don't they have kids?" Frankie frowned and shifted in his seat. Mama was reeling him in like a fat trout.

Mama leaned forward to pinch Frankie's cheek. "They were not blessed like me with two fine sons. Think what a tragedy it would be to the children to learn such things."

"So you want us to follow Al and get evidence so our good Catholic cousin can get a divorce?" Leo asked. He was not so easily seduced by his mother's arguments.

"Maybe she will use them to get him into some therapy, no? Once he knows she has her eye on him, maybe he will change his ways."

Lydia had never known Mama to be an optimist before. Perhaps this was her Catholic way of denying that she was assisting her cousin's daughter to get divorced. She wondered what kind of marriage Patricia and Al must have for him to seek satisfaction in the arms of streetwalkers. She thought of Glenda with a pang. Glenda had had the potential to be so much, but in the end she was a hooker who only cared about her next fix. Lydia didn't believe in making prostitution a crime, since it was usually the women who suffered, but she wished that Glenda had had better options and had made better choices.

Mama D'Angelo, after extracting a grudging promise from her sons to make Cousin Al's adultery their next case, zipped out of the office. It took them about thirty seconds to dig into the food she'd left: lasagna Bolognese, thick buttery garlic bread, calamari as a starter, and chocolate chip cannoli for dessert. Eleven thirty was a little early for lunch, but they had no trouble eating.

Once the feast had been reduced to crumbs, the three of them sat back in their chairs with a collective sigh. Lydia wished she could take a siesta. She hadn't gotten much sleep the night before, thinking about Glenda and her last moments. She wondered if it had been suicide or if Glenda had been too high to notice she was in danger. The third option, murder, scared Lydia, but Glenda's phone call took her thoughts again and again in that direction.

"So, you want to take first shift with Al?" Leo asked Frankie with a grin.

"Me? Why me? Why don't you do it? You used to have the hots for Patricia, after all."

Leo blushed. "I have plans."

Lydia stared at Leo in wonder. Leo's idea of a night on the town was playing chess with his buddies. Somehow she doubted that chess would reduce him to blushing. He definitely had a budding romance. Lydia couldn't imagine what Leo's type might be, or what kind of woman would find his dourness attractive.

"What kind of plans?" Frankie had a twinkle in his eye. He wasn't going to give up until Leo confessed what was more important than helping the family. Lydia felt sorry for Leo as his blush deepened.

"I could do it. Your cousin Al doesn't know me," Lydia offered casually. She didn't want to sound too eager, but the stakeout would be a great opportunity for her to be out at night photographing prostitutes and getting paid to do it. If Lydia had the assignment, she would be able to both photograph prostitutes for her own project and maybe find out if anyone knew anything about Glenda.

Frankie and Leo turned and gave her identical frowns. "It's too dangerous for a woman alone. You'd be on the waterfront at night all by yourself," Leo said.

"These people don't like having their pictures taken, and they could get violent. We wouldn't be able to live with ourselves if anything happened to you," Frankie explained.

Leo shook his head emphatically. "I'll do it and reschedule. I probably won't even have to get out of the car. And hopefully I'll get the pictures Patricia needs in one night." He didn't have to say "and get Mama off our backs," but that was implied.

Lydia opened her mouth to explain that she had self-defense training and could hold her own, but she could see that the D'Angelos weren't going to budge. She would just have to figure out how to continue working on her own.

Chapter 4

Half an hour later Lydia desperately needed fresh air. Since she had eaten her lunch at her desk, she felt justified in taking a break. She had a condolence call to make. The D'Angelos, distracted by a background check for a corporate client, barely looked up when she left.

The air was still and steamy, and there was no shade to be had as Lydia rode her bike east down Metropolitan Avenue. Summer was the one time when she wished the buildings in her neighborhood were taller and shaded more of the sidewalk and street. Everything was hot, and she tried to stay as far away as she could from idling buses and trucks at stoplights.

Lydia had once dropped Glenda off in a taxi at her mother's house. Susa lived in the projects in Bushwick, just twenty minutes from the D'Angelos' office, but it felt like a whole different country. Large brick apartment buildings with tiny windows towered over wide streets, and unemployed youths hung out on street corners with pagers and cell phones. Lydia locked her bike nearby with some trepidation. Usually her black Schwinn was too old and beat up for any robber to bother with, but there was always a first time.

This morning she'd known she was going to come and see Susa as soon as she could, but she hadn't told Jack she was going to. It really was just a lie of omission, but it made her feel strange. She knew he wouldn't approve and wanted her to stay away from Glenda's case, but she figured what he didn't know wouldn't hurt him.

The front door of the building was open and half off its hinges. She stepped inside, her eyes slowly adjusting to the darkness. A man was lying rolled in a ball in the dirty entryway. Lydia hoped he was sleeping. The elevators were broken, and judging by the yellowed sign, had been so for a long time. It was stuffy and not much cooler than the street.

She tried not to breathe in as she mounted the stairs, but the stench of urine was overpowering. She felt her clothes sticking to her back and grimaced. She was going to be a wreck by the time she got back to the office. Susa lived on the eighth floor, so Lydia was panting and even sweatier by the time she reached it. As Lydia opened the door to the hall, the scent of Caribbean cooking mixed with Pine-Sol washed over her. She could hear a baby crying as she knocked on Susa's door. She had the sensation of being spied on through the peephole before the door slowly opened.

Susa, a dark-skinned woman with her hair in curlers, peeked out cautiously. The noise of the crying baby intensified. Susa was small and skinny, but Lydia could see a hint of Glenda in her features. She was probably no more than forty, but she looked sixty. Her hard life had caught hold of her face and yanked it downward.

"You from the police?"

Lydia shook her head. "I knew Glenda. I did a portrait of her."

Susa stared at her. "She said she was going to be a star."

Glenda had never understood that the best-case scenario for her photograph was to end up on a gallery wall, not in a fashion magazine. "She called me yesterday. I went looking for her, but I found her body instead."

Susa shook her head. "They made me go to the morgue. I had to bring the babies with me because I don't trust no one around here to watch 'em."

"Would you mind if I came in?"

Susa shrugged and stepped aside. She was wearing a dirty tank top and shorts, and her clothes hung loosely on her thin body. The apartment looked as if a localized Category 3 hurricane had been through. Lydia had to step carefully to avoid clothes and toys covering the floor. A roach scuttled up the wall, and Lydia tried not to shudder visibly. Through a doorway she saw two small children, partially clothed, sitting on a bed and staring at a large color television blaring a cartoon soundtrack. The baby had stopped crying and sat on the floor chewing on a very dirty blanket. Lydia had never been particularly maternal, but her urge to offer some comfort, or at least a little bit of help with the cleaning, was overwhelming.

"That girl was beautiful but always so wild. I told her to stop chasing boys, but she never listened. She thought she was going to live forever," Susa said shakily, and began to cry. Lydia took Susa gently in her arms and hugged her, feeling so sorry for her lost dreams for Glenda that would never come true. It was like hugging a pile of bones. Lydia wondered if she was ill. She looked like a victim of starvation or an AIDS patient. She wondered what would happen to the kids if Susa died. They would probably end up in the foster care system, and she felt a profound sadness at the thought.

After a few minutes, Susa took a deep breath and wiped her eyes with a red cloth she'd pulled out from behind the sofa cushion. She blew her nose loudly. "You want some coffee? Not the watery stuff from the deli but the real stuff?"

"Yes, please, if it wouldn't be too much trouble."

Susa's eyes brightened. She shuffled into the kitchen. Instead of following, Lydia went into the room where the kids were watching TV. She thought it would be better not to see the kitchen that produced the coffee she was about to drink, judging by the state of the rest of the apartment.

The three kids glanced over at her and then turned their eyes back to the TV. They didn't seem to be at all curious about who she was. She wondered how they had felt about their mother. Glenda talked about her babies all the time, but Lydia didn't know how much time she actually spent with them. Lydia couldn't think of anything to tell them, so she simply sat down with them and watched a very violent cartoon featuring robots and monsters. Susa couldn't afford much, but she didn't scrimp on cable.

Susa at last shuffled back in with two mugs of coffee and a few dry-looking doughnuts. The coffee was hot and strong, and Lydia took a grateful sip. She didn't bother reaching for a doughnut. Luckily, Mama D'Angelo's offerings had filled her up.

"Glenda called me yesterday and she sounded scared. Do you know what was going on with her?"

Susa's eyes widened. "Gator Pinero is a no-good monster who kept my baby from straightening her life out. He knocked her around all the time. I wouldn't be surprised if he killed her."

"His name is Gator?" Lydia asked. She pictured a guy with lots of sharp teeth; half man half beast and definitely dangerous.

"Yeah. He runs all the business by the waterfront. And I heard he's started bringing in women from Mexico to work it." Susa shook her head in disgust. "But that wasn't enough for him. He had to destroy my baby, too."

Lydia was glad to have a suspect at last. "I'm so sorry for your loss. Is there anything I can do? Run out to the store?"

Susa nodded. "Now that she's joined the angels, I want my baby to have a funeral to remember."

Lydia made her escape fifteen minutes later with a lighter wallet and one possible suspect. She wasn't sure if the police had ruled Glenda's death suicide or murder. The only way she was going to find out was to talk to Romero. She checked her watch. She was pushing the whole lunch-hour thing, but she would just make up some story for the D'Angelos if they noticed.

The local precinct would never win an award for architectural beauty no matter who was judging. It was a squat white-brick building in a bad neighborhood, and it occupied the block like a silent and menacing guard on sentry duty. Inside, the cops had tried to brighten up the institutional green walls with posters in Spanish advising women to get help if their loved ones were beating them, others instructing people to not drive drunk and to look out for pickpockets, but sadly these efforts at decoration hadn't helped much. Visitors had to lean over and yell through a scarred hole in bulletproof glass to talk to an officer about their problems, and it was a wonder anyone had any faith in the system. Lydia took one look at the line and called Romero directly on his cell phone.

"It's Lydia," she stammered, feeling a fool for being embarrassed. "I wanted to ask you about Glenda."

"Tell me again how you knew the deceased." Romero didn't like to waste time. That was okay—she didn't have much of it to waste to-day, either. But if he thought he was going to trip her up by asking the same questions again and again, he was in for a surprise. She repeated her story.

"What have you learned about her death? Was she murdered?"

"It looks like she was strangled, but the autopsy is in the works." His voice sounded gruff, like he hadn't had much sleep last night.

"Strangled? I guess that couldn't be suicide or an accident then."

"Nope. We had a serial killer case a few years ago on the water-front, so we're looking into everything."

"The Brooklyn Strangler? The one who killed prostitutes? I thought you guys nabbed him."

"I did, too. But we're looking into everything and everyone that could be relevant."

Lydia decided to play her hand. "Have you spoken to Gator Pinero yet?"

There was silence on the other end. "How do you know Gator?"

Lydia tried to sound casual. "Her mother told me about him. Said he was violent. I was wondering if he could have been the one she called about."

Romero gave a quick bark of a laugh. "Pimps might slap hookers around, but they rarely kill a cash cow."

Lydia was annoyed. She wasn't that naïve or stupid. But not every-one acted rationally all the time. Gator could be a psychopath. "She said she was scared of someone. Maybe she was going to go to a dif-ferent pimp."

"Glenda looked like she was doing a great job killing herself. I don't know if she needed any help. But very likely her murder will join the long list of unsolved murders in the city, unless by chance some witness comes forward and tells us who did it."

Lydia had known him to be discouraged at times and fed up, but she'd never heard him sound so bitter. "You need a vacation."

"Thanks. I'll let the police commissioner know. You got anything else for me?"

"Not really. I should get back to work."

"That guy yesterday—is he your boyfriend?" Romero sounded indifferent, but she couldn't be sure. He was a good poker player.

"Yeah." Despite their differences of opinion the day before, Jack and Lydia had still managed to have a pizza party that ended very satisfactorily in bed.

"You should listen to him and stay out of this. Guys like Gator are not the type you want to mess with, okay?"

Lydia was stubborn and impulsive. She tried to think of these traits as assets rather than faults. But even she wasn't foolhardy enough to rush off and confront someone with the unfortunate name of Gator. She would leave this lead to Romero.

Chapter 5

Lydia checked her cell phone as she left the station and hurried back to her bike. The D'Angelos had left her a message, so she knew they'd noticed her extended break. She needed to get back fast. Her bike, unfortunately, had a flat tire. She let out a string of curses that would have shocked her mother, had she been nearby. Lydia was hot, tired, and crabby. She didn't need the added expense or hassle of a new tire.

She couldn't patch or change the tire right now. If it wasn't safe to leave her bike locked up in front of the police station, then she didn't know where it would be safe. She stepped into the street and waited on the shimmering hot pavement for a livery cab to drive by. No taxis drove this part of Brooklyn looking for fares, but car services abounded. She didn't have to wait long. She put out her hand and a Lincoln pulled over in front of her.

A young Jamaican man with a colorful woven hat over his massive dreadlocks lowered the tinted window. "Where you going, lady?"

"Lorimer Street. I'm in a hurry."

The locks popped open. "Then I'm your man."

"Are you sure you're nineteen?" It was the minimum age for a livery cab driver, but he looked more like seventeen.

"No worries, lady. You're safe with me."

Lydia hopped into the back. She noticed he hadn't answered the question, but he pulled out into traffic and appeared to drive quite competently. The car was air-conditioned, and she leaned back against the shiny leather seats with a happy sigh.

"You a student?"

"I'm a photographer," she said. There were times when she hated that she looked younger than her age. It was difficult to get people to take her seriously. Since she had just questioned him about his age, she couldn't exactly take offense. "But I work for a private detective agency."

"Private eyes? Like *Moonlighting*?"

Lydia smiled politely. He must watch a lot of reruns on cable.

"You undercover?"

Lydia remembered that she was in her sexy miniskirt outfit. Perhaps it had not been the best choice for the day.

"You ever need a car for a stakeout, lady? You call me. I work cheap." He glided up to a red light and then passed Lydia a business card. It read EMMANUEL JORDAN, CHAUFFEUR.

"Thanks, Emmanuel. My name is Lydia McKenzie."

"Lydia." He sounded like he was rolling her name around in his mouth to try out every syllable to see how it tasted. "I'll remember that. You just call me."

They were pulling onto Lorimer. "Drop me off at the corner. The office is just up a block that way."

Emmanuel surveyed the scene as though he would be tested on it later. Perhaps he would make a good private eye. Lydia tucked his card into her pocket as she stepped out into the heat of the street. Hoping that the air-conditioning was working inside, she went in to face the D'Angelos.

When the D'Angelos finally left at 5:30, she heaved a big sigh of relief. The day had seemed endless, and Leo had kept a special eye on her, as if he thought she might try to take another big break. She had to go pick up her bike and wheel it to the shop. And then she had to go home to put a few last-minute touches on her outfit before going out. Her best friend, Georgia, had a new band that was playing at a former roller rink turned disco. Jack was coming and was going to be meeting her friends for the first time. The notion made her nervous, but she was anxious to show him off. He was good-looking, smart, and artistic, and she reminded herself she was lucky to have nabbed him.

She wanted to take another look at Glenda's portrait. Unfortunately, Lydia wouldn't be able to get back into the darkroom until the weekend. Something was nagging her about the photograph, and she wondered if it was a potential clue. Maybe she would try enlarging the photograph and examine the details more closely. Glenda had helped her achieve that amazing portrait: Helping to find the answer to her death was the least Lydia could do.

The former roller rink looked like a warehouse from the outside, but inside it was all light and energy. The designers had installed light and kinetic sculptures that hung from the ceiling, but kept the original flooring. Customers could rent roller skates if they wanted to sail around the action instead of sitting still. A black woman who was over six feet tall with a long mane of Jheri curls and a huge pink-feather boa sailed around the room, lost in her own world. Lydia admired her style. Punk was definitely back with a vengeance. She counted six Mohawks and more piercings than she had fingers and toes. There were tattoos galore, and one guy had even had his face tattooed like a Maori warrior. Lydia shuddered to think what that procedure must have felt like.

The opening band was playing when they arrived, five guys in ragged jeans and T-shirts. They weren't good, but they were certainly loud. A loyal group of fans cheered them on and danced enthusiastically in front of the stage.

"C'mon. Let's find Georgia Rae." Lydia pulled Jack along behind her as she headed for the stage. Georgia was sitting on a speaker, impervious to the loud screeching noises, fixing her makeup. Georgia Rae was a jane-of-all-trades, specializing in hair and makeup (she had a salon), but also was a terrific singer and had worked in lots of bands as well as had a part in a musical theater production. Georgia lowered the mirror when she spotted Lydia and squealed. She was wearing a black catsuit that hugged her curves, and her hair was done exactly like Marilyn Monroe in *Some Like It Hot* except that the color wasn't blond but fluorescent blue.

"Lydia! You're pretty enough to stop traffic!" After ten years in New York, Georgia still had as strong a southern accent as when she first arrived. It was a source of pride for her. She hopped off the speaker and gave Lydia an enthusiastic hug and looked speculatively behind her at Jack.

"You look gorgeous, too," Lydia shouted over the music. "Are you a Bond girl?"

Georgia laughed and nudged her. "Introduce me!" she ordered.

"This is my friend Jack."

Georgia held out her hand, and she and Jack solemnly shook. Lydia bit her lip and tried not to think about what would happen if her best friend and boyfriend didn't get along. Divided loyalties were never comfortable. And she wasn't sure who she would choose at this point. She had a long history with Georgia, but Jack was something special.

"I've heard a lot about you. I'm looking forward to hearing you sing," Jack yelled. Georgia raised her eyebrows at Lydia as if to say, "Wow, he's got manners, too." Lydia tried not to look smug but it was hard.

"Thanks. I'm glad you could make it." Georgia smiled flirtatiously. "Oh, Lydia, there's someone I want you to meet for your project."

"There's something you should know about that. . . ." Lydia had to share the news about Glenda. Georgia had never met her, but she'd seen the portrait in progress.

"That's horrible! Do they know what happened?"

"The cops are looking into it." Lydia hoped that Georgia wouldn't mention Romero. She didn't want Jack to start getting suspicious about him. If he knew how well she had gotten to know the police detective months ago, he might get jealous. She told herself that Romero didn't mean anything to her, but she needed to keep in touch with him on Glenda's case.

"Are you going to drop the whole project? That would be too tragic." Georgia was one of her biggest cheerleaders, and had spent hours modeling for her for other projects.

"No. But I had high hopes for continuing to work with each subject. . . ." Lydia swallowed hard. She remembered seeing Glenda's swollen body come out of the river, and thought again what a waste her death had been.

The fabulous-looking woman with the feather boa sailed past again. Georgia waved at her enthusiastically. "Candi! Over here!" The woman smiled, her white teeth gleaming in the light from the disco ball as she glided over. It was only when she was a few feet away that Lydia realized she was actually a man dressed as a woman. Her Adam's apple gave her away. "This is my friend Lydia, the photographer I told you about."

Lydia shook the woman's hand gingerly, avoiding her extremely long press-on nails, and stared dazed into her face. Candi was the kind of subject a photographer only dreamed about. She could already imagine how her face would look lit and framed just so. "Can I photograph you?"

"Oh, darling. You flatter me." Candi giggled.

"I'm serious. I would love to do your portrait. I can't pay—"

Candi waved her hand as if to say this was of no importance and reached inside her pocket to pull out a card. "Give me a call and we'll set something up." Lydia took the card and watched as Candi sailed back into the crowd.

"She's amazing," Lydia said. She turned back to Georgia and gave her a big hug. "You're a genius. Thanks for introducing me."

"No problem." Georgia smiled, looking quite pleased with herself.

Jack plucked the card from Lydia's hand and studied it with a smile. "Candi Stick, she-male?"

"She-male? Let me see." Lydia took the card back and studied it. There was a sexy photograph of Candi showing off a pair of gonzo breasts for the camera. Below was a number for any interested johns to call to set up a date. "Isn't that when they get the boobs but don't have their penis removed?"

"I guess," Georgia said with a shrug. "You'll love working with

Candi. I've been cutting her hair for years. She has the soul of a cover girl and is one classy babe."

"A hooker with a heart of gold," Jack muttered. Lydia tucked Candi's card away, wishing Jack wasn't so negative. She didn't need a guy who wasn't supportive of her photography. She would rather be alone than feel diminished.

"Just be careful, okay?" Jack said, his charming smile back in place. "I wouldn't want anything to happen to you." He kissed Lydia, and she felt her annoyance melt away. Jack was just cautious, she told herself.

The band finally came to a crashing finale and leaped off the stage into their crowd of fans in a mock mosh pit. Luckily, the fans expected it and caught them easily.

"That's my cue," Georgia said brightly.

"Break a leg," Lydia called to her. It felt odd to speak in a regular voice again, but the music would start again soon and they would all be back to yelling. Georgia moved off to round up the band.

"Let's get a drink," Jack said. They made their way over to the bar, a former snack bar. The dark wooden counter was so scarred it looked as if it had been run over by a million roller skates. The woman behind the counter had a big ring in her nose and bright green hair. She was serving beers, popcorn, and candy at hyperspeed. The line never got long, and the cash in her tip drawer mounted fast.

They sipped their beers at the edge of the action on the floor. Jack saw Robert, a guy he knew from his studio building. After introducing him to Lydia, they got into a long discussion about escalating rents, broken elevators, and erratic trash pick up. Lydia, bored by the conversation, let her mind wander and watched the crowd. The place was starting to fill up and warm up. The fans mostly wore a uniform of black T-shirts and jeans, but a few had on interesting outfits. One woman was wearing a turquoise prom dress with biker boots, and another had on a top made out of peacock feathers.

Lydia thought about suggesting that they rent roller skates, but she hadn't done it in years. She would probably fall all over like a klutz, which was not the kind of impression she cared to make with Jack. She watched enviously as a few women sailed effortlessly around the rink, neatly dodging other people. She imagined how wonderful it must feel to go so fast but be completely in control. Finally, Georgia's band took to the stage.

"We are the Pileated Woodpeckers, and we're here to rock this place!" Georgia screamed into the microphone, and the band launched into its first number. The drummer hammered away, and the guitars and bass blended into one loud noise. Lydia wondered if the last band had actually been okay, but the sound system just sucked. There was suddenly no one in front of the stage, and Lydia didn't want Georgia to feel like no one was enjoying the music.

"Let's dance," Lydia suggested brightly.

"To this? There's no beat," Jack complained.

"We'll make our own." Lydia took Jack's hand firmly. "Excuse us, Robert." Lydia dragged Jack onto the dance floor. They rocked for a moment to the music, then began to gaze into one another's eyes.

"I'll have you know that my test of long-term boyfriend material is a willingness to get up and make a fool of yourself," Lydia shouted in his ear.

"Does this mean karaoke is in my future?"

"Oh, no. Just the chicken dance at some second cousin's wedding."

"Then I'm your man." Jack leaned down and kissed Lydia. He was an excellent kisser, and she returned the kiss enthusiastically. When they finally broke apart to catch their breath, Jack gave her a considering look. "How many songs do we have to stay for?"

"Why? You have to get up early tomorrow?"

"No. But I think I have to get to bed early tonight." Jack smiled sexily down at her. Knowing Georgia would forgive her as long as she got all the details, Lydia left with Jack after just six songs.

Chapter 6

That man never gets tired! He ran around until 3 A.M. picking up women." Leo sounded thoroughly disgusted, and the dark bags under his eyes looked even more pronounced than usual. Lydia smiled. Since she had been dying to do Al's stakeout herself she couldn't be too sympathetic.

"Did you get any good shots?" The D'Angelos were not great photographers, but they usually managed to get the photos they needed. Lydia would have added a little more pizzazz to hers, cooler details and sophisticated angles and depth of field, but she couldn't fault them for accuracy. And clients usually didn't care that it wasn't pretty. They just wanted results.

"I don't know. Can you download them for me? I need another espresso."

"Sure." Leo handed Lydia the camera. He hadn't even bothered to check his e-mail. "But bring me back an espresso, too." Leo waved as he went out the door, seeming not to mind the extra order. She had

had a long night as well, and if he didn't want her to fall asleep over the computer he had better supply her with some serious caffeine.

The fifty shots on Leo's camera were big files and took awhile to download. The computers in the office were several years old, and it seemed like computers these days became antiquated as soon as they were carried from the store. She had friends who were always waiting for the next big thing before they bought electronics, and so ended up never getting a nice computer or camera. In her opinion, the strategy of waiting was counterproductive in both electronics and love.

Lydia's first love was film. She would have been happy to stay away from digital for the rest of her life, but she had to admit digital photography made their job at work far easier. The results were instantaneous, and there was no waiting for the photo lab to finish up the job. She had had to learn a lot about the computer software since she began working for the D'Angelos, and she found the work almost as satisfying as the darkroom when she managed to get a nice image.

At last a pop-up on the screen announced that the task was finished. Lydia was curious to see what Al had been up to on his late-night prowls. She quickly discarded forty-five of the fifty shots because they were pictures of the dashboard or because they were out of focus or too dark. The remaining ones repeated a few times, so she was left with just two usable shots. Neither was particularly exciting. One shot was presumably of Al talking to a prostitute through his car window. His face was in shadow and unidentifiable. She put it aside to massage later in Photoshop. The other shot showed a shadowy Al locked in an embrace with a hooker in his maroon SUV. The license plate was readable, but perhaps he could argue in court that someone had borrowed his car. The haul was disappointing, and Lydia was convinced she could have done better.

Leo came back a few minutes later with the coffees and a bag of Danish. "How'd they look?"

Lydia took a big sip of her espresso before answering. "There's one I might be able to work on so we can see his face. . . ."

Leo shook his head in disgust. "It was so freakin' dark down there, I had trouble finding the guy half the time through the camera."

That explained why there had been so many shots of the dashboard. "It's too bad prostitutes don't ply their trade in well-lit areas."

Leo took a giant bite of a Danish and chewed for a minute. "Mama is going to be seriously upset if we mess this up. But I just can't face following him around for another night. Besides, I have another engagement tonight."

She had guessed Leo was seeing someone before, but now she was convinced it was true. Usually life in general took a backseat to his work, and the fact that this new woman made him reprioritize was big.

"Why don't you let me try?" Lydia asked casually, and took another sip of her coffee. The caffeine was making her blood sing, and she was feeling brave.

Leo frowned. "We already discussed it. It's too dangerous."

"I've been down there to photograph prostitutes for a series I'm doing, and I've never had any problems. Why should this be any different?"

"You're not just getting a pretty shot here. You're stalking someone and trying to catch him in the act." Leo stuffed the rest of his Danish in his mouth. "You know the most violent people I've ever had to deal with? Not criminals, that's for sure. No, sir. It was the party at fault in divorce cases. They think if they break your camera—or worse, kill you—they'll make the whole thing go away. They're totally nuts." Lydia sat silently, letting him finish. Leo drummed his fingers on the desk. "Besides, you don't even have a car. Were you planning to sail by on your bike and shoot from the hip?"

Leo and Frankie were clearly against her becoming more active in the business. She wondered how long she could continue being just a secretary and drudge. She knew she could do what they did, but they weren't willing to give her a try.

"Let me know if you change your mind. I'd like to try," she said. She decided it was best not to argue, but to act with as much dignity as possible in the face of their sexism.

Leo snorted. "It's definitely Frankie's turn." He sounded almost gleeful at the thought of his brother chasing around their sex-starved cousin-in-law.

To make herself feel less like a mindless worker bee and more like an artist, Lydia called Candi's number to try to set up a photo shoot with the beautiful transsexual. She reached an answering service. Lydia left a message that she wanted Candi to call her back as soon as possible. The expressionless voice on the other end probably assumed she was an anxious customer. In a way, she supposed she was. Only she wanted to photograph Candi, not sleep with her.

Candi called back a couple of hours later and sounded pleasantly flattered to have her portrait done. "Can you come by tomorrow morning?" It was a Wednesday, and technically Lydia had to work. But she couldn't resist catching Candi on film as soon as possible. Besides, she didn't feel very much loyalty to the D'Angelos at the moment. She'd just call in sick and come in late.

"It's a date," she said.

On her way home from work, Lydia found herself walking back down to the waterfront. She felt like she finally understood why moths battered themselves against lights until they expired. Some danger was addictive. She was drawn to the water, hoping somehow she would find an answer beneath its choppy surface. A group of guys lingered with their beers in the shadows, hiding from the cops. They didn't seem dangerous, just intent on having fun.

During the day, it was easy to look past the occasional needle or used condom and forget that hookers and drug dealers occupied the streets in the evening. It looked like an industrial wasteland bordered by a busy waterfront. Tourists swept by on the Circle Line boat tours, and commuters buzzed past on the ferry headed up to midtown or down to Wall Street. She sat down on a bench and tried to think.

Glenda was dead. What had her last moments been like? Had she gotten in the car with a stranger or a repeat customer? Was it a serial killer?

Lydia thought of Susa and the three little kids. She didn't know what to do. Should she give up? Let the police do their jobs? Or should she try to sniff around and see what else she could uncover? She couldn't decide. She hated giving up on anything, but she wasn't sure where else to go with the case. None of her friends or acquaintances knew Glenda so could they not offer anything new.

She started to get hungry. She got up and started walking home. Just as she got to Wythe a black SUV hurtled down the avenue, startling her. As it zoomed past she was able to read the license plate clearly. It said GATOR.

Chapter 7

"Oh, darling. Come on up," Candi Stick said through the intercom. Her voice sounded bubbly even through the crackling intercom. The glass door of the building buzzed, and Lydia pushed her way inside. The lobby floor was marble and the walls were a pale peach. A handy mirrored wall by the elevator revealed to Lydia that her outfit looked both intelligent and sexy. She was channeling Audrey Hepburn in *Funny Face*. She had on slim black pants, ballet flats, and a tight red T-shirt that managed somehow not to clash with her hair. She had taken the bus so as to look cool and comfortable despite the mounting temperature outside. Inside her black messenger bag was her camera, tripod, extra rolls of film, and a notebook.

The elevator dinged discreetly, and Lydia got inside. Hooking had to be pretty lucrative. The prices they were advertising for the luxury condominiums by the park were beyond outrageous. Candi lived on the top floor and was sure to have a view of Manhattan

The hallway was clean and plain, and Lydia wondered how long the cheap construction would last. They put up the buildings so fast, she wouldn't have been surprised to find out that they'd forgotten something essential like plumbing. Lydia pressed the buzzer on #5L and waited. The door opened and Candi posed in the doorway in a flowing pink robe edged with fuchsia feathers on the neckline and sleeves.

"Darling! How lovely to see you!" They kissed the air next to each other's cheeks, careful not to mess up Candi's hot pink lipstick. Lydia caught a whiff of expensive perfume. She was clearly in the wrong line of work.

After arranging the photo shoot, Lydia had fretted over whether Candi's beauty had come only from her style. Perhaps the darkness of the nightclub had hidden her flaws. She was relieved to see that, from her bright pink toes to her perfectly coiffed hair, Candi did not disappoint in the harsh light of the daytime.

"Come in. I've just made a pot of jasmine green tea. They say it's chock full of antioxidants, and I need a big detox today."

Lydia followed Candi into the apartment. The temperature was a cool sixty degrees, and the heat of the city street seemed far away. She felt a little dazed to be in the presence of such glamour. Every piece in Candi's apartment looked as if it had been carefully selected for its unique style and expensiveness. The sofa was a Louis Quinze knockoff in red velvet, or at least it didn't look to Lydia's untrained eye like an original. If it were that old, Lydia would feel too guilty to sit on it. The paintings on the walls were originals, though, some from well-known modern artists, and the rug looked like an oriental heirloom.

Candi followed Lydia's gaze to an African figurine above the fireplace. "You like sculpture?"

"I like that one." The dark wooden figure was crouched with his arms bent in front of him. He had a scowling death-mask face. She could see the carving marks on his face and easily imagine the hands that had created him.

"It was something I picked up on my travels. I spent a lot of time in Africa and Asia." Candi smiled as if her mind had slipped across the sea to another continent. "I actually considered a career in diplomacy."

Lydia could not stop her jaw from dropping in an undignified fashion. A hooker who had aspirations to be in the government? Nothing added up where Candi was concerned.

Candi laughed at Lydia's expression. "I attended college and majored in foreign policy, you know."

"Then why . . . ," Lydia began. She was beginning to feel like the worst hypocrite in the world. She had set out to photograph and understand prostitutes and prostitution, but the more she dug, the more she discovered that her expectations were far off the mark.

"There was no room for me to be who I really was in the State Department. I felt like a woman trapped in a man's body, and that world is completely unforgiving. There was no way I could have a sex change. It was either quit or commit suicide." Lydia had ridden the subway during rush hour in Washington, D.C. It had felt like everyone was a government worker wearing a beige trench coat over a suit. Candi Stick must have felt like a peacock among pigeons there.

"But surely there were other things you could do." Lydia was usually great at brainstorming, but on this one she was drawing a blank.

"Sure. Be a rock star, but I can't sing. Be an actress, but I can't act." Candi tossed her hair over her shoulder.

The world seemed very small and horrible suddenly. Candi was so beautiful and smart, but the world had marginalized her. She could have offered so much, but instead she was stuck in the sex trade. At least Candi was smart enough not to get addicted to drugs, and to pour her money into real estate and decorating. She looked like she had amassed a tidy nest egg for when she retired.

"I think you're a terrific model. I guess it's lucky for me that no one discovered you yet."

Candi smiled back and checked her small gold watch. "I have an appointment in an hour. Can we get the photograph done by then?"

Lydia hated to work with time constraints. She got so nervous she always forgot something silly, like taking off the lens cap or readjusting the f-stop after she changed the lights. But she was willing to do whatever she could to get some pictures of Candi, who had a face that made a photographer's job easy. "Sure, no problem. I hope you don't mind if we talk while I set up."

"Not at all." Candi settled down on the velvet sofa, then looked up. "Do you mind if I sit here?"

"That's fine." The light from the large windows would have been too bright on a clear day. Luckily, the day was a little overcast. Lydia tried to work with natural light for her portraits as much as possible, but sometimes there wasn't enough for a good exposure or there was too much and her subject looked washed out. "Is that what you'd like to wear?"

"This old thing?" Candi gestured to her feather robe. "I thought I'd put on something a little more dressy."

"Only if you want to. I like the way it looks."

Candi shrugged. "You're the photographer."

Lydia smiled. She wished all her subjects were as docile. She quickly took a few shots, looked, considered, readjusted, and changed her angle and repeated. Candi started to look dreamy and lost in her own thoughts. It might have worked on another subject, but Lydia preferred to see Candi's eyes look sharp and alert. She lowered her camera and considered how to reengage her subject. She belatedly remembered her other goal for the visit.

"I was wondering if you knew the woman who was killed on the waterfront, Glenda."

Candi grimaced. "Because I'm a hooker, too?"

Lydia remembered the many times someone had asked if she knew so-and-so who was a photographer in New York City. Strangely enough, in such a big city, she often did know them. New York was a strange grouping of tribes and neighborhoods, like a mishmash of small towns all smushed together in a huge city. "I don't know. Some worlds can be small."

Candi arranged the feathers on her sleeve delicately with one hand. Her nails were painted in gold and black stripes. It must have taken someone hours to do them. "Actually, I did know her."

Lydia could tell Candi wasn't going to dish if she thought Lydia wanted to know the details simply out of ghoulish curiosity. "I was doing a portrait of Glenda before she died. She called me the day she disappeared and asked for my help. I feel guilty that I didn't answer the phone."

Candi watched her carefully. "She called a lot just wanting to borrow money. I ducked a call from her the day before, too."

That was curious. Maybe she hadn't been looking for a private eye after all. Maybe she had just needed a friend. "Do you think her pimp or dealer killed her?"

Candi shook her head. "They both got more from her alive than dead. I doubt Gator would kill one of his girls. Beat them severely perhaps, but killing one of them would be like a rancher killing a healthy heifer."

Lydia nodded. Candi's eyes were focused again so she snapped a few quick shots.

"On the other hand, Gator is, I suspect, insane. And insane people are not rational. He wants the girls frightened and afraid to leave him. He wants them to believe that it would be dangerous for them to leave him and go to another pimp. He could conceivably have killed Glenda as a way to frighten the rest. Everyone agrees that murder on the waterfront hurts everyone's business. No one wants to go where you might get murdered."

Lydia lowered the camera. "What do you know about Glenda?"

"Glenda—she was a lifer. She had the soul of the hooker. She might have stopped briefly if she had a boyfriend who picked up the bills, but she always would return to it."

Lydia thought sadly about the three kids in the apartment in the projects. "Was there a rival pimp who was trying to scoop up the women on the waterfront?"

"I did hear rumors about a guy named Sammy the Sauce. He had been working farther down near the navy yard, and word on the street was that he wanted to expand northward. He might have killed a few girls to make them feel unsafe with Gator and come to him for protection."

Lydia wondered how anyone managed to find one of these guys with no last names. But she supposed they were deliberately making it difficult for them to be found. That way they couldn't be arrested.

"You're awfully curious about her death, aren't you?" Candi said.

"I found Glenda's body," Lydia told her.

Candi winced. She had probably read the details of the death and knew that Glenda had been a floater. "I've known Glenda for years. I worked on the waterfront briefly when I started out and found out firsthand that it was really dangerous. Glenda helped me at a time when she didn't really need to." Candi smiled at Lydia's incredulous expression. It was hard to imagine Glenda helping anyone but herself. "She was a little more together back then. So when I finally escaped to a house, I was determined to go back someday and help all the women working out there."

Candi had a militant look in her eye that Lydia liked. She shifted, refocused, and took a few quick snaps of Candi framed by the window. The feathers had a warm glow around their edges that intrigued her. "I founded a nonprofit with a social worker and a doctor. We bought a bus and we go to places where prostitutes are as many nights a week as we can afford. We offer counseling and condoms, give information on literacy programs, drug treatment, and housing, and we test them for sexually transmitted diseases."

Lydia lowered her camera, amazed. She had instantly recognized that Candi was a powerful and interesting person, but she had no idea she was such a force for good. She certainly had not let the sex trade bring her down. "So that's how you saw Glenda regularly."

"Yeah. She came by a lot. Glenda was always trying to get anything she could. We all lent her money at one time or another before I said 'enough.' Now I'm sorry I was so harsh."

Lydia thought about her sessions with Glenda. When Glenda had talked about her dreams for the future, she had a softness about her.

"Despite everything, I really liked her," Lydia began. "There was something special about her." She had had a strange charisma and beauty that were hard for Lydia to describe. Glenda could have lived such a different life under different circumstances, and it was a real shame.

"She was like a chameleon. She always kept me off balance. I never could figure her out."

Lydia looked down at her camera, realizing she'd forgotten all about taking pictures. Their discussion seemed much more important. "Do you take volunteers on the bus?"

Candi sighed, and Lydia now saw the sleepless nights etched in her face. "We take anyone who's willing to hand out condoms, label blood tests, and help people fill out forms. But we rarely use guys, since they make the women nervous. We prefer former sex workers because they can tell it like it is."

"I've never been a sex worker, but I'd like to volunteer the next time you go out." Candi raised an eyebrow at Lydia. "I ducked Glenda's call, and I can't help feeling sort of responsible, you know?" And guilty.

Candi nodded. "Those girls need someone looking out for them. We'll take you with us, if you want to start tonight. But be careful, girlfriend. Okay?"

If anyone knew about the danger of the streets it would be a transvestite hooker. Lydia promised to be very, very careful.

Chapter 8

Lydia wasn't sure what the other bus volunteers would be wearing, so she went through her clothes collection anxiously. She didn't want to look too conservative or too sexy. She decided comfort was the best strategy. She dug out a jean skirt, a black short-sleeved blouse, and a pair of flats.

As instructed, she walked to the corner of Bedford and Metropolitan. She had brought her camera just in case, and she fingered it in her bag as if it was some kind of talisman. She had made sure that she told Jack where she was going. She didn't want to argue about whether or not it was safe, so she left a message on his cell phone while he was at work. She could have called his office line and had a chance to talk to him, but she took the easier route.

Painted with rainbow stripes, the school bus that lumbered up Metropolitan Avenue was not at all what Lydia had expected. It looked like it would fit in better at Burning Man or a Grateful Dead concert. She guessed they had gotten a good deal on it, and poor nonprofits couldn't be too choosy. The doors swung open, and Lydia advanced toward it, hit by a wave of heat emanating from the vehicle. There was definitely no air-conditioning on the bus. The driver, a woman in her seventies with a messy bun held up on top of her head by something that looked like a digital thermometer, peered down at Lydia from her perch.

"Lydia?" When Lydia nodded, the woman gestured impatiently for her to come aboard. "Hop in, dear. I'm Dr. Iris Whitfield." Dr. Whitfield was wearing cargo pants, a white T-shirt, and clogs. Lydia was glad she hadn't put on something too dressy.

Lydia climbed aboard, trying to ignore the heat. She was pleased to see that the inside had been stripped of the rows of black seats she remembered from her childhood. The front had two conversation areas with comfortable benches covered in red fabric. The back was curtained off, presumably to hide some kind of an exam room. Flowered curtains framed the windows, and the effect was somewhere between a doctor's office and day care center. Overall, it felt homey and comfortable—the kind of place where a working girl could put up her feet.

Candi Stick was in close conversation with an earnest-looking blonde in her forties and an African-American woman in her twenties. She smiled when she saw Lydia and gestured for her to come over. Lydia made her way over, clutching at the benches as she passed. The shocks on the bus were bad, and the doctor alternatively braked and accelerated as they bumped over potholes. Lydia landed breathlessly in a seat beside Candi after they hit a big one.

"Sorry, my dears!" Dr. Whitfield called out cheerfully.

"We're going to be parked for most of the night, right?" Lydia asked.

Candi laughed. She was looking elegant in a simple black shift with just a few pieces of chunky gold jewelry. "Iris is the only one of us who was determined to get her bus driving license, so we rely on her to get us down to the water. But after that, she can just be a physician. And she's much better at that."

The blond woman smiled. "I'm Sarah—the social worker. Thanks for coming to help us out." She shook Lydia's hand. She came across as both businesslike and sweet, and Lydia was sure that's what made her successful in counseling.

"I'm looking forward to it."

Candi broke in again. "And this is Lakisha. She's an intern from City College. She's studying the sex trade, and I'm going to be one of her thesis advisers." Lakisha smiled shyly at Candi, looking as if she had a bad case of hero worship, and nodded at Lydia. She didn't look very happy to have more help on the bus. Perhaps she enjoyed being the only volunteer and thought Lydia was going to steal her thunder.

"We're headed for Kent now. We always set up over by Grand Street Park. Everyone knows to look for us there."

It took a lot of cranking of gears, lurching back and forth, and chipper apologies from the front to get the bus parallel to the curb by Grand Street. Lydia used to love coming to the park, but now it was hard for her to be there. In her mind she kept seeing Glenda's body floating just below the surface. The park no longer felt like a restful safe haven.

As soon as the bus was parked, the women all leaped up and began to bustle about. Iris started rummaging in cabinets, Sarah began sorting papers onto clipboards, Lakisha started assembling a large black coffeepot, and Candi began talking on the phone. "What can I do to help?" Lydia asked, to no one in particular. She didn't want to sit and be useless.

Iris waved her back. "Come to the back and help me sort out my equipment. I never do a good job of packing it at the end of the night. We're always too exhausted."

Lydia obediently sorted sealed bags of tubes ready to take urine samples and tubes for blood, and she untangled the cords for a blood pressure machine. After a few minutes, Sarah came down to their end of the bus. "Can I borrow Lydia to help me with paperwork?"

"Certainly, dear. I'm ready for customers now."

Lydia followed Sarah to the front of the bus. A shivering teenager sat at the front. She was beautiful with her black hair scraped back from a perfect oval face. But her cat-shaped dark eyes already looked flat and dead. She might only be sixteen, but she was clearly a veteran on the streets.

"This is Josefina," Sarah said gently. "We're going to help her apply for Section Eight housing, and I'm going to call around to some shelters to see if they have any beds."

Josefina's eyes darted out onto the street. Lydia couldn't tell if she was looking for an escape route or afraid of someone who lingered outside. "I ain't decided yet." Josefina's voice was flat and lifeless, as if she had given up on hoping for a happy ending a long time ago.

Sarah smiled. "It doesn't hurt to apply. Meanwhile, I hope you won't mind if Dr. Whitfield takes a few samples of blood and urine? We want to make sure you're healthy."

Josefina shook her head. "I got a powerful itch . . . down there," she said. This was apparently the symptom that brought her to the bus. An itch "down there" would undoubtedly interfere with business. Lydia suddenly understood how the health care the bus provided was a real lifeline for these women. How else would they find out if the streets had given them any diseases? Lydia wasn't sure if Josefina was really ready to leave her life as a streetwalker, but she resolved to fill out the paperwork for Josefina as well as she could.

They were in the process of figuring out what to put down for her address and full name and salary when Iris came out and called Josefina's name.

As soon as Josefina disappeared behind the curtain, customers began coming fast and furious. The vat of coffee Lakisha kept filled to the brim attracted them, as did the doughnut holes she kept supplied on the plate, but they also clearly felt at home with the women who worked the bus. They poured out their troubles to Candi and Sarah, complaining of men in jail they couldn't visit, kids lost in the foster care system, and bad working conditions. And then one by one they went back for a little exam with Iris, ostensibly to check out a blister or strained muscle, but really to get blood and urine tests to make sure they were disease-free.

Lydia caught another quick glimpse of Josefina as she wolfed down a few doughnuts, but before she could help her finish her housing application, she was gone.

Lydia showed the application to Sarah. "We didn't have a chance to finish it before she disappeared," she complained.

"That happens a lot," Sarah said cheerfully. "We'll just hold on to it for the next time she comes by."

Lydia had to admire the women for keeping their spirits up. She found it terribly disheartening that once Josefina had received her medicine, she had hit the streets again.

In the crowded lounge filled with spandex and sparkles, Lydia tried to sort out who was who. Everyone had to sign in, and she slowly figured out that Anna was the small, delicate woman whose face was transformed by a big smile when she talked about her husband and two kids. Big Wanda was as wide as she was tall. She had skin that was a deep golden color marred by acne scars, and her hair was caught back in a long ponytail that fell halfway down her back. Princess was a slim woman in her twenties, and she was dressed tough in tight jeans and Timberland boots. She had delicate, classically beautiful features marred only by a long white scar above one of her eyebrows. Cilla was a curvy woman with a wide, flat nose that looked as if it had been broken several times. Her hair was in cornrows, and her jeans were large and baggy.

All the women appeared to be close friends, and the conversations between Candi and Big Wanda, Sarah and Princess, and everyone else were going at a mile a minute. Lydia began to lose track of who was a hooker and who was a volunteer. If everyone had been wearing bunny slippers, she would have assumed she had stumbled into a sorority. In the middle of it, Iris cajoled the women back behind the curtain for their exams, and Sarah got them to apply for WIC, housing, and literacy programs without ever disturbing the atmosphere.

But the conversation, not unexpectedly, turned to the murder of Glenda. "I say it was an ex. Ain't it always?" Big Wanda said.

"Yeah, yeah, but everyone knows . . . ," Cilla began and then broke off.

"That she was with Gator?" Princess finished. "Sure. But everyone knew she played around on her own, too. Anything for drugs."

"She didn't deserve it," Anna said, softly picking at her sleeves. "No one does."

They all nodded in agreement. No woman did. But that didn't mean it didn't happen over and over again. Violence was clearly a daily occurrence in these women's lives.

Lydia worried that if she spoke up, she would frighten them all into shutting up, but in the end she couldn't resist. "Was Glenda frightened of anything or anyone?"

Big Wanda laughed, a humorless bark from deep in her chest. "Just of missing her next fix."

"She loved her kids," Anna said. Maybe she was saying it out loud just to convince herself it was true or maybe she believed it. Lydia guessed leaving her kids with her mother constituted taking some kind of responsibility for them. "She wouldn't have wanted anything to happen to them." Anna looked around nervously, as if she was frightened of saying the wrong thing or of being overheard.

As Lydia moved to refill Anna's coffee cup, Anna's sleeve fell back to reveal a small horseshoe tattoo.

Lydia gasped. "That horseshoe! Glenda had it, too."

Anna quickly pulled down her sleeve to cover the tattoo, looking embarrassed. A silence fell over the women on the bus.

Lydia suddenly realized she should have been subtler. She'd scared Anna and the rest with her overreaction, and now they were all staring at her. "I'm sorry. I'm just curious about what it means. Is it good luck?"

"Sure didn't work that way for her." Big Wanda cracked her knuckles, and the rest of the women looked away.

Lydia opened her mouth to ask in another way when a black SUV pulled up across the street. "Damn! What's he doing here?" Big Wanda said as the women gathered by the window.

"Checking on us," Anna said. Her face had gone pale.

"Send out Cilla," Big Wanda said. "He never stays mad at his cousin."

"If he knows I'm here, he'll get mad," Cilla said, looking a little frightened herself. But under pressure from the women on the bus, she finally went out to his SUV.

"Who is it?" Lydia whispered to Sarah, peering out the window.

"Gator," Sarah said, shaking her head. "He 'permits' us to give his girls free health care, but he checks up to make sure we're not helping them get a better life."

"Is he everyone's pimp?"

"Nah. Some of them are with Sammy the Sauce, but Gator pretty much owns the rest."

"Owns? Can't they leave him if they want?"

Sarah shook her head. "He ties himself to them emotionally, taking them on when they're super young. And then he abuses them when they think of straying. He's got them all convinced that if they try to stop hooking, he'll kill them."

"Do you know if he marks them?" Lydia asked.

"The horseshoe tattoo?" Sarah had heard her exchange with Anna. "I don't know. But I wouldn't put it past him."

Lydia watched the SUV thoughtfully as Cilla spoke through the crack in the window. Gator was looking better and better as a suspect. He was mean, controlling, and violent, and considered the women his property. Maybe Glenda had gotten tired of hooking, and when Gator found out that she was leaving, he'd killed her. He had promised to do it, so it wasn't a real stretch. She was determined to find out more about Gator.

Chapter 9

Presenting the incredible Ruby!" An anonymous voice boomed from behind the curtain, breaking through the chatter at the bar of the Bank. The crowd quieted as a drumroll sounded. Lydia tore her eyes away from Jack to turn to the stage. There was a puff of smoke from a smoke machine, and Lydia's friend Ruby, dressed like Carmen Miranda, stepped onto the stage. She wore an enormous hat that looked like a fruit platter.

It was the Bank's weekly burlesque show. The Bank was a trendy art space and watering hole with a huge waterfall behind the bar. It had the stark look of a loft, appropriate since it was a former coffin factory. Hipsters had discovered stripping but only liked it if it was carefully veiled as art with a heavy dose of irony. Women of all shapes and sizes, tattooed and pierced—and even the occasional man—created an artful program that was not always about beauty but was supposed to be about attitude. It always ended with the performers taking off their clothes to the hoots and whistles of the crowd, but that was just part of the irony.

Ruby shimmied around the stage. She was a talented modern dancer but had just recently discovered burlesque. After three or four e-mails promoting her new act, Lydia had made it to the Bank to support her friend. She whistled and hollered as Ruby took off each piece of fruit provocatively and tossed it into the crowd. Ruby peeled a banana and slipped it in and out of her red lips, much to the delight of the audience. But when Ruby slipped off her frilled top and cupped her breasts, Lydia went silent. The crowd's growing frenzy suddenly bothered her. She looked over at Jack, who was whistling, and wondered if he was turned on by the display.

What made burlesque different from stripping? Intention? Placement? Payment? Lydia wasn't sure. She did know that stripping often led to prostitution when women were lured by bigger returns. And just because a hooker said she did it for fun, it didn't mean that selling her body was any less dangerous or demeaning to women. Lydia had an overwhelming urge to jump up on the stage and carry Ruby away before she finished taking off her clothes, before she somehow fell down the slippery slope. Ruby didn't need to take off her clothes to feel beautiful or desired. Someone had brainwashed her into thinking the experience was somehow empowering.

Finally the performance finished and the curtain dropped. "Let's hear it for the fabulous Ruby!" the voice boomed, and the crowd cheered. Lydia clapped for her friend, wondering how long she had to stay.

After Ruby's performance, another woman took the stage. She was dressed as a spider and was pretending to devour her prey, a life-sized male doll. The audience loved the act, especially when she began to take off her clothes. They whistled and stomped, but Lydia tuned it out, turning her back to the stage to nurse her drink. The faces of the audience had turned into grotesque caricatures to her, like Romans cheering for gladiators.

Fifteen minutes later, Ruby came out to the bar area. She had changed into jeans and a ruffled blouse. She had a glowing self-confidence that made her look especially beautiful, although her makeup was overdone because of the stage. Lydia felt bad for thinking that her show was lacking. She jumped up and gave Ruby an enthusiastic hug and introduced her to Jack.

"Great performance!" Jack said, holding Ruby's hand just a shade too long. "I always had the hots for Carmen."

"Really?" Ruby said. "Me, too." They laughed together and Ruby ordered a beer.

Lydia watched them both and felt annoyed all over again. She had to ask her question. "Don't you feel a little bit demeaned stripping?"

"Oh, Lydia," Ruby said with a laugh. "I choose to do it. It's fun. It's empowering."

"Climbing a mountain is empowering. Getting appointed head of a corporation is empowering. How come men don't see taking their clothes off as empowering?"

Jack cleared his throat while Ruby shifted in her seat. Jack put his arm around Lydia's shoulder in what felt like a paternalistic way. "Don't you think you're acting a little like a puritan?"

"Maybe. Or maybe I just have gotten to know women who sell their bodies, risk disease and violence all because they have no choice. Maybe I feel like the irony is a little like giving them the finger. We have tremendous advantages, and instead of using them to better society, we strip our clothes off in order to titillate a bar crowd. Doesn't that seem wrong to you?"

"But Lydia, it's my choice to do it," Ruby protested. "Burlesque is a lot of fun. Women who've never felt really sexy before, simply because their body types aren't considered fashionable, now have a chance to feel like a bombshell. It's their turn to be Marilyn Monroe. Now that's empowering."

Marilyn Monroe had died of a drug overdose, alone and depressed. Wanting to replicate her life seemed more than a little depressing to Lydia. She didn't want to sound like a party pooper, but it seemed as if there should have been a better outcome to the feminist movement than college girls wanting to ape impoverished and exploited sex workers.

Lydia took a sip from her drink. She felt outnumbered, but she wasn't finished yet. "How is burlesque really that different from stripping?"

"It's not just taking off your clothes or doing a lap dance. It tells a story with a beginning, middle, and end. It's ironic and silly and beautiful all at the same time. Weren't you even watching?"

"I'm sure a feminist theoretician could write a thesis about that other performer who did the whole spider-eating-the-man act. That was frightening," Jack said with a fake shudder and a laugh.

Lydia frowned. Considering there was a whole industry for men who wanted to be humiliated and whipped by sexual objects, she didn't think the idea was that original. She was also annoyed at Jack for being such a guy about the whole thing. He was supposed to be on her side. She didn't expect him to agree with her about everything, but she could have used a little moral support.

Ruby was called away by another table of friends, and she gave them an absentminded wave as she left. Lydia was probably going to have to apologize to her tomorrow for attacking her art form. She didn't mean to make her feel bad. She just wanted to work out the swirling confusion in her brain about the hookers she had met.

Suddenly the air felt stale and close inside. The show was about to start again, and Lydia had no desire to see more. "I'm ready to go. Are you?" Lydia asked, standing up.

"What's the rush?" Jack complained. "I was going to order another beer."

"I need some air," Lydia said. She grabbed her purse. Without watching to see if he was following she went out the door. She knew it was rude, but she had to get out.

Outside, the air was steamy, but at least fresh. She filled her lungs with oxygen and felt her brain clear. She leaned against the wall and waited. She was mad, but she wouldn't leave without Jack. She would give him a chance to say he was sorry for not listening to her argument.

Down the block she saw two women in high heels wobbling along on the sidewalk. A dark SUV slowed down next to them, checking them out. It accelerated ahead toward Lydia, then slowed down in front of where Lydia stood. Lydia grimaced. The driver thought she was a hooker. She wasn't dressed particularly provocatively, and she certainly wasn't strutting around. But she was a woman alone, and on a dark side street, so the driver had concluded that she was available for purchase. The scenario played itself over and over again across the world.

Lydia wondered what she would do if the driver spoke to her. Laugh? Yell? Call 911? She didn't have a chance, though, because the door to the Bank opened and Jack came out. He put an arm around her waist, and the car accelerated out of sight. The driver of the SUV had seen she was "taken" by another man and not available. She felt both relieved and angry.

Behind the car she saw a blue sedan inch along and was surprised to catch a glimpse of Frankie D'Angelo at the wheel. What was he doing here? Then it hit her. Frankie was following the errant husband. Patricia's husband, Al Savarese, had just checked her out—he had been the man in the dark SUV.

Chapter 10

Stuck in a long line of cars on the Long Island Expressway in ninety-five-degree heat with no air-conditioning would make anyone grumpy, Lydia reasoned. She and Jack had been sniping ever since they had jumped into his car for a getaway weekend at the beach house of some friends of Jack. She was still a little mad at him for not backing her up last night at Ruby's performance. And in the light of the day, her overreaction to the burlesque seemed overblown.

They had planned to leave early Saturday morning to avoid traffic and the worst of the heat, but somehow they had gotten off to a very slow start. Jack had to run some errands and buy wine for their hosts. Lydia had to pack and decide what on earth to bring. She imagined brokers were slightly more conservative than Williamsburg artists, and she didn't want to look like an exotic bird among sparrows. At the same time, she didn't want to dress like a preppie. Besides, she didn't own any J. Crew, Land's End, or Eddie Bauer kind of clothes. So she just went for simple, clean lines. She had a pretty yellow sundress that tied around her neck and came discreetly to her knee. She packed her jean skirt, a few cotton blouses that she thought looked okay and didn't appear to have any noticeable holes.

Lydia was not a huge fan of the beach. She liked the idea of getting out of town and cooling off. But she hated the sand and disliked swimming in the ocean. She had seen *Jaws* at a particularly impressionable age and found it disconcerting to always be searching the water for any sign of a fin. She also was suspicious that New York's sewers were dumping into the ocean, and thus always felt dirty.

Nonetheless, Lydia was looking forward to escaping Williamsburg, oppressively hot and sticky in the summer, and to looking at something else for a few days. Summers in the city were a cacophony of sounds—ice-cream truck tunes, loud salsa music, car alarms, honking horns, and yelling. And there was also a mix of horrible smells. The trash began to stink as soon as it left the building. Everything was overripe. And riding the subway meant being mashed up against someone else's strong body odor.

A quick glance at Jack revealed the heat and traffic were darkening his mood. Although they had cheerful music on the iPod, he was cursing under his breath and making ridiculous moves to change lanes. Clearly no one was going anywhere fast. Lydia's last overture to stop for a bite to eat was soundly rejected. She had resigned herself to silence and spent the next half an hour looking outside the window wishing they were there already.

Inexplicably, just as suddenly as the traffic had snarled, it opened up after an entrance to a mall. Could all these people be going shopping? A hot summer day at the mall eating Cinnabons and watching a movie in air-conditioned splendor sounded more appealing than a traffic jam on the LIE, Lydia had to admit.

"Tell me about your friends that we're staying with. You knew them in college?"

Jack nodded. "Chad and I met freshman year. He works in finance, too—just with a different firm. And Adam and I got to be friends through Chad."

Lydia admired how Jack juggled his art life and his work life. It must be hard to be with people all day who didn't think that art was a particularly admirable occupation. Sometimes Lydia wondered how Jack did it. She thought that she would probably become too schizoid. It was hard enough to get her photography done after working with the D'Angelos all day, and her job had nowhere near the intensity or responsibility that Jack's did.

"And their girlfriends will be there, too?" Lydia wasn't particularly concerned about the guys, but the women worried her a bit. She would probably end up hanging out with them, and the weekend had the potential to evolve into her worst memories of junior high. Popular girls usually didn't like girls who were smart.

Jack shrugged. "Probably. I haven't met the latest."

That meant Chad and Adam were serial daters. Not good news. It would have been nice if one of them had been married or at least in a long-term relationship. Lydia was trying to keep an open mind, but she was beginning to wonder what the group would be like.

After following some very confusing directions through some quaint Hampton townships, they at last pulled up in front of a "beach house." It looked like a normal suburban house and appeared to be quite far from the beach. A BMW and a Mercedes were parked outside.

Sweaty and hot, Lydia and Jack hefted their bags and a few bags of groceries out of the car. The ocean had never sounded so good to her.

She was dying to put on a bikini and lower her core temperature by twenty degrees.

The house was quiet when they entered the unlocked front door. "Hello!" Jack called out.

"Maybe they went to the beach," Lydia said, but Jack barged upstairs without listening. Lydia went into the kitchen and began to put away some of the food and wine. She heard a murmur of voices a few minutes later.

Jack entered the kitchen a few minutes later, followed by a tall, handsome guy with a blond crew cut. "Lydia, this is Adam."

"Hi, it's nice to meet you."

"Likewise," Adam said, shaking her hand with exactly the right amount of pressure and lingering on the eye contact just enough to make her feel comfortable. The guy was smooth. "We were just having a siesta. Late night at the clubs last night."

"You dogs. You couldn't wait for us?" Jack grinned.

"You should totally have come yesterday," Adam said. "This place is unreal."

"It looks gorgeous," Lydia said. "Thanks for having us."

"No prob. The girls should be down in a sec."

"I want to go the beach and try out my new board," Jack said. "Have you been out yet?"

"Nope. It was dark by the time we got here. Let me show you where you're staying." Adam led them down the hallway to a small back bedroom. It was neat and clean, and Lydia felt cooler and calmer by the second.

"Get changed and we'll hit the beach." Adam yawned and disappeared.

Lydia reached over and gave Jack a big kiss. "I'm sorry I was so grumpy."

"Isn't this place great?" Jack enthused. "I can't wait to get in the ocean."

Lydia changed into her 1950s-looking bikini—brown-and-white-striped boy shorts and a halter top. She tied a brown patterned sarong around her waist and put together a quick beach bag: sunscreen, a paperback of *Lady Chatterley's Lover,* a hat, and a beach towel. Then she slipped into some sandals.

When they came out into the kitchen, the whole gang had assembled. Lydia quickly met Sarah, a tall, skinny blonde with a deep tan, Carrie, a small brunette with a curvy figure, and Chad, a handsome, stocky guy who looked like he might be Hawaiian or Filipino. Everyone was friendly, and Lydia quickly relaxed. On their way to the beach (which turned out to be about four blocks away), Lydia learned that Carrie worked in marketing, and Sarah was an executive assistant.

At the beach, the guys all plunged into the water with surfboards while the girls sunned themselves and talked. "How long have you known Jack?" Carrie asked.

"Only about six weeks."

"Wow. Chad talks about him all the time. He was kind of a lady-killer in college."

Lydia was not surprised, but she wondered what the point of the conversation was exactly. She couldn't decide if it was to make her feel good or bad about dating him.

"How long have you known Chad?" Lydia countered.

"Six months. No ring yet," Carrie said cheerfully, but her eyes looked a little desperate.

Carrie appeared to be one of those women with marriage on their minds. Lydia wouldn't mind getting married someday, but she had determined a long time ago that she didn't need a man to make her happy. "Have you guys talked about marriage?"

"Oh, no. But I've dropped lots of hints." Carrie said, checking her tan line under her microscopic black bikini.

"I think Adam might propose soon," Sarah said, examining her fingernails.

"Really?" Carrie squealed. "How do you know?"

"I think he took one of my rings to get it measured the other day. I pretended not to notice."

Lydia hoped it was true, for Sarah's sake. But she could see lots of other explanations for a missing ring. It could have fallen down behind something and gotten lost, for example.

Marriage was something, in her eyes, that should be discussed. Marriage was a partnership, not a fairy tale. And too many women got caught up in the trappings of marriage instead of seeing it as something that would be challenging. They focused on the ring, the gown, and the wedding but didn't think about who was going to do the dishes, earn the money, and raise the kids.

Did Lydia daydream about marriage? Sure, but then she got over it. It would be nice to have someone to lean on. It was, she corrected herself, nice to have a boyfriend to lean on these days. But she wasn't anxious to jump into something neither she nor Jack were ready for and become yet another statistic.

Jack came out of the water and hollered up the beach. "Come on in—the water is great!" Sarah and Carrie shook their heads, but Lydia got up gratefully and went to the water. She still needed to cool off.

Later that night, stuffed full of lobster and wine, Lydia laid her head companionably against Jack's shoulder and listened to the conversation swirl around her. It was nice to be out of the city and hear the sounds of a country summer evening. She could smell the sea in the air combined with the sharp smell of mowed grass. They had gone outside after dinner to look at the stars, and Lydia had been amazed at how many there were in the sky. She had become used to the city sky with barely Orion visible and often just the moon.

She felt a strong sense of relief that made her body feel relaxed. She had met Jack's friends and they seemed to like her. Jack had met Georgia Rae and they had gotten along. Their relationship was going okay. Maybe, just maybe, they would make it.

Chapter 11

I'm the client, and I want some results!" Mama D'Angelo had swooped in on them first thing on Monday morning, suspecting that they were not doing everything in their power to help Patricia. Frankie and Leo's reports and photographs, out of focus and underexposed, did not appease her.

"But Mama," Leo whined, "I followed him around for hours. It's hard to get good pictures in the dark."

Frankie mulishly crossed his arms. "I'm not going to do it again, either." The brothers were both reverting back to their two-year-old selves. Lydia rolled her eyes discreetly behind the computer monitor.

"What will I tell Rose? Patricia needs evidence, not attitude!" Mama watched too many daytime talk shows on TV. It was funny to hear her use psychobabble with an Italian accent.

Lydia took a deep breath. She could see this was her big chance. If she wanted to return to the waterfront and find out what was happening, she had to act now. "I'm sure I could get some good photographs for her," she said. "I've done night photography before."

Leo and Frankie turned and glared at her. Lydia had just disobeyed and gone to a higher power, which was not acceptable in their eyes. "We said it was too dangerous—"

Mama cut Leo off with a wave of her hand. She leaned closer to Lydia. The smell of garlic on her breath was particularly strong today. "You are a good photographer. But the waterfront is not safe for a girl alone."

Lydia remembered the card she had saved from Emmanuel, the car service driver, who had offered to be her private chauffeur in just such a circumstance. She pulled the card out of the side pocket of her bag and waved it.

"What if I hired a guy to drive me and hang out with me at night? If anything happened, he'd be able to provide some muscle."

"Who? Your boyfriend?" Mama had met Jack once and had been very impressed. He had been dressed for work in his broker suit and tie. Mama had fawned over him in a way that had been highly embarrassing, rolling her eyes at Lydia and pinching her arm. Lydia had half expected her to ask his intentions to her or something.

"No. He's a car service driver who wants to be a private eye. He's street-savvy, and he would make sure I was never alone." At least Lydia assumed he was. She was also pretty sure she could take care of herself, too. She'd done a pretty good job for the last twenty-eight years.

Leo scowled at her, but Mama clapped her hands with glee. "That sounds perfect!"

"Mama, we don't come over to the restaurant and order your dishwashers to do the bookkeeping . . . ," Leo began, flaring his nostrils.

"But I am the client, Leo," Mama said sweetly, patting Leo's hand.

She had clearly forgotten they were working for her for free. Or at least just for lasagna and cannoli barter. "And I demand satisfaction. I think Lydia will do a beautiful job, and she will stay safe with this gentleman helping her."

Lydia suddenly got nervous now that the case was within her grasp. "Let me see how much he'll charge. I doubt it would be much since he wanted to work a stakeout. And I could even call in regularly to someone if you want to make sure that I'm okay."

Mama nodded enthusiastically, so Lydia grabbed the phone to call Emmanuel before Leo could protest. Emmanuel was available, he was eager, and he was willing to work for a measly sum.

When Leo heard how cheap it would be, he reluctantly caved. After all, the case wasn't for a paying client but for family. However, he was still full of advice. "Don't get out of the car. Don't let him see you following him. Just record where he goes and try to get as many shots of him as possible."

"Got it." Lydia knew her job was to smile and nod. The D'Angelos felt uncomfortable, and she had to make them feel like it was going to be okay. But she really couldn't see how she could do a worse job than they had done. They had a bunch of dark shots that any divorce lawyer could have dismissed in seconds.

A more difficult task was telling Jack about her new case. They were back to being happy after they had made up in a satisfying way at the beach house. They had never really talked about Lydia's discomfort over burlesque or his enthusiasm for it, and Lydia had tried to shake off her discontent. She had had a good time with his friends and felt that he had made a big effort to make her feel included. They weren't going to agree about everything, so it was best for her to let it go. She decided to overwhelm him with her enthusiasm for the new project until he could only be happy for her.

She called him on his office phone. She could picture his tiny cubicle on the thirtieth floor of the brokerage exactly since she had been by once to see it. He had a photograph of a gorgeous waterfall pinned up on the gray cubicle wall next to his computer, and unfortunately that was as much of a view as he was going to get for a while. Lydia hoped he kept his priorities straight and stayed unambitious at work. If he embraced the late hours and the generous bonuses at the brokerage house and tried to make vice president, she was pretty sure it would ruin his artistic career.

"I can't make it tonight for drinks. But you'll never guess why!"

"You've got another date?" Jack asked dryly. She heard people talking in the background. She wondered if his coworkers were listening in. She hoped Jack wasn't trying to show off for them.

"No, silly. The D'Angelos are sending me out on a stakeout!" Her voice sounded artificially bubbly to her own ears.

"At night?"

"This guy picks up prostitutes and his wife wants proof so she can dump him. I'm going to follow him and take pictures."

Lydia could hear Jack breathing on the line. Lydia guessed he was thinking of the best way to express his misgivings without bursting her bubbliness. "That sounds . . . unsafe."

"I know what you're thinking. But I'm hiring a car service driver to drive me around all night, and I'll stay in the car the whole time. It's totally perfect for my new series."

Jack probably had a million questions but didn't know where to begin. "How late are you going to be?"

Lydia tried to imagine how long Al could go. She really had no idea how old he was or if he took Viagra. "I'm not sure. Leo was out until three-ish last night."

"I don't like the sound of this. . . . "

"Well," Lydia said, trying to sound conciliatory, "if you want, I can call in regularly to let you know that I'm okay."

"That would help." Jack sounded relieved. "I would hate for anything to happen to you, sweetheart. And I'd offer to go with you, but . . ."

"But you have to work tomorrow, I know," she said. "It's okay. I'll be fine." Lydia reached out and couldn't resist knocking on wood.

Chapter 12

Preparing for a stakeout was a little like planning for a jungle expedition or a trip to the North Pole, depending on the climate. Thirst, hunger, a full bladder, and getting too cold or hot all had the potential to make a detective bail out and endanger the assignment. Running out of batteries on her phone or camera also could be a potential problem she needed to prevent. Lydia began by filling up a large bag with all sorts of essentials. She sacrificed her flair for fashion and instead grabbed comfortable layers from her closet: a pair of brown pants with big pockets, a cotton shirt, and comfortable black Converse high-tops.

Emmanuel pulled up in front of her building promptly at six. She slipped into the backseat clutching a bag containing her camera, notebook, snacks, and water. Emmanuel turned back in his seat and gave her a big grin.

"Where to first, Ms. Fletcher?"

Lydia grinned back, even though she knew she was nothing like

Angela Lansbury. She was excited, too. She was finally going to follow someone, and it felt like uncharted territory. "We need to head over to Al's house in Jackson Heights. The D'Angelos said he always comes home from work and grabs his car before he goes out on the prowl."

Emmanuel steered the car out into traffic. "Oh, man. He must be crazy, sleeping with hookers when he is married. My girlfriend would kill me if she caught me messing around."

Lydia wondered what Emmanuel's girlfriend was like, and what she thought about the stakeout. "Some people like to live on the edge. And if everyone was a law-abiding citizen, we wouldn't have very much business at work."

"True, true." Emmanuel paused briefly at a red light, but when the other direction looked clear he continued straight on red. As she clutched the door handle, Lydia was starting to have a few doubts about Emmanuel's driving ability. But it was too late tonight to make another plan.

"Hey, remember to drive carefully, okay? We can't afford to get stopped for a ticket. It would call too much attention to our stakeout."

Emmanuel glanced back and grinned at her in the rearview mirror. "I thought private eyes broke the law all the time."

"Only the ones who go to jail." Lydia grimaced and shut her eyes briefly as he turned onto Meserole Street in front of a speeding garbage truck. But soon afterward they screeched to a stop behind a long line of traffic waiting to get on the highway. The BQE, the snaking highway that connects Brooklyn to Queens, was bumper-to-bumper as usual. She was a little relieved to not be moving, but also anxious about missing Al's departure.

"I go to jail, I get deported," Emmanuel said, shaking his head. "A friend of mine got caught with less than an ounce of ganja, and he's back in Kingston for good. They don't mess around."

Lydia had heard that they were cracking down on illegal immigrants and even shipping young people who had been in the United States since they were small children back to their country of citizenship if they broke the law. It was extreme justice, but bureaucracy rarely operated with moderation. The country was glad to see extreme criminals go, but to kick out hardworking folks for minor offenses seemed ridiculous.

She fished around in her bag until she found her notebook. She opened it to the first page and started her log for the evening. She wrote, "Picked up at 6 P.M." She would make a note of their arrival time when they got to Al's house. After she was done with her log, she would type it up and deliver it to Mama's cousin Rose with the photographs she had taken. She hoped it would give Patricia a clear picture of her husband's movements, and would become evidence that could be presented in court.

Al lived in a suburban area of Queens with small 1950s-era houses. The neighborhood had changed over the years as immigrants had moved in, and the group of kids playing basketball in the driveway of one of the houses resembled a miniature United Nations. "It's number 15437," Lydia said, leaning forward over the seat. "When you see it, just drive by slowly. We'll find a place where we can safely watch the house."

Finally, she spotted the correct address. As they cruised slowly past, Lydia scanned the small white house with lacy molding and a wide driveway. The yard looked a little bereft without a collection of toys and bikes like the neighbors had, and neither Al nor Patricia Savarese appeared to be avid gardeners. The bushes leaned sadly, as if they hadn't had a good stiff drink in a long time, and the grass had large bare patches. The Savareses' matching Ford Explorer SUVs sat in the driveway, one maroon and the other dark green. They clearly weren't lacking the cash to hire a gardener, so they must really not care.

"Good. He hasn't left yet."

"Where should I park?" Emmanuel asked as he inched forward.

"Go down to the end of the block and do a U-turn. We'll park across the street, farther down, in front of that house without a car."

Emmanuel looked back and forth like he was nervous. The suburbs, even when they were within city limits, did that to people sometimes. Hanging around in a car on her block would be no problem, but the suburbs had organizations like a neighborhood watch that inspired residents to call the cops when they saw suspicious people, especially persons of color with dreads who appeared to be casing a house.

They did a turn and pulled up in front of a small brick house across the street. It had a FOR SALE sign in the yard and looked empty. "Perfect," Lydia said, satisfied. "If anyone asks, I'm waiting for a realtor to show me this place." She took out her camera, turned it on, and waited.

"What do we do now?" Emmanuel shifted in his seat and turned around to look at her.

"We wait for Al to go out." She couldn't wait to nab him, then wave the pictures triumphantly in the D'Angelos' faces. They hadn't been able to get anything, but she was going to get amazing shots of the adulterer.

Emmanuel put back his seat and got comfortable. He turned the radio on low to a reggae station. But Lydia sat up straight, alert for any movement. The D'Angelos had reported that Al was a creature of habit, and left the house at almost the same time every day.

After twenty minutes of staring at Al's house, Lydia was beginning to feel a little fatigued. She checked the time on her cell phone for the thirtieth time, wondering if he would pick this night of all nights not to go out on the town. It would be a bummer to have come all this way and not be able to get any photos. Maybe he had even started to suspect he was being followed and had decided to change his ways.

At last she saw a man come out of the house. He was of medium height with dark hair and a potbelly. He was wearing a white T-shirt and jeans. He didn't even glance in their direction, just hopped into the maroon SUV.

"There he is!" Lydia tapped the seat. Emmanuel sat up and brought his seat upright. He quickly started the car as the SUV backed out of the driveway and headed down the street toward them. Lydia instinctively scrunched down in her seat, but she caught a quick glimpse of his face as he went by. As a kid he'd had a bad case of acne that had left scarring, and he had those eyebrows that looked like one continuous line of hair.

Lydia straightened up, feeling a little silly. Al didn't know her, and there was no reason for him to recognize her. "Turn around and follow him. But not too close."

"Got it," Emmanuel said as he quickly pulled out, did a three-point turn, and sped off after Al. At first Lydia thought they'd lost him, but then she caught a glimpse of maroon as the SUV made a quick right. Like most New Yorkers, Al drove fast and didn't use turn signals. He was going to be hard to follow.

"There he goes. Turn right up there." Lydia pointed. Emmanuel turned, sped up a little, and nearly caught up with the SUV. Lydia felt a surge of panic. "Drop back! Drop back! We don't want him to see us."

Emmanuel slowed down and allowed another car service driver to butt in between his car and Al's. Lydia sat back and relaxed for a moment. She reminded herself that one car service car looked very much like another. They were almost all dark colored and always seemed to be Lincolns. If Al looked back, he would think they were just another car service car following him and hopefully wouldn't connect them with the car parked on his street.

Al drove back roads all the way to Greenpoint, avoiding a backup on the BQE. Some of the back roads that wound through tiny wooden row houses and sprawling warehouses were almost devoid of traffic. He picked up speed, but they had to let him get farther ahead so he wouldn't notice them.

Emmanuel reached up to adjust his rearview mirror. "Uh-oh," he said under his breath.

"What's the matter?"

"We're being followed."

"What?" Lydia turned and craned her neck. She saw a few cars behind them, but nothing that seemed menacing.

"There's a red Volkswagen Beetle that's been on our tail since Queens."

Lydia spotted the Beetle weaving in and out of traffic behind them and frowned. "Why would someone be following us?"

Chapter 13

The red Volkswagen looked completely harmless, but somehow that made Lydia even more suspicious. A black Cadillac would have invoked shades of mobsters gunning from the windows and might have caused her to call off the expedition. But a red Volkswagen was the kind of car favored not by dangerous hit men but by blond sorority sisters at the University of Dayton. It was the kind of car you could imagine someone trying to stuff a hundred clowns into for comic effect. A happy car.

They could be following Al, too, and she wondered who else would be interested in him. Another relative of Patricia's who had become suspicious? An enemy of his who was also after photos? A jealous mistress? But then she remembered how protective the D'Angelos had been of her. They didn't think she could handle the assignment at all. Their mother had insisted that they give her a chance, but they were reluctant up until the end. Perhaps they had decided to follow her to make sure she stayed safe.

She should have been touched by the thought of the D'Angelos' concern, but instead she was annoyed. She didn't like to be second-guessed or have her actions double-checked for no reason except that she was a woman. She had taken a self-defense class with a real hard-ass named Martina, and she knew that when push came to shove, she could probably do some damage to someone's kneecaps. And she was smart enough to call the cops when a situation got dangerous. After all, she had a homicide detective in her cell's phone book. Lydia turned around and glared at the car. As if sensing her anger, the car dropped back slightly. She was unable to tell who was driving, Leo or Frankie.

"He's slowing down." Emmanuel sounded a little on edge. Lydia turned back to face front. Al pulled over to the edge of the road in Greenpoint where some scantily dressed ladies were showing their wares at dusk next to a desolate overgrown lot.

"Whatever you do, don't rear-end him," she warned. Emmanuel slowed down quickly. "Just drive past slowly. We'll pull up a little farther along and hopefully he won't suspect we're following him."

Emmanuel snorted but drove slowly past. Her mind off the Beetle, Lydia put her camera up to her eye and took several quick shots of Al's car and the ladies coming up to it. Two of the women—one in tight stonewashed denim from head to toe, and the other in a red leather dress that left little to the imagination—approached Al's SUV. The light was pretty bright, and she could make out their garishly made-up faces through the viewfinder.

Emmanuel pulled up half a block away, next to a small apartment building with a broken banister on the stairs and a peeling paint job. She hoped no one would question them there.

Lydia guessed they might look a little suspicious, but she hoped Al was so focused on the hookers he wasn't watching for a car service car.

And certainly not for one to have followed him all the way from Queens. He very likely didn't suspect that his wife was on to him.

Lydia turned around and knelt on the seat and in rapid succession snapped another ten shots of Al and the hookers. The photos she was getting certainly weren't going to be enough to prove infidelity, but it might make him feel guilty enough to give his wife everything she asked for. She then previewed them quickly in the camera to make sure they were in focus. It was a difficult to tell what was going on. She supposed Al could say to the judge he was lost and was just asking for directions. She hoped she could get a shot of a hooker jumping into his car. When she lowered the camera and waited for them to do something else, she was relieved to see that the red Volkswagen was nowhere in sight. Maybe it was just a lost coed after all.

The ladies were either too ugly or too expensive for Al because he peeled away from the curb alone a few minutes later. The one in denim gave him the finger. Lydia didn't blame her. She ducked down quickly as Al went roaring by.

Emmanuel slammed the car's gearshift into drive and would have sped after him if Lydia hadn't shouted, "Slowly, slowly!" Emmanuel waited a second and then pulled out leisurely from the curb. With any luck, it would look as if he had just received a call from the dispatch and was now on his way to pick up a customer.

Al drove erratically down the street, slowing down for single ladies and accelerating whenever the road got busy. But the fact that he seemed oblivious to anyone but his quarry, and impervious to the honking horns of other cars, made it possible to follow him with impunity. Once in Williamsburg, Lydia could guess more easily where he was going, and even suggest shortcuts so they could meet Al on the other side rather than staying on his tail the whole time. The hookers were generally by the bridge and the water, so Emmanuel swung around and waited for Al to pass by. When he did, they picked him up again. This time, though, they appeared to have picked up an SUV as their tail.

"Who's that?" Emmanuel asked, checking the rearview mirror.

"I don't know," Lydia said. She wondered if the new tail was another figment of her imagination, or if the red Volkswagen had known it was spotted and bailed for another car. She was too new at the whole business of tailing and stakeouts to really know the ropes. She hoped she could get some tags off the dark colored SUV behind them. She preferred to have some proof before she confronted the D'Angelos about their mother-hen behavior. Or find out who else could be tailing her.

"He's slowing down again," Emmanuel said. He slowed down, too. He was picking up her strategy quickly, and Lydia was glad he was the one driving her. They sailed past Candi's rainbow bus, and Lydia suppressed the urge to wave at her new friends. It looked like they had a few customers already.

Three women stood on the corner of Kent and North Fourth Street. They all looked Latina, and each was wearing clothing that screamed hooker: a red micro mini, tight leopard-print pants and stilettos, and a black leather dress. Al jerked his wheel to the right and pulled up next to the women at the curb. The smallest one in the red mini was already swaying her way to Al's door as Emmanuel and Lydia slipped quietly past. Lydia took photographs as they drove by, hoping again she was getting something good. The woman's hair covered her face so Lydia couldn't tell what she looked like.

"Pull around the corner where he won't see us," she whispered to Emmanuel. "I think he's found himself a keeper."

Emmanuel signaled and turned left. They could still see Al's car, but she couldn't see enough to get a good shot. Fortunately, Al made his selection quickly and drove off with the small one in the red mini-skirt. The corner was a little too public even for him to have sex.

"They're moving!" Lydia cried out, and Emmanuel did a quick il-legal maneuver that would definitely have alerted Al to their presence if he were paying attention at all. Luckily for them, he seemed to be so focused on his libido that he was oblivious. He hung a left onto a side street, then took another left onto Berry Street. They were headed north again to Greenpoint. Lydia was so preoccupied with keeping track of Al that she forgot to look for the SUV tailing them for several blocks. When she did scope out the rearview mirror she wasn't sure if it was still following them or not. The streets were now getting dark, illuminated by headlights and the occasional streetlight.

About nine blocks later, Al apparently decided that the streets were deserted enough and pulled onto a side street next to a new condo development. Lydia guessed that his hobby was going to become more difficult in a few years when all the condos were built and oc-cupied. She wasn't looking forward to the overcrowding of the neigh-borhood, but that one side effect cheered her considerably.

"Should I get right behind him?" Emmanuel asked as he slowed down.

"No. It'll only spook him. He's looking for a quiet place to knock boots. Stay around the corner and I'll go back on foot."

Emmanuel did as he was told and pulled up quietly and efficiently. He turned in the driver's seat to watch Lydia as she readied her cam-era. She planned to rest the camera on top of her purse, hidden under a flap. She hoped to just reach inside and take a photograph without being too obvious.

"What if he spots you?"

Lydia was nervous about that, too. "Hopefully I'll look like I'm just out for a walk."

"But what if he sees you taking pictures?" Emmanuel sounded truly concerned. He was taking the bodyguard portion of his job seriously.

"I'll run as fast as I can back to the car," Lydia assured him. "And I'll wave my arm if I need you to come rescue me."

The answer appeared to satisfy him. "Okay. Wave your arm if you need help. I'll be watching."

Lydia wanted Emmanuel to feel that he was a special part of the team. "Thanks, Emmanuel. You've been doing great so far. I really appreciate you coming out with me."

Emmanuel gave her a big grin. "Are you kidding? This scene is totally cool."

Lydia smiled as she opened the car door and got out. It was definitely the right move to hire someone who wanted to be a private eye.

The humidity and heat outside was shocking after the air-conditioning in the car. It took her a minute to catch her breath.

She casually looked behind her to check the street for the SUV but didn't see any sign of it. There were vans, cars, and SUVs of other colors, but not one like she'd seen following her earlier. Satisfied, she fished in her pocket for a scrap of paper and pretended to study it as she walked. She hoped she looked like someone who was searching for an address. She crossed the street and first walked down the side opposite Al's car. She stopped across from his car, studied her paper, and reached into her bag with her other hand to press the button on her camera. It was set for a long exposure because of the darkness, and she didn't use a flash so she wouldn't alert Al to her presence. She had to stay still so the photograph would be in focus. She tried not to look directly at the car, but from the corner of her eye she could see that it was rocking rhythmically.

Lydia walked down the block a little way, crossed the street, then walked back toward Al's car. She had scooted her bag to rest on her stomach and stopped repeatedly to take a few shots as she pretended to study the paper. Next to the car was a small building. Lydia went up and knocked on the door, hoping the occupants were all out. If they answered she would ask for someone who she knew didn't live there. She stepped back to study the address and took another two photos of the car as she pretended to survey the street.

She felt exposed standing right by the car, so she walked away from Al's car and away from Emmanuel so she could do another circuit on the block. She was lingering near a small alley when she suddenly felt someone watching her. Lydia froze and felt a trickle of sweat on the small of her back. She turned slowly around, wondering if Emmanuel would spot her if she waved. Just then, a small black-and-white tuxedo cat trotted out of the alley. She let out the breath she was holding. It was only a cat.

The cat came up to Lydia and meowed. She smiled and relaxed the tension in her shoulders. He was small but friendly, and he wound around her legs like she was his only friend in the world.

"You're probably hungry, huh?" She reached down and petted him. He purred and butted his head against her hand. His black fur felt soft and looked shiny, and his stomach and all four of his paws looked like they had been dipped in white frosting.

She'd never had a cat or a dog when she was growing up because her father had been allergic. And as an adult, they always seemed to be a liability if you were interested in moving to another apartment or traveling. She liked animals but had never seen the point in sharing her living space with one. She had hundreds of items of clothing in her apartment, and each one was precious to her. She would hate to see a cat ruin something irreplaceable.

She gave the cat another pat and continued on her way. But the cat refused to let her go. He trotted along next to her, meowing hopefully.

She was afraid he would call attention to her presence and blow her cover.

"Go home," she whispered to him. He paid no attention and rubbed against her leg. He didn't have a collar and looked really skinny. "I've got to go. I'm sorry."

Lydia decided to cross the street and hope that he went back to where he lived on his own. She was stepping into the street when the cat suddenly let out a strange shrieking meow and ran in front of her legs to dash underneath a nearby parked car. She stopped to see what was wrong with the cat just as an SUV hurtled out of nowhere and came just inches from hitting her as it sped down the street.

Chapter 14

Lydia twisted and jumped back onto the sidewalk, trying to get away from the vehicle. The SUV did not stop but continued zooming down the block. She stayed down between the cars where she fell, taking stock of her injuries. She had probably bruised her shin when she'd fallen across the curb, and the palms of her hands burned from getting scraped against the concrete. Anger boiled up inside her at the driver of the SUV. Had he not seen her? Or had had he been aiming for her?

If she had stepped out any farther into the street without looking, she would have been killed. She didn't think it was an accident. It looked like the same SUV that had been following her before. If so, who wanted to kill her? She knew the D'Angelos had no reason to run her down, so it must be someone with a grudge. She wondered if it could be Gator. He drove a black SUV and may have heard that she was asking questions about him.

She got up slowly a few minutes later, making sure the coast was clear. The cat that had warned her so kindly now appeared out from underneath one of the cars and rubbed against her again. He seemed to be inquiring how she was feeling.

"Thanks for the heads-up," Lydia whispered, petting him behind the ears. He meowed softly. He looked hungry and didn't have a collar. She wondered how he was surviving on the streets of Williamsburg. It must be tough for a small cat. She felt as if she owed him something for warning her that the car was coming. She picked him up and he relaxed in her arms. She decided she would take him to a shelter where he would be warm and well fed and they would find someone who wanted a kitty at their house.

"Good kitty, nice kitty," she told him as she walked back to Emmanuel's car. She was limping slightly and still feeling angry.

As she slid into the seat, Emmanuel looked at her, surprised. "What's that?"

"A Good Samaritan kitty," she told him. "I nearly got run over by an SUV, but the cat warned me. Did you see the car?"

Emmanuel shook his head. "Next time I think I should come with you. I couldn't see anything from inside the car. And it's too dangerous."

"If there is a next time," Lydia said. She was regretfully beginning to agree with the D'Angelos. Stakeouts were dangerous. Her knee ached. She was tired from the tension of waiting and trying to get good photographs. It was late.

"Did you get good pictures?"

For a moment Lydia had forgotten all about Al and his new friend. They were presumably still in Al's car. "I don't know. I'll have to check when I get home."

She had forgotten all about calling and checking in with Jack, too. There were two messages on her cell phone on the seat. He must be worried. She didn't bother listening to the messages but called Jack immediately.

"Where are you?" He sounded more concerned than angry.

"On Wythe, not far from home."

"How did it go?"

"Okay. But I'm exhausted." Her near-death experience with the SUV was too hard to explain on the phone. She still felt shaken.

"Do you want me to come over?"

Suddenly she did want him to come over very much. She wanted to banish the images of cheap sex and violence that kept running through her brain. She wanted someone to minister to her hurts and hold her tight. "If it wouldn't be too much trouble." Her voice sounded pathetic even to her own ears. She cleared her throat and tried again. "I seem to have acquired a cat and have no food or litter."

"A cat?" Jack sounded baffled. Lydia was baffled, too.

"I'll take him to a shelter tomorrow, but I need to put him up for the night."

"I'll bring some food over. But you can make a litter box with just a cardboard box and some shredded newspaper."

Jack was such a handy boyfriend. She knew nothing about cats except that they were pretty self-sufficient and didn't need to be walked. "Thanks. I'll see you at my apartment then."

Emmanuel drove her up to her front doorstep, and she counted out his earnings for the evening. "You did a great job tonight. Thanks again for all your help."

He took the money and studied it for a moment. "I would have done it for free, you know."

Lydia smiled. "We have a paying client, and I think we both earned the cash tonight."

She wished him good night and carried the cat carefully in her arms. Walking through the scarred door of her large brick tenement building, she was surprised at how calm the cat was. He looked around with curiosity but appeared willing to go with her anywhere. She felt honored to be trusted so completely by another being. Perhaps his instincts, which had kept him alive so far, had taught him to know who to trust and who not to.

Lydia wondered if she should tiptoe past her super's door. She couldn't remember the rules for animals in her building, but she knew her neighbor had a cat, so she hoped she wouldn't get into any trouble for violating her lease. The last thing she needed was to get evicted. Her apartment wasn't much to look at, but it was cheap, convenient, and snug. She had meant to move ages ago, but she had never found anything better that she could afford.

Lydia walked in and set the cat down in her living room. Her clothes hung on both walls, forming a walk-in closet, and were protected only by curtains. The cat looked around and sniffed the air. Lydia knelt down in front of him. "My clothes are very important to me. Lifesaving skills or not, if you scratch the clothes I'll throw you back out onto the street, okay?"

The cat didn't answer but began to walk quietly around the apartment, sniffing everything delicately. He seemed to have understood.

"You're probably hungry. The food and litter box are on the way. I hope you can hold it until then."

Satisfied that the cat was entertained with exploring, Lydia went into the bathroom to take care of her scrapes. The cabinet over the sink had an old bottle of peroxide and a tube of antibiotic cream. She fished around under the sink to find a bag of cotton balls, then got to work cleaning and disinfecting her hands and knees. The problem with skinned knees was that they were so childlike. There was no way that a skinned knee could ever look sophisticated. They definitely felt even worse than they looked.

She changed into a cotton sundress that fell above her knee and went back to the kitchen. She had received a postcard from her parents, and it was sitting on the counter, unread. There was a picture of a giant potato on the front that looked like an obvious fake. On the other side, a small description extolled the great beauty of Idaho and the size of its potatoes. Her dad had scrawled something about going to the scene of the birth next. He frequently wrote strange puzzles for her to decode on the postcards. But she had no time to speculate about what he meant because her phone rang. Jack was downstairs.

"I'll be right back," she told her new roommate, now settled on the sofa cleaning his whiskers. She liked having someone to talk to, but she reminded herself not to get too used to it.

She went downstairs and let Jack in. He was carrying a big bag of cat food and a cardboard box. She gave him an enthusiastic hug and kiss. "You're a hero!"

"They didn't have any small bags of food."

"That's okay. I'll just donate it to the shelter, too. I don't think this cat is going to have any trouble getting adopted. He's a real sweetie."

Jack came up to the apartment and greeted the cat gravely. The cat sniffed his fingers and allowed Jack to pet him, although not with the same enthusiasm with which he greeted Lydia, she noted with a strange satisfaction. She reminded herself that she was not going to get attached to the cat as she took a cereal bowl from the cabinet. She poured food into it and set it down on the floor. She watched him run over and eat the food hungrily, as if he hadn't had a good meal in a long time. He was just a temporary visitor, but she felt happy to be taking care of him. She had done the right thing rescuing him from the street.

Jack took newspapers from her recycling bin and shredded them into the box for the cat. The cat inspected it solemnly, got in, and quickly did his business. She marveled at his efficiency as she stifled a huge yawn.

"How did tonight go?" Jack asked. He hadn't guilt-tripped her about not calling in, but the question did make her feel some remorse.

"I didn't have time to preview all my pictures yet," she told him. She wasn't going to tell him about the SUV that nearly hit her. She didn't want him to worry now that the danger was over.

Lydia stripped off her dress and got into bed. Jack stripped down to his boxers and climbed in next to her. He picked up one of her scraped palms and kissed it. "How did this happen?"

"Oh, I tripped and fell being stealthy in the dark. Silly of me, huh?"

"Did you put anything on it?"

"Yes. I hope it stops stinging soon. It's like having a paper cut. You hate to complain, but it hurts all the same."

Jack kissed her tenderly. "Are you tired?"

Lydia smiled at him wickedly, forgetting her hurts. "Not too tired for what you have in mind." And she wasn't.

After forgetting to set an alarm, Lydia and Jack accidentally slept late the next morning. The sky was cloudy, so the sun didn't wake them up. Jack didn't have clothes at her place yet, so he had to run home to change before work. The morning called for the kind of clothes of a hot, humid day. Lydia dug out an A-line red skirt and sexy peasant blouse to wear to work. She had some terrific black ankle strap sandals that she managed to find and that looked great with the outfit. She put on some bright red lipstick and admired her reflection in the mirror. Having sex or a regular basis had a way of making one feel remarkably feminine, she found.

She was eager to get to the office and download her pictures of Al. She was hoping that using a long exposure had paid off. A flash would have revealed her presence, but a long exposure was tricky, since one move could put the whole shot out of focus. She couldn't face the office without a large coffee and some food, though. Her closest café, a badly run hipster hangout with erratic hours, was miraculously open. The woman behind the counter had dreadlocks down to her waist, despite being a blue-eyed redhead, and a nose ring that made her look like a bull. She moved at the same glacial speed as all the staff there, so Lydia didn't bother with a cappuccino or anything cooked. She asked for a large coffee with milk and pointed to a blueberry muffin that she hoped hadn't been sitting there too long. With her prize in hand, she sprinted for Lorimer Street and the D'Angelos.

Leo and Frankie were there waiting for her. Instead of being angry because of her late arrival, they looked strangely relieved to see her.

"Lydia!" Frankie cried and came over and hugged her—coffee, blueberry muffin, and all. Lydia almost spilled her coffee down his back.

"I'm sorry I'm late, but I overslept after last night . . . ," Lydia said, puzzled, when he finally released her. She had expected growls, not hugs.

"What happened last night?" Frankie asked. "You weren't alone, were you?"

"Oh, no." Lydia sat down with her coffee. She opened her blueberry muffin and told an edited version of the events of the evening before between bites. "I did think a couple of times I was being followed. You guys weren't checking up on me, were you?"

Leo smiled fleetingly. He wasn't going to confirm or deny her suspicions. "What did the woman look like who got in his car?"

"She was small, Latina I think, and wearing a small red miniskirt. I can plug in my camera if you want to see for yourselves."

Leo and Frankie exchanged glances. "I think that would be good. The police may be interested in what you have."

"Why?"

"You haven't seen the news, then," Leo said gravely.

Neither she nor Jack had turned on the TV or radio this morning in their haste to get out the door. And the hipster coffee bar near her house didn't have newspapers except for the zines. She fortified herself with a large sip of coffee. "What happened?"

Frankie shook his head. "A prostitute was murdered last night on the waterfront."

Chapter 15

Another woman was dead on the Brooklyn waterfront. Lydia couldn't suppress a shudder. She wondered if there was some kind of sick serial killer out there killing prostitutes. None of it made sense. "Do they know who she is?"

"Her name is Anna Cortez."

Lydia remembered the small woman on the bus. She had a sweetness about her that had attracted the other women to her. She remembered that Anna had also shown pictures of her kids. Lydia's heart sank. She wanted to make sure that it was the same woman, though.

"How did they describe her?"

"Just as you did—as a small Latina woman wearing a red miniskirt."

She was also the prostitute that Al had picked up last night. Lydia had never gotten a clear shot of her face. "What about Al? Is he okay?"

Frankie nodded. "We called Rose. She checked with Patricia that

Al came home okay." Frankie took a big fortifying sip of coffee and mopped his face with a handkerchief. "Rose wanted to know how we were coming with the pictures, and we told her that after last night we were pulling the plug on the operation. It's getting too dangerous."

Lydia wondered how much the family really knew about Al. He was lying to his wife and seemed to have uncontrollable sexual appetites and a thirst for danger, considering the likelihood of catching a terrible disease from the streetwalkers he picked up regularly. Could he also be a violent psychopath? It wasn't that improbable that he had had sexual relations with Glenda. And he certainly had with Anna on the same night she was killed. It was highly suspicious. She wondered what had happened after she had hurried home, shaken by her close call with the SUV.

In the morning light, she had decided that she had probably magnified the incident with the SUV the night before. There were thousands of SUVs in the neighborhood. It could have been an outraged boyfriend of Anna's or possibly her pimp. Or just some guys joyriding. Just because the vehicle had almost hit Lydia didn't mean that it was intentional. But the murder of Anna put the SUV back into the sinister and suspicious column. The behavior of the driver had been odd, and he hadn't swerved away or slowed down after nearly hitting her. It was only luck and the interference of a certain cat that kept her from becoming a road pancake.

She wondered if she had managed to capture any distinguishing features of the SUV following her while she was shooting. There was only one way to find out. She set to work downloading the photographs. While she waited, she called the local animal shelter. She was determined to find a good home for the cat after his heroism.

"He's not feral, is he?" the vet inquired.

"No. He's very friendly. Is anyone missing a black-and-white tuxedo cat?"

"We don't have any notices, but I'll check. Why don't you bring him in so we can look him over? Say five o'clock?"

Lydia wondered if she could leave early for the day to fetch the cat and make it over to the appointment in time. She figured she could tell them she had a bad headache after running around after Al the night before and dealing with the stress of nearly witnessing a homicide. The D'Angelos would have to let her go. "Sure, five o'clock is fine."

Lydia looked up and was happy to see that her photographs were ready. At times like this, she was overjoyed to be part of the digital revolution. The instant gratification was very satisfying, even if the images didn't have the rich quality of film. She quickly flipped through her photographs. She had taken three hundred, so there was a lot of junk to be deleted. A few of the photographs were visually appealing, despite their lack of information, and she couldn't resist sticking them in a folder with her name on it to look at and perhaps use another time for a future project.

The photographs of Al and Anna were better than Leo's but still not terrific, she noted as she paged through them. Anna and the other women on the streets were identifiable, which was good news for the cops and her case. A lot of her shooting from the hip with a long exposure had given her dark fuzzy shots, but she had managed to get one excellent picture of Al's face lit by a streetlight and locked in an embrace with Anna. Bingo. If Patricia should pursue the case, they had him.

She also found a shot she'd taken of the back of the dark SUV that had been following them. Using the Photoshop tools to zoom in on the photograph, she could barely make out the license plate. It had a few letters she could read, an X and a Y, but the rest was unreadable, which was disappointing. She wondered if the SUV could belong to Gator. He had a personalized plate, but he could have easily have switched it out or driven another car. Too bad she had no proof.

She wished Romero would tell her what was going on. She would offer him the photographs and see if he might return a little information in kind. She wished Glenda were still alive. She would have been the perfect one to ask about the rumors on the streets. But she was gone, and it was perhaps her loose lips that had led to her death. She tried to think of who else she could talk to, and Candi Stick's face popped into her mind. Candi was a prostitute, and although her customer base was different from those on the waterfront, she knew what was going on. Besides, Lydia was anxious to start her portrait.

Lydia returned to studying the photographs. Here and there she caught glimpses of Anna's face. She remembered that Anna had a real freshness about her face. She didn't look worn and tired like Glenda. Lydia wondered if Anna had been working the streets for less time than Glenda, or if Anna simply hadn't succumbed to the lures of drugs and alcohol to help her get through her work.

She remembered Romero mentioning a killer in Brooklyn awhile ago. She opened her browser and typed in "Brooklyn prostitute killer." After a few minutes searching through articles, she found what she was looking for. Vincent Johnson, a homeless crack addict, had strangled five prostitutes in Williamsburg some years ago. Could he have committed these crimes, too? She wondered if he was still in jail or back out on the streets. She had to check with Romero about his status.

The pile of paperwork on Lydia's desk beckoned. She dove in and tried to clear a space for the D'Angelos to pile more. A few hours later, she resurfaced to find that it was almost 4:30. She was going to have to sprint home to fetch the cat if she was going to get him to the shelter in time for their appointment. The D'Angelos were already gone for the day, so Lydia locked up. It wasn't until she was halfway home that she remembered she didn't have any kind of cat carrier. He had been well behaved in the car, but she wasn't sure how he would feel about riding her bike. She could put him in a cardboard box, but that would be difficult for her to carry.

Inside her apartment, the cat ran to the door to greet her and wound himself around her legs. Lydia scratched him behind the ears in the place she knew he liked and was rewarded with a loud purring sound. She was glad he was such a nice cat. "I'm sorry I'm not a pet owner. There are some people who love pets. I'm just not one of them. But I'll make sure you get a good home."

She had noticed lately that people in Williamsburg with small dogs had begun wearing them in slings and harnesses similar to the ones in which people carried small babies. Lydia went to her closet to see what she had that might work for a cat. She had a few long scarves, but she was afraid he would fall out. She found a canvas messenger bag that she occasionally used for shoots. The cat might not stay inside, but she would be unlikely to get scratched through the thick material.

It took a few tries to convince the cat to climb inside, but with a few nudges and scratches behind the ears he was putty in her hands, and she put him right where she wanted him. The cat watched as she fastened the buckles, but remained calm as she petted him and talked to him. "It's okay. We're just going to visit the vet." She didn't tell him it was a one-way trip because she had the feeling that he understood everything.

She wrapped the bag strap over her shoulder and across her back and struggled to her feet. He was surprisingly heavy for such a skin-and-bones cat. He would definitely add to her workout when she biked over to the vet. She hoped she wouldn't end up a totally sweaty mess. She ran downstairs and unlocked her bike from the NO PARKING sign. She had only a few minutes to get there. Mindful of her cargo, she set out slowly at first and then began to speed up. Alarmed by the speed, the cat meowed a couple of times and clawed at the bag.

"It's okay, it's okay," Lydia told him again and again. She couldn't pet him because she had to keep her hands on the handlebars, but he eventually calmed down again. She sped up but still arrived late.

The receptionist at the shelter frowned at her when she arrived. Her hair had been dyed black and was most unflattering on her. The frown didn't help, either.

"I'm sorry I'm late. I didn't have a cat carrier." Lydia showed her the cat's face peeking out of the bag.

The receptionist, obviously a real animal lover, melted at the sight of him. "What a sweetie. What's his name?"

"I don't know. I found him on the street last night."

The receptionist stretched out her fingers and let him sniff them. "You're going to keep him, then?"

"I can't." The receptionist frowned at her again. Lydia felt guilty enough as it was.

"Your landlord won't let you keep animals?"

"It's not that . . . ," Lydia began. She had no idea what the rules were in her building, but she wondered if she should just lie to get them to help her.

The phone rang and the receptionist nodded coldly at her. All her earlier friendliness had disappeared. "Dr. Weiner will be with you in just a moment."

Lydia slunk over to look at the magazines in the waiting room. Unfortunately, there wasn't a single trashy celebrity rag among them. They were all about the joys of pet ownership. Cat, dog, and hamster eyes looked out beseechingly from the pages and made Lydia feel even more uncomfortable. The nameless cat in her bag watched her expectantly.

Finally Dr. Weiner, a blond Polish woman, came in. "Miss McKenzie? You have a cat?"

"He rode in my bag." Lydia held it up for her to see.

"He is an unusual one. Most cats wouldn't stand for that." Lydia felt a little glow of pride. She imagined it was similar to the one a parent feels when her child is praised. But she squashed the feeling. He was not her cat. "Come in and let's take a look at him."

The cat was relaxed and curious about the vet and her examining room. He hopped out of Lydia's bag when she opened it up and sniffed around the table. The vet ran her hands over him, a quick exam disguised as a petting session, and the cat purred and rubbed back.

"He is a little thin."

"I found him on the street last night. I don't know if he has a home or not."

"Doubtful, in his condition. But he clearly lived with someone at some point because he likes people."

Lydia nodded. "Should I put up signs about him?"

"If you want to, but pet owners who lose their cats in the neighborhood usually contact us. We haven't heard about anyone losing a tuxedo cat so you're welcome to keep him."

"But I can't keep him! I just wanted to find a place in a shelter for him."

The vet crossed her arms and looked much less friendly. Lydia didn't want to be guilt-tripped into pet ownership. She had done a good deed, rescuing the cat. Now she wanted someone else to take him on. "There's no room in our shelter. You're welcome to take him to the city one. But I would say he had a better chance on the street. Adult cats don't last a week there."

"What do you mean?"

"People adopt kittens. But the people at the shelter usually euthanize cats when they're not adopted quickly. And they don't have much room."

Lydia was filled with a rush of protectiveness for the cat. He had saved her life after all. She didn't want to sentence him to death in return. "Maybe I'll put up signs to see if anyone wants him. He's such a cool cat."

"That's a great idea. Meanwhile, I'll give him his shots. And you should make an appointment to get him fixed."

The vet quickly took care of the painful part, and the cat only complained a little bit. He was happy to crawl back into the bag. Lydia paid the bill, balking only a little at the high price. It would be easier to find a family to adopt him if his shots were all up to date, she reasoned. And she did owe the cat something for acting as her guardian angel.

Back at her bike, she checked her phone for the time. She had never had a chance to call Romero, and she might be able to catch him still at the office. She wanted to e-mail him the photographs and see if he was more willing to share information about Anna Cortez than he was about Glenda. She moved over to take advantage of some shade from the building, and carefully avoided some scattered broken glass.

Romero did not sound thrilled to hear from her, but at least he answered the phone. As soon as he did, the cat let out a strange yowl, maybe a late reaction to all those needles.

"What's that?"

"A cat," she said, and tried to soothe him by petting him with her free hand.

"You don't own a cat." Lydia forgot sometimes that Romero was intimately acquainted with her apartment since he had been over there several times when she was robbed and stalked. He had seen her when she was a basket case and afraid of her own shadow. She had gained back her confidence and preferred not to remember the sensation of being vulnerable in her own home.

"I rescued him last night and the shelter wouldn't take him."

"Then I guess you have a cat now," Romero said with a laugh.

"It's just temporary. I'm going to get someone to adopt him," Lydia protested.

"Uh-huh."

Lydia opened her mouth to protest that the cat was not her pet, but she decided for once it was worth it not to argue. She belatedly recalled the purpose of her call.

"Do you think this killer could be the same as the one who was called the Brooklyn Strangler?"

"Vincent Johnson? Nah. We thought of him first, but he's still in jail. He got life in Clinton."

Lydia processed this for a moment. She wondered if the killer was a copycat, or familiar with his case, but she guessed the cops were looking into that, too. "Did you know that Glenda and Anna both worked for Gator?"

"What do you know about Anna Cortez?" His voice sounded sharp, and she could almost feel him frowning through the phone.

"I met her the other day and then saw her last night with her last john before her death. Or her second-to-last john."

Romero cursed. "I told you to stay away from there! This is no game."

Lydia smiled smugly, glad he couldn't see her face. "I was sent there for work. A certain wayward husband goes there all the time, and I was following him to catch him in the act."

"Name?"

Lydia wondered how much trouble she could get in for not

answering his questions, but she gave it a shot. "You give me something first."

"You've got this on film, I assume."

"Digital."

Romero wasn't happy with her and Lydia didn't care. She wanted to find out what was going on. Someone was killing women she knew, and she wanted them stopped.

"And you've got the victim on camera?"

"In all her Lycra glory."

"What time?"

"About ten o'clock. Now you give me something."

Romero was silent for a moment. Lydia knew that he hated to reveal anything, but she didn't care. She wanted to know what had happened to Glenda. "Both victims are Latina. They were also killed by strangulation. Glenda was dumped in the water, but Anna was left in an alley. So yes, we are looking into the possibility that the killer might have been the same person in both crimes."

Lydia was pleased her hunch was correct. Despite her scare with the SUV, she was anxious to get back out and find some answers. If the D'Angelos weren't going to fund her investigation, then she was going to have to find information on her own.

"I'll send you over the photos I have."

"So who is this guy anyway?"

"Our client wants it confidential."

"He could be the murderer."

Lydia said nothing. The D'Angelos would be furious if the cops started sniffing around Al and Patricia.

"You've got pictures of his car in there?"

Lydia ran the images through her mind for a moment. "Yeah."

"I can trace him from the license plate then."

She sighed. The D'Angelos would be angry, but she could honestly tell them that she didn't reveal Al's identity to the cops. "I think that would be best. If this guy finds out we're following him, his wife's court case could be ruined."

"Send me those pictures right away."

"Will you let me know if you find anything? It might, er, help our client's divorce suit."

"In your dreams." Romero hung up on her.

Lydia frowned at the phone in her hand, wondering why she even bothered. Anna's murder might or might not be separate from Glenda's. The department was overwhelmed by murders and might just declare it unsolvable. If Glenda was going to get justice, Lydia was probably going to have to dig on her own.

Chapter 16

Lydia was snuggled in Jack's warm embrace when her phone rang. Normally she turned off the phone before she went to bed, but lately she had been a little distracted. Speeding SUVs, murdered prostitutes, and a new roommate with pointy ears had thrown off her regular routine. The phone rang again. She opened one eye and found herself staring into a pair of yellow eyes just inches from her own.

"You don't answer phones?" The cat stared at her from her pillow. Apparently the question was too silly to require an answer. Jack stirred, releasing his hold on her. She slipped out from under his arm, wiggled out from under the covers, and scooted past the cat to get to her cell phone. It wasn't easy, but she wanted to get the phone before it woke Jack. She stood naked in her kitchen, staring at the readout. The number was unlisted. The time was midnight. It was probably just a wrong number, but she decided to answer it in order to get rid of them faster.

"Hello?"

"Yo, you Lydia McKenzie?" The voice was pure Brooklyn street. She was reminded of Glenda and all her bristling attitude. Glenda's aggression had masked a sensitive and defenseless woman, but you would never have known at first glance. She swaggered like she had a knife strapped to her leg and she wasn't afraid to use it.

"Yes, this is Lydia speaking." She felt prim and proper using correct grammar, but she didn't think the caller would find it amusing if she "yo'd" back.

"Come down to our crib. We got a proposition for you."

"Your crib?"

"Yeah. The clubhouse, 210 South Second Street. In the basement." Their clubhouse was only a couple blocks away, but in the dark it seemed like miles.

"I'm sorry, but I was in bed. . . ."

"We're the Golden Horseshoe Gang."

Lydia wondered what on earth a gang member would want with her. Then she remembered. The horseshoe tattoo. Glenda. The other women on the bus. "Who is this?"

"Big Wanda." Lydia remembered a large dark woman who cracked jokes. She was scary, but not as scary as if she were a stranger.

"You want to see me now? It's really late . . . ," Lydia began, thinking of the naked man in her bed. She was curious but would have felt better meeting them during the day.

"Come in fifteen. It's a matter of life or death."

Lydia stood for a few minutes holding her dead phone. A matter of life and death, Big Wanda had said. The last time she had ignored a cry for help, Glenda ended up dead. She didn't want another death on her conscience.

But the last thing she was going to do was go out to a midnight rendezvous on her own. She wasn't crazy. She nudged Jack awake.

"What?" He said in a thick voice, confused.

"I need you to come with me," Lydia told him, and explained the phone call.

"You're crazy. Why can't it wait until tomorrow?"

"She said it was a matter of life and death. And I can't go alone." Lydia was already throwing on clothes in the dark under the watchful eye of the cat. He didn't look like he approved of her outfit, and she didn't blame him. Half of it she'd retrieved from the floor, and the rest she'd grabbed at random from her closet by feel. She probably looked like a mess.

Jack slowly swung his legs out of bed with a sigh. "I'll come with you, but this better be quick."

Lydia hoped sincerely it was. She was tired herself. But the adrenaline was already pumping. She watched as Jack put on clothes. She was tempted to pull him back to bed and skip the whole thing. He looked good even all rumpled and tired from sleeping. It wasn't fair.

Out on the street, a rat scuttled across the sidewalk a few feet in front of them and she grabbed Jack's arm. He laughed. "It wasn't even a five-pounder."

She rolled her eyes but still felt nervous. The traffic light on South Second had a short, and the red light hissed and blinked on and off. Every corner and crevice looked dark and scary, and Lydia was glad she wasn't alone. Still, she wondered what she was doing. It was stupid to walk into a situation she was unfamiliar with just because she was intrigued. There was no reason to believe she was any safer just because her caller had been a woman or because she herself had a man with her. The girl gangs were reported to be just as violent as the boys and sometimes even more vicious. The whole thing could be a setup to knock her off so she couldn't investigate the case.

"Where is this place anyway?" Jack asked. He sounded annoyed.

"Two ten," Lydia said. But none of the street numbers were legible in the dark, so Lydia continued on her way, scanning for a basement club that looked obvious. "If it looks too weird, we won't go in. We'll just go home, okay?"

The street looked fairly well cared for. The stairs on the stoops were clean and were garnished with decorations for Easter. The sidewalk had been swept and neatened, and the trash was laid out in strong bags for the garbage pickup the next day.

Suddenly a shape stepped from the darkness, a big woman dressed all in black. It was Big Wanda. "Who's that?"

"My boyfriend, Jack."

"We thought you were coming alone."

"He likes to know that I'm safe."

Big Wanda appeared to consider her answer for a few seconds before she jerked her head to the left. "Follow me."

Big Wanda turned and walked down a staircase under one of the stoops. Full of trepidation, Lydia followed her with Jack's warm hand on her back. The cement steps were small, and Lydia had to go slowly in order not to fall. Big Wanda had bounded down them quickly and waited impatiently in the dark hallway below. A single lightbulb overhead illuminated her hostess's strong and serious face. The hall around her was covered with fake mahogany paneling, and the floor was linoleum in a brick design.

Big Wanda turned and walked pigeon-toed like a sumo wrestler down the hall. She suddenly turned into an open doorway. Lydia stepped forward and peeked inside. The club was a dark, dingy hole in the wall with small tables, a full bar, and a pool table at the back. Every bulb was red, and the walls were hung with scenes of Puerto

Rico. Twenty women sat at tables and at the bar, and they turned to stare at her. A few she recognized from the bus, but most were strangers. It was daunting to say the least.

"This is the Golden Horseshoe Gang," the big woman muttered. "And this is Lydia McKenzie. And Jack."

Jack blinked as he looked around the room. He looked large and rumpled, like he'd just rolled out of bed. One of the women whistled.

"Back down. He's her boyfriend," Big Wanda growled.

"At least offer them a drink, Big Wanda," someone shouted from the back.

Big Wanda blushed and turned to Lydia. "You want a Coke or something?"

"Thank you, I would." Lydia didn't want to drink it, but she thought it might be good to have something to do with her hands. And if worse came to worse, she could use the glass as a weapon. "Jack?"

Jack shook his head. He didn't look nervous, just wary.

Big Wanda signaled to the bartender, a teenager in a low-cut blouse. The teenager poured the drink and passed it to Princess, the strikingly beautiful woman Lydia remembered from the bus, who slid off her bar stool and approached. She was dressed tough, with a leather jacket and Timberland boots.

"Why don't we sit down?" Princess indicated a nearby table, and Lydia slid into a seat with Jack next to her. Princess sat opposite them and set down the Coke in front of Lydia. Her sleeve fell back to reveal a horseshoe tattoo on one of her wrists. Lydia guessed all the women had the same tattoo Anna and Glenda did.

"Glenda was part of your gang, right?"

Princess exchanged glances with Wanda. "She tell you that?"

Lydia shook her head.

Princess nodded. "We heard from Candi that you're smart. There's a murderer out there killing our girls and we want him stopped."

"Your girls?"

"Anna was one of us, too."

Lydia nodded. She wondered if Anna and Glenda's deaths had really been gang-related. If a rival gang wanted to go after them, it would make sense that they would target the most helpless members. Prostitutes would get into any potential customer's car, they worked on lonely waterfronts, and they were easily isolated and attacked.

"We want it stopped. And we want the killer found and punished."

"You tell her, Princess!" an older woman said loudly from the bar. Princess nodded her head regally in the older woman's direction.

Lydia had no interest in finding out just how tough this gang was. In fact, she would have preferred not to know of their existence. The women in the room were of varying ages and sizes, but they all looked like they were mad enough to kill. Jack touched her back lightly, as if to remind her that she was not alone.

"The police have asked me not to interfere. They said they're handling it."

Princess snorted. "Like they care about us. They just keep the white people from getting mugged. Any of our girls goes down, they act like we deserved to get everything we got. It's not justice."

Princess had a point. "If I were to investigate for you," Lydia told her, "I would not be interested in the revenge part. The suspect should be turned over to the police for them to deal with."

Princess and Big Wanda exchanged glances. There was some murmuring from some other women in the room until Princess held up her hand for silence. "We understand. You won't be involved with that. And we'll help you find out anything you need to know."

"I need to talk to Anna's family. Glenda called me before she died, scared of something. I was wondering if Anna was scared, too. Maybe she told her family or friends what was going on. Did she tell any of you?"

Princess shook her head. "I was her closest friend and she said nothing. Her family didn't know she was hooking, and this is killing them. Killing them."

"Would they be willing to talk to me?"

"If I took you there."

Lydia nodded. She could deal with that. It would definitely help to open doors. Especially if Anna's family didn't speak English. Her Spanish was limited to *hola, agua,* and *tortillas,* so she definitely needed help. They settled on the next day at five o'clock.

"What about Gator? Anyone here know him?"

The room became unnaturally still. "Why do you need to talk to him?"

"He was the pimp for both women. Could he have killed them?"

A few young women began to whisper among themselves until Princess once again held up her hand for silence. It was like some kind of dictatorship. Lydia was losing patience. "I'm not going to do this job if you won't let anyone speak. I need to know about their lives. If you're going to demand that everything be censored, I might as well quit right now."

The room fell silent again. Perhaps no one dared to talk back to Princess. Belatedly Lydia remembered that gang members very likely carried weapons, and that she had walked into their place unarmed and with only her tired artist boyfriend to protect her. She didn't dare look at Jack to see if he was furious with her. But she reminded herself that she must start speaking up, if she intended to carry through with the investigation. Allowing them to walk all over her at the beginning meant that she would be hampered constantly and probably would learn nothing new.

With a bravado she no longer felt, Lydia forced herself to stand up. "Well?"

"Sit down, sit down." Princess waved at her impatiently. "I don't like gossip here. It just starts people fighting."

Lydia returned to her seat. "Gossip is one of the main tools in any investigation. If no one shares what they think might have happened, there's no way for me to find leads to follow. So if no one shares with me the rumor that Glenda was thinking of taking up with Sammy the Sauce, then how do I know that could be a motive for her death?"

Princess whistled. "You've done your homework, girl."

"You don't want a lazy private eye." She was not officially a private detective, but she doubted the women cared very much about the legal technicalities of certification.

"That's right. Okay. How about you stick around here for twenty minutes, and anyone who has information can come over and talk to you about it personally. As long as it's not gossip that gets passed around, but information, you understand?"

Lydia understood.

Lydia sipped her Coke. She winced at the sweetness on her tongue and waited to talk to anyone brave enough to venture over with Princess sitting only a foot away.

Jack leaned over so his lips were touching her ear. "Are you out of your mind? I thought we were going to hear what they said and go home."

Lydia hushed him. Her eyes were on a curvy woman with a wide, flat nose that looked as if it had been broken several times. Her hair was in cornrows and her jeans were large and baggy, and she had just gotten the courage to come forward.

"I know Gator," she announced.

"This is Cilla," Princess offered. Lydia vaguely remembered her from the bus.

Cilla chomped on a toothpick. She didn't look like a prostitute, but one never knew. "Do you know him very well?" Lydia inquired delicately.

"He's my stepcousin. I don't see him much, but he would meet me if I asked."

Lydia nodded. "Just let me know when we can meet him. I'd like to know what he thinks about the killings."

"He wants to kill the bastard who did this, same as us," Cilla announced.

"Right," Lydia said with a sigh. Cilla sat back down.

The next woman was small and superskinny. She had big brown eyes and hair pulled back tight into a pigtail. Her name was Deena. "I hear Gator is bringing in foreign girls now."

"You mean illegals?"

"Yeah. He don't have to pay them nothing. Maybe he killed Glenda and Anna 'cause he didn't need them anymore."

It wasn't much of a motive, but Lydia nodded in encouragement anyway. If Gator had been the one to die it would have made more sense.

"Thanks, Deena," Princess said, and Deena slunk back to her seat. It didn't look as if anyone else was going to be brave enough to approach. Lydia was so tired she could barely see, and Jack was getting impatient.

Lydia took out a stack of business cards and placed them on the table. "If anyone thinks of any other information that might be helpful, please feel free to call me. My office number is on the cards."

"I'll pick you up at your office tomorrow at five, okay?" Princess said gruffly.

Lydia nodded and picked her way through the darkness toward the exit with Jack's strong hand at her back. Outside, the windows were dark and the air smelled like the sea.

"This is crazy. You're going to help them, aren't you?" Jack sounded more tired than annoyed.

"I'm going to try." Lydia couldn't explain why she felt so compelled to help. She knew she wasn't an experienced investigator or a cop with the resources to uncover the truth. But somewhere out there was a killer, and a whole group of women wouldn't rest until he paid. If no one else would help them, she would do her best to find him.

Chapter 17

Lydia and Jack didn't crawl back into bed after their late-night excursion until after 2 A.M. The cat decided to play energetically with a grape on the kitchen floor at 5 A.M. Then Jack jumped out of bed at 7 so he could get back to his place and change, and Lydia lay in bed feeling like she hadn't slept at all. She decided she would have to be more proactive about finding a new home for the cat and getting some peace and quiet back into her apartment. It seemed less trouble than dumping her boyfriend or turning off her cell phone. She decided to treat herself to a large cappuccino from Dave's coffee shop to help her get through the day.

Leo and Frankie were already in the office when she arrived, and a mousy-looking woman was sitting in the armchair they reserved for guests. Except for the occasional client, Mama D'Angelo, and Lydia, no other women crossed the threshold of D'Angelo Investigations. It was strictly a guy's-only kind of place. But there, sitting next to Leo's desk chair, was a woman with lanky brown hair dressed in a tan skirt and a gray blouse staring at Leo adoringly.

Lydia smiled into her cappuccino. She knew something was up when Leo had started going to the gym. A girlfriend would be good for him if she could get him to relax.

Leo looked up and saw Lydia's speculative stare. "This is Lydia McKenzie, our administrative assistant. Lydia, this is, uh, Caroline Powers."

Caroline blushed and nodded at Lydia.

Lydia put down her coffee and walked over to Caroline. "It's nice to meet you, Caroline. Do you live around here?"

"No," she whispered, and stared at the rug. It was an ugly gray rug, and Lydia tried to avert her eyes from it as much as possible.

"She lives in Queens," Leo said proudly, as if her shyness was some sort of sign of her virtue. Lydia imagined that coming into the office as Leo's date would be a bit intimidating, but wondered if Caroline ever said anything.

"How nice," Lydia replied. "Welcome to the office." She retreated to her desk and tried to make it look like she was not spying on her while she did just that. She wondered if Mama knew about her. Or better yet, if the shrinking violet had met Mama yet. That matchup was no contest. Mama might like having a daughter-in-law she could railroad, but that game would get old quickly. She knew it was hard for the D'Angelos to have such a forceful mother, and she wondered if it would ever be possible for them to have another woman in their lives.

Lydia's extension rang. She picked it up absently as she scanned the e-mail messages in her inbox. There were offers to see pictures of Britney Spears naked, chances to buy Viagra cheap, and a note from a college friend who was helping to solve the problem of world hunger in Africa. Lydia deleted everything except the note from the friend, and decided to read it later when she felt less fatigued and more sympathetic.

"Lydia," hissed Mama D'Angelo. "Is she there?"

Lydia chuckled to herself. She swore sometimes that Mama was a witch or that she had planted microphones in their office. Mama always knew what was going on. She glanced over at Leo and Caroline. Perhaps they had arranged a rendezvous at the restaurant and Mama just wanted to check and see if it was going to happen. "Yes, she is."

"Oh, such trouble. I brought this down on my sons' heads. I know I did." Mama moaned theatrically.

Lydia kept her voice quiet so she wouldn't be overhead. "She seems nice to me. Just a little mousy."

"Cousin Patricia? Mousy?"

Lydia frowned. "Wait—who are you looking for?"

"The police picked up Al and questioned him at the station. He saw the pictures that the boys took, and now he and Patricia are on their way over there," Mama announced. "Now, who were you talking about?"

"Oh, no one," Lydia stammered. She didn't want to get the D'Angelos into trouble. "I'd better warn Leo and Frankie and call you back later."

But just as Lydia hung up the phone, the door opened and hit the wall with a bang. They heard Al Savarese before they saw him. "You sons of bitches! You trying to get me the electric chair or something?"

Al marched in like a boxer into the ring and kicked the filing cabinet by the door as hard as he could. It was a giant four-drawer one. He howled in pain and clutched his foot. Leo and Frankie jumped up, and Leo moved Caroline behind him protectively. Lydia thought about cowering under her desk in case he started throwing stuff, but she didn't want to miss any of the action.

Patricia ran through the door after Al. She was a vibrant dark-haired woman who looked as if she had been very beautiful at eighteen, but Al's sexcapades had aged her. Time and trouble had caused furrows in her face, giant bags under her eyes, and a permanent scowl. She wore a wrap dress that looked designer, and her fingers looked like red talons as she clutched at Al's sleeve.

"Al—it's not my fault, I swear. My mother was the one who called the D'Angelos and begged them to help. She said the boys would help you find counseling. . . ."

Al shook Patricia off, and she fell back against the wall with a sob. Lydia couldn't stop herself from flinching. Al advanced menacingly and pounded on Leo's desk with his fist. "I demand that you apologize for violating my privacy and putting my life in danger! I'll sue you so fast your head will spin."

Frankie stood frozen in horror, and Leo had turned a strange purply red color that couldn't be healthy. Caroline was cowering behind the chair. Lydia's fingers itched to dial 911, but she didn't think the D'Angelos would appreciate her bringing in more strangers to witness their family scandal. She wondered if Rose had consulted with Patricia before calling Mama. The whole situation was a mess.

"Get out of my office immediately!" Leo spat out each word like a little stab of a knife. Al paid him no heed, grabbing a file box and overturning it on the floor. They all watched in horror as their client files spilled out in a messy muddle. Lydia knew who would be cleaning up this disaster. Her blood came to a brisk boil. She hadn't had enough sleep or coffee to deal with this kind of crap. She got up and marched over so she was toe-to-toe with Al.

"Stop behaving like a juvenile delinquent or I'll call the cops. Then you'll be up for violation of private property and assault so fast your head will spin."

Al stopped grabbing things off Leo's desk. He turned and stepped in an intimidating fashion toward Lydia. "Who the hell are you?" His eyes were dark brown. His face looked puffy, as if his lifestyle had started to affect his health. She remembered how he had aggressively shopped for sex and how he had had sex with Anna in a public place. He was neither a nice guy nor someone easily intimidated.

Lydia almost took a step back, but she let her own anger keep her in place. "I work here, and that's all you need to know," she said. "Frankie, help your cousin take Al home. If he's going to beat this rap, he needs to say out of trouble. Leo, take Caroline out for coffee, and I'll clean up this mess."

Everyone stared at her, not sure what it would mean if they followed her instructions. She had never bossed them around like that before, and she technically should have been following their orders.

Caroline was staring at them all, horrified. Lydia wondered if there was any hope for the new relationship between Leo and Caroline.

"You can't order me around, bitch! You haven't seen the last of me!" Al shouted at her. But Frankie had at last become unfrozen, and he had already moved his reassuring bulk between Lydia and Al.

Lydia shooed them all with her hands. "Go, or I call the cops! And don't think I'm not cranky enough to do it because I am!"

They all started moving. Frankie took Al and Patricia by the arm and escorted them out the door. Leo took Caroline's hand and guided her gently out of the office.

Lydia breathed a sigh of relief as the door to the office finally shut and there was silence. Then the phone rang again. It sounded shrill. Lydia answered it reluctantly only because she knew it was Mama D'Angelo again, and that she would come over personally if she thought her chicks were in danger. Lydia explained as quickly and succinctly as she could what had happened.

"Patricia is blaming this all on her mama? She's crazy. She takes after my crazy great-aunt who always walked around in her night-gown during the full moon."

"She said it so her husband wouldn't leave her," Lydia said, feeling sorry for a woman who was that desperate.

"But Rose says she wants to leave him."

Some people didn't know what they wanted. "Leaving and being left are fundamentally different," Lydia said. She wished she had bought two large cappuccinos this morning. She could barely focus her eyes, she was so tired.

"Huh!" Mama snorted. "I'm going to call that girl and give her a piece of my mind. That's the last favor we do for her side of the family."

Lydia hung up. She wondered if Al was the the one who murdered Glenda and Anna. He certainly had a bad temper. She wondered what he would do next. Someone needed to watch him. She wished she could tail him, but now he had seen her up close and that would be impossible. She needed someone he didn't know. She picked up the phone and dialed Emmanuel's number.

Emmanuel was delighted at the idea. "I'll drive up there right away. I'm not busy at all."

"I can't afford much," Lydia began. She could probably find a way to get the D'Angelos to pay, especially if she could show that Patricia was in danger.

"I'd do it for free. If he's the murderer we'll get a big reward for catching him, right?"

Lydia doubted it, but it was always good to dream. "Call me if he heads to the waterfront. I'll hop in the car with you and see if I can get some photos of him."

She hung up and looked around the office in dismay. Although technically it was never clean, at least she usually knew where to find stuff. Everything looked hopelessly scrambled. But it was going to be worse once the D'Angelos got back, so she reluctantly got to work picking up the scattered paperwork. Some of it was so mixed up that it was impossible to tell which case it belonged to. The cases were all several years old, and she hoped that no one would ever really need the information. She started shoving the papers into random files just to get it all off the floor.

Today was definitely the kind of day that would have been better spent in bed, if her home hadn't been occupied by a noisy animal. With the floor back in order, she moved over to her computer to make a sign for the cat. She was not a cat person, and it was time for him to find a new home.

As Lydia worked on her poster, she wished she had a picture of the cat. She just tried to describe his coloring (tuxedo) and personality (easygoing) as best as she could. It wasn't a particularly good sign, but if someone had lost him maybe they would recognize him from her description. She decided to take a long lunch hour to hang her signs up on Bedford Avenue near the subway and near the spot where she had found the cat. After Al and Patricia's visit to the office, a break was the very least that she deserved.

Walking outside on a beautiful summer day felt wonderful, and her mood lifted like magic. There were lots of cute clothes, cute guys, and tons of cute dogs. There were babies in carriages and backpacks and carrying packs. The world felt sunny and happy.

After hanging up most of her signs on light poles, Lydia stopped at a French sidewalk café to treat herself to a cappuccino and a Caesar salad. She sat with her face in the sun and watched the pedestrians parade past. Instead of just dull New York black, people were wearing bright colors to beat the summer heat. She enjoyed watching some of the more adventurous hats and costumes go past. Someone had hung a sign with a name and Web site around a stump, claiming it for an art project. A juggler had set up his act across from the café and was tossing a boot, baton, beanbag, and flip-flop in the air. Everything everywhere felt alive, and she was able to forget about death for a while.

Rain, another photographer Lydia knew from the darkroom, walked down the sidewalk with her head down. She dressed like a hippy, with flowing caftans and crazy curly hair, but she always had her own personal storm cloud above her head. Lydia almost said nothing to stop her, but it felt uncharitable on such a nice day. In the end she waved.

"What a beautiful day, huh?"

Rain came over and stood awkwardly next to the table. "It could be a little cooler. And less humid."

It was a bit warm, now that she mentioned it, but Lydia had been doing a great job ignoring it. "I'm enjoying the sunshine."

Rain reached over and picked up one of Lydia's signs from the table. "You lost a cat?"

"No, I found one."

"Seems like a nice cat. Why do you want to get rid of it?"

Lydia felt her anger rising, as it always did in Rain's presence. She wished Rain weren't so aggressively negative. "I'm not a cat person. I never wanted one."

Rain smiled—perhaps for the first time all week. "You'll change your mind soon enough."

Lydia remembered belatedly that Rain was a cat person in a major way. She had five cats or something, and gave them the run of her house. They were always sleeping and shedding everywhere, and the furniture had all been clawed to shreds. Rain loved them, though, and took endless photographs of them, which she sold on the street with her sentimental Twin Towers pictures.

"Know anyone who's looking for a cat?"

Rain shook her head. "Been to the darkroom recently?"

Lydia almost said not since Glenda died, but she stopped herself. She didn't want to talk about Glenda with Rain. She wouldn't understand. Lydia had a few rolls of film from her shoot with Candi that she wanted to develop. "Not in a week, but I have to go back soon."

"Maybe I'll see you there. I almost sold out last weekend, and my reserves are low."

Lydia was glad to see Rain finally walk away toward the subway. There was something nice about being at an outdoor café and seeing people you knew, but on the other hand, she wished Rain hadn't come and burst her happy bubble. Now she felt irritated. Although she would never want to trade places with Rain, she was a little jealous of Rain's ability to live off the proceeds from her photographs. It was disheartening to have to go back to the office and deal with the D'Angelos and Al's whole mess. She didn't have to be anywhere until five o'clock, when Princess would pick her up. So she sat back and closed her eyes. She was in no hurry to get out of the sun.

Chapter 18

Princess may have acted a little controlling and stuck up when Lydia had first met her, but she couldn't fault her for being late. She pulled up in front of the office promptly at five o'clock in a green Range Rover. Wow, Lydia thought, crime does pay. She had no idea what the members of the Golden Horseshoe Gang really did, but she somehow doubted it consisted of contributing to the economy in legitimate ways.

Lydia opened the door and hopped in. The car had that new-car smell that was both overpowering and attractive. Princess's radio blared salsa music, but she thoughtfully turned it down a couple of decibels.

"Does Anna's family know we're coming?"

Princess shrugged as she weaved through traffic. She appeared to think she was a NASCAR driver. Unfortunately, the car was not equipped with helmets or a steel cage. "Isn't that going to be awkward?"

"They know about you," Princess said, keeping one hand on the wheel. "Anna and I were in and out of each other's houses since we were both in diapers. Her family is like mine." Lydia fought the urge to close her eyes as they turned a corner without slowing down. She wished she had arranged to meet Princess at Anna's house and ridden her bike there. "Just don't push them too hard, okay?"

Lydia didn't bother being offended. Her job was to ask hard questions. The first suspect in a murder investigation was always the spouse and family. They might be closest to the victim, but they usually had the most to gain from the death.

"Who is going to be there?"

"Roberto, her husband, Brandy and Marcos, her kids, and Eva, her mom. There might be some of Roberto's family there, and maybe some cousins or something. I'm not sure."

"I'd really like to talk to Roberto and Eva. They're probably the most likely to have heard something." Lydia was half expecting Princess to drive them to the projects, and she felt a little ashamed of herself when they pulled up in front of a neat little row house.

Princess must have read her mind. "Eva was a lot smarter than my mom. She borrowed from all her relatives and bought this place thirty years ago, when everyone thought the neighborhood was a dump. Now she's sitting on a gold mine."

"Why did Anna . . . ?" Lydia began, but couldn't finish.

"Keep on hooking? Her mom owns the house. She still has to pay rent and feed her kids."

"What about Roberto?"

"He worked in one of the factories that closed down last year. He hasn't been able to find more work. He does day-labor stuff when he can, but it doesn't pay very much."

Lydia had to hold on to the door to hop down since the ground was so far away. She followed Princess up to the front door. Princess rang the bell, and it sounded a happy little electronic salsa melody. It was nice to hear the first time, but Lydia could imagine it would drive you crazy after the next one hundred times.

An older woman with sad eyes and a disheveled short haircut answered the door. She was small and round, and wore fuchsia leggings and a black tunic. "Princess," she began, then burst into tears. Princess murmured to her in Spanish and helped her back into the house. Lydia decided that she must be Eva. Lydia followed behind them, carefully shutting the front door behind her.

Princess walked Eva to the immediate right into a family room. The gold living room sofa and chairs were encased in clear plastic, the white walls were covered with family portraits, and the plants in the dim room looked too green and lush to be real. A television in the corner was turned to a Spanish soap opera.

Princess and Eva sat down on the sofa side by side. Lydia sat down across from them in an easy chair without waiting to be asked.

Eva cried into a tissue and spoke Spanish to Princess. Lydia wished she hadn't had visions of Paris floating in her head when she made her language choice in high school, but had chosen something more practical instead.

Lydia exchanged a quick glance with Princess. She looked a little teary, and Lydia interpreted her look to mean that she wanted Lydia to delay her interrogation. Lydia studied the family pictures while she waited. There were rows of cute kids with teeth missing in Catholic school uniforms turning into awkward teenagers with braces in the same uniforms, morphing into brides, grooms, and in one case a marine. Lydia spotted Anna in white at her first communion and then again as a bride smiling shyly at the camera. The pictures of her life told a sanitized tale, and one a stranger would never guess would end in murder.

After a few minutes, Eva sat up and blew her nose. She spoke Spanish to both of them. Princess turned to Lydia. "Eva apologizes for her lack of manners and wants to offer you a cup of coffee."

Lydia knew better than to refuse, even though this was the time of day when she usually switched from caffeine to cocktails. "If it wouldn't be too much trouble . . ."

Princess jumped up and waved Eva back in her chair. "I'll get it, Mami."

"*Gracias,* Princess." Eva sniffed and tried for a watery smile.

Lydia wasn't sure whether Eva spoke any English. So as soon as Princess left the room, Lydia leaned forward. "I'm so sorry to hear about your daughter."

Eva nodded politely but said nothing. No dice. Lydia was going to have to rely on Princess for translation. Luckily, the coffee was already made, and Princess returned shortly with three mugs, each with images of angels on them. Eva spoke rapidly to Princess, and Princess frowned.

"Eva says Anna was always a sweet girl, and she wants you to know she's sure she's an angel in heaven now."

Lydia wasn't sure if the Catholic Church believed that prostitutes had the right to enter the pearly gates, but she hoped so.

Lydia took a sip of her coffee and nearly choked. Princess had poured in milk and sugar rather liberally.

"It's okay?"

"Perfect," Lydia managed to say. "Just went down wrong." She cleared her throat and changed the subject. "I don't know if Princess told you, but Anna and Glenda's friends asked me to help out."

There was a quick consultation on the couch. "Eva doesn't think you look old enough to be a detective."

Lydia smiled. "I work for private eyes, and I've spent some time on the waterfront."

"No one in her family will rest until the killer is caught." Princess's English translation was delivered deadpan, without the hand gestures and drama of Eva's statement. Lydia wasn't sure if Princess believed it.

Lydia let that comment pass since Anna was dead. She had seemed sweet when Lydia met her, but she also worked as a hooker. "Do you know if Anna was afraid of anyone or if anything bad happened to her lately?"

Eva hesitated. She seemed to know something but was reluctant to share it. After a minute she said something hesitantly and Princess translated. "She hadn't been looking so good lately, like she wasn't sleeping. But I don't know if she was scared of anyone."

Lydia nodded. She handed Eva her card. "If you think of anything else that might help, please don't hesitate to call me. Even the littlest thing might help." She hoped that Eva would think it over and decide to tell her whatever was on her mind.

"Roberto is in the kitchen," Princess told her.

Lydia nodded, putting her cup down gratefully. She remembered that "Roberto" was the name of Anna's husband. "I'll go and pay my respects." She didn't bother asking where it was; the smell of fish wafted from the back of the house. She followed her nose past the bikes, skate-boards, and basketballs parked in the hallway. The kitchen was small and filled with short, chubby women talking all at once in Spanish and stirring various pots on the stove. Sitting at the kitchen table was a glum-looking man with a receding hairline and a potbelly. He had a little girl on his lap. The girl looked too old to be sucking her thumb, and her eyes looked blank, as if she'd checked out for the duration.

The aunts ignored Lydia. No doubt visitors had been stopping in ever since they'd heard the news. Lydia touched Roberto gently on the shoulder. He turned. His dark eyes were the saddest eyes she had ever seen.

"I'm Lydia. Princess brought me here," she said. "I'm so sorry about your wife."

Roberto nodded. "I thought she was still working in the sewing factory and getting bonuses for being so fast."

"I'm sorry," Lydia repeated. The words seemed inadequate, but she didn't know what else to say. The family was living in an extreme state of denial if they professed not to know about Anna's career.

"The police have no idea who killed my Anna." Roberto hugged his daughter tighter.

"I'll do my best to help out," Lydia promised. "But I didn't know Anna very well so I need some help. Did she mention anything or anyone in particular in the week or so before her death?"

Roberto shook his head. "She reminded me to pick up some clothes from the cleaner but I forgot. I still have the ticket in my pocket."

Probably a woman who kept her profession secret from her husband wouldn't be too forthcoming about other matters. Lydia wondered what Roberto would have done if he'd discovered that his wife was a prostitute while she was still alive. Would he have been angry enough to kill her? Roberto appeared to be genuinely sad, but she'd heard that Arab men who killed their daughters or sisters for dishonoring the family grieved for them, too.

"I was happy to take the money she brought home, but I didn't know what it was from. I didn't know."

Lydia patted him on the shoulder and tried smiling encouragingly at the little girl. "It wasn't your fault," she told him. Unless, of course, it was.

Lydia walked from Anna's family's house to her darkroom. The distance was only about six blocks, but it felt like another planet. She paid a reasonable fee to belong to a communal darkroom. In exchange for an iffy neighborhood, the group got a spacious loft in which to work. She was eager to trade in the grief-stricken house for the comfortable familiarity of her darkroom, where she might run into a few friends with no problems more pressing than paying their Visa bill or finding true love with a metrosexual.

Her friend Emily was at the printer, bopping her head to the music on her iPod. Lydia peeked over Emily's shoulder to see what she was working on. Emily was printing copies of a ten-by-twelve-inch picture of a miniature dachshund posed with a stuffed fish.

"Is the picture bigger than the actual dog?" Lydia inquired loudly.

Emily spun around, removed her earbuds from her ears, and gave her a big hug. "Lydia! Where have you been?"

"Oh, around," Lydia said mysteriously.

"Okay, who is he?" Lydia and Emily could go for weeks and months without seeing each other, and somehow always pick up exactly where they'd left off. Emily's family had never known what to make of their adopted Asian daughter, and Lydia always thought it was too bad. She, too, had felt like a swan being raised by ducks during her own childhood.

"I'll have to introduce you." Lydia took out her rolls of film from the shoot with Candi. She removed a black bag from under the counter, took out two spools, and put them inside the black bag with her film. Then she reached in through two light-safe armholes to begin to roll the films onto the spools. After that, she dropped them in a canister with developer and began the process of finding out what was on the film.

Emily filled her in on the latest details of her work life. A poodle had bitten her last week, and the owner had refused to pay for shots. She had taken pictures of what she thought was a sleeping Persian cat only to discover an hour later that the cat was actually dead. The owners were devastated but paid her handsomely for Jonesie's last pictures. As usual, she had nothing new to share about her social or love life. Emily, although always wonderfully friendly and outgoing, had never dated anyone as long as Lydia had known her. She had a hopeless crush on another photographer, Stuart, but neither one of them ever did anything to advance that relationship.

Lydia gave Emily a brief sketch of Jack, and then, as she poured out the developer and filled the canister with stop bath, she gave her an edited version of the events that had occurred over the past few weeks on the waterfront.

"I read about that in the paper. You were there? You knew that prostitute?"

"A little," Lydia said. She was finding that the more she learned about Glenda and Anna, the less she felt she had known them. "I've been trying to figure out what happened."

"Be careful," Emily warned. "I heard they suspect a serial killer. Maybe even one from years ago."

"The original killer has been in jail for years," Lydia said. "He was a homeless drug addict with a mother fixation."

Emily shook her head. "I hope you're not going down there alone."

"No way. I hired myself a bodyguard." Lydia was glad Emily had never caught a glimpse of Emmanuel. She hoped Emily pictured him as an enormous weight lifter, instead of the skinny, laid-back Jamaican that he was.

Lydia had finished the fixer stage and rinsed the negatives. She shook them out over the sink and hung them up to dry on the line. She couldn't help peering at the frames to see the images in the dim red light.

"You can flip on the light if you want," Emily offered. "I'm done here."

Lydia flipped it on and together they studied the negatives from the shoot with Candi. Since it was a negative image, Candi's eyes were white instead of dark, and the window was dark instead of light. It was eerie even when you were used to it.

"I'd watch out for that one," Emily said. "She looks dangerous to me."

Chapter 19

The afternoon of Glenda's funeral was rainy and steamy. Susa had arranged for it to be held at a local funeral home, Funeraria Vega, on Havemeyer. Lydia scrounged up a simple black dress and pumps, and set out reluctantly under a big golf umbrella.

The funeral home was built like a large gray mausoleum and had a sober dark brown awning. Lydia stepped underneath and gingerly shook out her umbrella. Once she was inside, her pumps sank into deep blue plush carpeting. It was like an icebox inside, and she felt herself drying and getting chilly right away. She bent and scrawled her name in the book. There was only a short list of mourners ahead of her. She hoped, for Susa's sake, that more showed up.

The door to the chapel was open, and Lydia walked in. Thankfully, Susa had chosen a closed casket. Lydia had seen enough of Glenda's body as it was. A large framed photograph of Glenda sat surrounded by flowers next to the coffin. It was a posed fake-looking portrait, and

Glenda looked about fifteen. Her face lacked the character it had when Lydia photographed her, but she also looked innocent and untouched.

Susa sat stiffly in the front row with Glenda's three kids. As she walked up to pay her respects, Lydia noticed that Susa had bought little blue suits for the boys and a frilly white dress for the girl.

"Hi. I'm Lydia. We spoke the other day. I'm so sorry. . . ."

Susa grasped Lydia's hand like a lifeline. Her eyes looked vague and unfocused. Lydia wondered with a sinking heart if Susa took drugs as well. Those poor kids didn't stand a chance. She wondered if Susa even knew who she was until she whispered in a raspy voice, "Have they found him yet?"

Lydia's heart sunk as she shook her head. She had no good news to pass on to the grieving mother. The police apparently had no real suspects, no definite leads, and the killer seemed unstoppable.

Susa turned her gaze back toward Glenda's portrait. The kids next to her were remarkably subdued. They were probably scared to death and had no idea what was going on.

Lydia went to sit in one of the middle rows where she could scope out the other mourners. Princess and some of the other women she'd seen from the clubhouse came in and sat in the row reserved for family. Lydia was glad to see Princess lift up the little girl and hold her in her lap. Those children needed all the friends they could get.

A few minutes later, Candi strutted in with a handsome man on her arm. She looked as if she had stepped from a *Vogue* cover, circa 1983. She had on a tight dress that was white on one half and black on the other, a tiny hat with a black veil and a large black feather that curled around her chin. Lydia admired her style and was rewarded with a small, subtle wink as Candi sashayed by.

Someone sat down next to her. Turning in her seat, Lydia found her nose just inches from Romero's. Embarrassed, she scooted back. "Hello, Detective."

Romero sat back and unbuttoned his jacket, making himself at home. He took up more than his share of the bench, and his arm felt warm against her bare, goose-pimpled shoulder. "You turn up any more red herrings you want to share?"

She smiled sweetly through gritted teeth. "Those photographs were the best leads you had all week, admit it."

Romero shrugged. "A signed confession would be better."

Lydia snorted. "You're just lazy. When I start getting the equivalent of an NYPD salary with benefits, maybe I'll be willing to do your job for you." She felt safe in this taunt, because they both knew that Romero worked insanely long hours seven days a week when his job called for it.

"Hah." Romero ran a hand through his hair. He looked exhausted. She wondered if he'd slept at all lately.

"What did you learn from Al?"

"He says he's innocent. Despite your photographs, he insists he's never had sexual relations with prostitutes."

Lydia snorted. "What's his explanation?"

"He's converting the ladies to Catholicism."

Lydia had to bite her lip from laughing out loud. They were in a funeral home, after all. It didn't seem polite to let out a belly laugh or even a chuckle. Romero turned to her and they grinned at each other. She hadn't felt this close to him in ages, like they were finally on the same team again. It felt wonderful.

She heard a slight stir and a murmur from near the door, and she turned to see a tall black man in a long black leather coat. From his pointed cowboy boots outlined in gold thread to the gray silk shirt peeking out from below his collar, he was all style. His hair was teased into a giant Afro, seventies style, and on his fingers he wore several flashy rings. Around him were several other men dressed almost all identically, but none of them pulled off his style quite so effectively. The smile faded from her face. He had to be Gator.

She turned back to Romero and noted that he was also watching Gator's entrance. "Is it true that the killer usually comes to the funeral?"

"We wish they would," Romero said. "It would make them easier to catch."

"Have you talked to Gator yet?"

"Oh, yeah. He's got an alibi list as long as his Afro is high. And he swears that he's prostrated with grief."

"Hmm. More like greed." She watched as Gator made the rounds of the room. Everyone looked scared of him, but they nodded their heads politely because they couldn't afford to offend him. Even Susa nodded solemnly at him, and he pressed a wad of bills in her hand. It was the least he could do, and he probably was doing it for the benefit of the audience. Lydia doubted any of them were fooled.

Gator, as if sensing her stare, turned and looked straight at her. She felt a chill on her spine. He might or might not have killed Glenda and Anna, but he looked capable of violence toward her. She wanted to shrink down in her seat and disappear, but she knew she would have to talk to him at some point. She had promised the gang that she would follow all the leads. She made herself sit up straight and return his gaze without flinching. She watched as Gator's eyes slid to Romero next to her.

Romero nodded at the pimp, and Lydia watched in amazement as Gator nodded back.

"You know each other?" she whispered out of the corner of her mouth.

"We went to high school together," Romero said, knocking a piece of invisible dust off his sleeve.

Lydia's jaw dropped. "You did not."

"We're both local boys."

Lydia just shook her head. She couldn't imagine either of them as teenagers.

"We also tend to get to know the guys on the other end of the law better than the average citizen who stays out of trouble. They spend more time in my car."

"Except for me," Lydia said with a grin.

"I wouldn't put you in the category of the average citizen who doesn't get into any trouble."

He was flirting with her again. They were both either sparring or flirting, and she felt a slight pang of guilt when she thought about Jack. Jack was exciting, handsome, and sexy, but he wasn't exactly enthralled that she was investigating Glenda's death. Maybe she and Jack were too different to make it work. Not that she was interested in Romero, she assured herself, ignoring her crazy hormones.

The funeral service began. The minister clearly had no idea who Glenda was. It wasn't surprising. Lydia doubted that she'd set foot in a church since she was a kid. He read off remarks prepared by Susa about her angelic nature and sweet disposition. Lydia stared at the photo of Glenda and wondered what she would have thought of all of it. She probably would have loved it. The notion that she was misunderstood—a good mother and a good daughter—this was part of her mythic belief of herself. Facing reality would have torn all of it apart.

She felt a vibrating sensation next to her hip. She shot Romero a dirty look, and he raised his eyebrows at her. He made no move to answer the phone. She suddenly realized it was her phone vibrating, and her face flamed up like a firework. She had forgotten to turn it off. Answering your phone during a funeral would have violated all the principles of Miss Manners and Emily Post, and she wasn't about to try it. She was just grateful it wasn't blasting some loud corny tune.

Lydia took it out of her bag and pushed the button on the side to make it stop. She couldn't help but read the caller ID. Emmanuel was calling. Her heartbeat accelerated. His call could only mean one thing. Al was back on the prowl.

Chapter 20

When Emmanuel pulled up at the corner of Metropolitan and Havemeyer, Lydia was ready. She leaped into the backseat before he even stopped. She'd barely closed the door before he zoomed off again.

"Did you lose him?" Lydia asked breathlessly, clutching her camera. She was grateful she'd brought it to the funeral in her bag.

"We know where he's going, right?" Emmanuel passed a cement mixer with about six inches to spare.

"Right." It seemed a bit early in the day for Al to be out. Usually he waited until dark. Maybe he had stored up so much energy from staying at home and out of trouble for the past few days that he couldn't help himself.

Emmanuel raced down Metropolitan toward the river. At Wythe he turned left and went south.

Lydia peered anxiously out the window. The rain had stopped and the sun was threatening to come out from behind a dark cloud. "Isn't he going to Kent?"

"I want to catch him going the other way so he doesn't suspect that we're following him." Lydia widened her eyes, impressed. She was amazed at how sneaky he had become in such a short time.

In the Hasidic neighborhood, he dodged a large family of girls in identical blue-and-black-striped dresses clinging to the side of a pram. He turned and drove one block to Kent and made a right. He drove slowly back as they both scanned the side streets for a sign of Al's car. Lydia tried to be optimistic. She trusted Emmanuel's instincts, but now that Al knew he was being followed, she couldn't believe he wouldn't have learned to be more devious.

They drove past a small backhoe digging up the sidewalk, splashing through an enormous puddle. They passed a car carrier unloading impounded cars into the police lot for auction. And they almost missed Al's maroon SUV parked between two minivans at the Grand Street Park. The park was the tiny piece of land on the river next to the Domino factory, and it was right where she had found Glenda's body. Lydia shuddered as Emmanuel slammed on the brakes.

"This is perfect," Emmanuel muttered as he pulled in. They rolled slowly past the parked cars and Lydia scrunched down in the seat. A dark SUV suddenly backed out of one of the spaces, and Lydia flinched. She knew there were a million of them, but it seemed like a coincidence to see one again so near Al. The SUV drove off, and Lydia was glad to see it go.

Lydia peeked out the window at Al's car as they eased past. "Careful he doesn't spot us."

"No worries. Lots of car services park here while they wait for a call." Three other cars with limousine and car service plates were idling on the side road leading to the park. Emmanuel pulled in behind the last one. There was only one problem with their great parking space. They couldn't see Al's car at all.

"We don't even know he's in there," Lydia said, frustrated. "And I can't walk by because he knows who I am now."

"I could do it," Emmanuel suggested.

Lydia looked at him doubtfully. He'd proved adept at learning how to follow cars, but she wasn't sure how he'd do on his feet. It took a special skill to pretend you were doing nothing while snooping like crazy on someone. "Are you sure you feel . . . ready?"

"Ya. I could take some pictures if you want."

Lydia violently shook her head no. No one else touched her camera. No one. "My camera is a bit complicated. If you see anything come right back and we'll figure something out."

Emmanuel slipped out of the front seat and shut the door with a bang. Lydia grimaced. She hoped his snooping technique would be a bit subtler. He moved out of sight, and she sat back in the seat with a sigh. It was difficult for her to relax, but Al had seen her now and would know she was trying to catch him in the act. She had no choice but to let someone else handle the surveillance.

The shadows were lengthening across the park. The families headed home and couples arrived at the water, then drifted into shadowy corners to neck. Lydia craned her neck to see if Emmanuel was returning. He'd had time to cross the Williamsburg Bridge and back by now.

Finally he reappeared next to the car, opened the door, and slid in. "I walked by his car, but nothing's going on in there."

"Is he inside?" She wondered if Al had given them the slip.

"Two people are in there, but I couldn't see much with the reflection on the glass." Emmanuel seemed nervous, maybe because it was the first stakeout he'd done where he had done more than drive. She didn't blame him for being nervous. She'd witnessed Al's temper firsthand and it wasn't pretty.

"The sun is going down. Maybe that'll help."

They sat in the car and waited. Lydia took her day planner from her bag and started to go through it. She entered phone numbers from business cards and scraps of paper she had in the bottom of her bag. She always threw notes in the bottom of her bag until she had time to go through them. Emmanuel cycled through the radio stations until he finally found one he liked. It was some sort of Caribbean call-in show. The voices sounded musical. Lydia had a hard time understanding what they were saying, but she got the gist of it. A woman was having trouble with her cheating man. The DJ said that his cheating ways could be a death sentence for her. The woman began to moan and cry. Then Lydia just caught the word *condoms* in the DJ's fiery lecture. It was difficult not to think of Al's wife, Patricia.

Lydia was curious what Emmanuel thought about it. "Do you think she should just leave him?"

"That woman?" Emmanuel shrugged. "Depends on how many kiddies they have at home. Some women do the leaving and then they have no one to feed the children."

Lydia guessed that not every country's child-support laws were as stringent as they were in the United States. She wondered what he thought about Al's cheating. Too many cultures believed it was a man's right, despite the suffering it caused the wife and children.

The sun sank behind the skyscrapers of Manhattan across the river in a ball of red-orange. The sky was streaked with purple and pink. The whole scene would have been peaceful if the notion of Al having crazy sex with a prostitute in a neighboring car hadn't nagged at her. She didn't mind the sex part so much as her inability to take pictures that would nail him in court. Patricia deserved to have the chance to marry a man who respected her as a woman and didn't endanger her life. Lydia's camera sat looking forlorn and alone on the seat next to her.

"I'm going to walk by," Lydia announced when she couldn't stand it anymore.

"I thought you said he knew what you look like."

"He does. But it's dark out here, and I don't think he expects me to show up." She would have to hide her camera so she didn't jump-start his memory.

"Maybe you could wear a hat or something," Emmanuel suggested.

"Do you have one?" He rummaged inside his glove compartment and pulled out a giant rainbow macramé beret that looked like it was made for a reggae Smurf.

"That's not exactly subtle." Everyone in the park would be staring at the weird hat.

"It'll hide your hair and face." Emmanuel looked hurt by her rejection, so she snatched it from his hand and took it with her. Outside the car, she started to feel a little defenseless again. The park was open and exposed. She had no bushes to lurk behind. She put the hat on her head, covering the side of her face that was closer to Al's vehicle. There was no way even her mother would recognize her in the hat, Lydia assured herself.

Lydia strolled by, looking deliberately away from the car and at the river. She watched a small sailboat make its way back to its dock. The sky had now turned a deep purple. When she had gone a few feet past the car, she pivoted and turned her uncovered eye toward Al's SUV. As Emmanuel had said, there was no movement inside, but she could see two figures. Had Al turned over a new leaf and begun to convert the prostitutes to Catholicism? It was highly unlikely. But perhaps he was with someone who wasn't a prostitute. Lydia strolled toward the water and pretended to take a few quick photos of the Williamsburg Bridge. It was far too dark, and she knew there was no way they would come out. The sight of the water reminded her of Glenda and her tragic end. The poor woman had been murdered and was being buried today. If the man in the SUV behind her was the murderer, he needed to be stopped and punished.

Lydia turned and walked back toward the parking lot. The glare was now gone from the windshield, and a streetlight had come on next to the car. Lydia could see the two figures in the car much more clearly now. They were sitting awkwardly, tilted in their seats as if they had fallen asleep. The head of the woman in the passenger seat had fallen forward. Lydia quickened her pace, her breathing accelerated. No one except a long-haul trucker fell asleep at six o'clock. Something wasn't right.

Despite the risk of getting caught, she had to get closer. She marched forward as if she were headed for the car next to Al's, then veered right by the driver's window. She turned her head when she was parallel to Al's window and looked inside. She was afraid to meet Al's eyes initially, but now she was afraid of something else. She saw the blood first and then she knew. Al was not the killer. He had just become another victim.

Chapter 21

The flashing lights of the assembled police cars and ambulances turned the brick building next to the park a pulsing blood red. Men and women in blue uniforms swarmed all over the park, having evicted all the necking couples. It was déjà vu all over again. Same park, different victim. When it looked like it was going to be a long night, Lydia gave Emmanuel some money to run up to the bodega on Berry and get them sandwiches for dinner. The cops would want to question them both, but first they had to take care of Al and the other victim. She wondered if anything on her camera might identify the killer. She had searched through the photos on her camera over and over again and could see nothing on her tiny screen that might help.

Between quick bites of her Italian sub, she thought about what she did know. Al had driven himself to Grand Street, so he had to have been killed at the park. There hadn't been much time between when he had arrived and when Lydia and Emmanuel had followed him there, but that had to be when he was murdered. There was maybe a five-minute window. Or it could have been after they arrived, since they hadn't had a clear view of his vehicle.

She tried to remember all the people they had seen enter and leave the park while they waited, but none of them seemed remarkable. Just families, people walking dogs, a few cars, and couples strolling in and out. Who could have done it? Who had wanted him dead? The only thing that made sense was that the same person who had killed Al had also killed Glenda and Anna.

An unmarked police car pulled up to the entrance at an angle, and Detective Romero got out and surveyed the scene. One of the cops approached him, a tiny African-American woman who had questioned Lydia earlier, and he tilted his head down to her as she clearly filled him in on all the details. When the cop pointed toward Emmanuel's car, she saw him frown. Lydia was afraid he was going to be more upset to have her involved again in one of his cases than happy to have a witness to Al's murder. Romero stalked over to the car. He hadn't even peeked at Al's body. She was definitely in trouble.

Lydia finished the last bite of her sandwich and quickly wiped her face with the tiny napkin that was more like a tissue. "Get ready," she told Emmanuel.

Emmanuel peered through the windshield. "You know that cop?"

"Oh, yeah," she said.

Romero rapped on the window with his knuckle. Lydia tried for a smile as she pressed the button on the window, slowly lowering it. "Hello, Detective."

Romero glanced around the car, shooting Emmanuel a quick assessing glance. He would probably be able to pick him out of a lineup later if he had to, but right now his focus was on Lydia. "McKenzie, I thought I told you to stay out of this mess."

"I guess I'm not very good at following orders. Perhaps if you said please . . ."

Emmanuel watched their exchange with an open mouth. She guessed that he had learned at an early age that it didn't pay to mouth off to officers. It was too bad she hadn't learned the lesson, too, but this wasn't just anyone.

Romero's face tightened and he looked as if he was about to say something that he was going to regret. Instead, he sniffed the air. "What's that smell? An Italian sub?"

Lydia stuffed the napkin into the paper bag and nodded.

Romero threw back his head and laughed. The other cops looked over, appearing only mildly surprised to hear a detective laugh at a crime scene. "You took a look at those bodies and then ordered dinner? I gotta tell the guys that."

"It was dinnertime." Perhaps some people thought it was disrespectful to eat at the scene of a murder, but Lydia had been starving. She had missed the snacks at the funeral home, and she had no desire to pass out before they could be questioned.

Romero slapped the side of the car. "We'll make a cop out of you yet."

Lydia tucked the rest of her trash neatly into a paper bag. "So do you want to know what we saw or not?"

"Sure." Romero opened the door. Lydia had to slide over so he could get inside. He waited for her to resettle herself and start talking. Lydia started from when she got the call from Emmanuel and gave the details of the chase.

"You had Al followed?" Romero looked at Emmanuel, but Emmanuel had shrunk down in his seat.

"I thought he might be guilty. He certainly was upset when he found out that we'd taken pictures of him."

Romero twitched as though he wanted to tell her to let him do his job, but he knew it was no good. "Did you see anyone approach the car?"

Lydia gestured in the direction of Al's car. "We didn't exactly have a clear view. And there were those few minutes before we even arrived at the park. I think the murderer could have struck then. What time does the medical examiner say?"

"It's not such an exact science as that. They can just give us a ball-park."

Lydia was sorry now that they hadn't searched for a better place to park. If they'd known that Al was already dead or was about to get knocked off, they never would have bothered to hide.

Romero pointed at Lydia's camera. "You took some photos, didn't you?"

"Of course. This was a stakeout." She was surprised he would have to ask.

"Then I'll need to take the camera."

"What?"

"It's evidence."

"Now just a minute . . . ," Lydia began. She tried to help the NYPD as much as she could, and this was the thanks she got? "I need that camera. I have to take pictures for work."

"Borrow another one."

"No way." Lydia crossed her arms. "You'll have to talk to my lawyer." She was afraid she was actually going to have to get one.

Romero shook his head. "I'll borrow it for a couple of hours and download the pictures. After that, you can have it back."

"I'll send you the pictures like I did before."

"What are you so afraid of?"

"One, my camera won't come back to me. Two, the pictures haven't been edited yet."

"You don't want us to see any duds, huh? Or do you have naked pictures of your boyfriend on there?"

Lydia ignored his last comment. "I would prefer to just send you the few select ones that illuminate the murder of Al."

Romero looked over the scene in front of them, his mind clearly already on the task ahead. "By the way, do you know the woman who was with Al Savarese?"

Lydia remembered the woman's body in the car and swallowed hard. Her sandwich suddenly wasn't sitting so nicely in her stomach. "No, I don't think so. But I didn't take a close look."

Romero shrugged. "You seem to know every other person we carry out on a gurney, so I thought I'd check."

Lydia snorted. "Why don't you go figure out who she is and stop leaning on me to do your job?"

Romero opened the car door and slid out. "Send me those photos by ten o'clock or I'll come collect that camera personally."

Lydia waved a hand at him dismissively and wished she had the guts to give him the finger. She couldn't help watching him move purposely over to Al's car. The guy certainly knew how to take control of a crime scene.

Her phone rang. Jack was calling.

"Hello?" she answered, wondering what kind of mood he'd be in. Just then a police car pulled out of the park and let loose its siren.

"Where are you?" Jack demanded.

"Uh, Grand Street Park."

"Are you in trouble with the cops again?"

Lydia bit her lip. She tried to make it her policy never to lie in relationships. She sometimes didn't mention things that might disturb or worry the other person, but when faced with a direct question, she couldn't tell a lie. "I'm with Emmanuel. Al Savarese was murdered and we found his body."

"You were following him again? I thought you were done with that case."

"Sort of." There was a long silence. Lydia wondered what it would take for him to relax and trust her. He seemed convinced that she was putting herself in mortal danger just by sitting in a Lincoln and doing her job.

"You forgot, didn't you?" Jack's voice was petulant. Lydia wracked her brain. Today was Thursday. She'd had Glenda's funeral to go to, and then what? Uh-oh. She just remembered that she'd promised to go out to Lulu's with Jack and some friends from work to celebrate his best friend's promotion.

"You got started without me, right? I think the cops will let me go if I ask."

"We've been here an hour already," Jack said. He clearly wasn't willing to give up laying on the guilt.

"I can be there in fifteen minutes. Emmanuel can take me right over the bridge." The last thing Lydia wanted to do was go to a bar. She felt tired and grubby. But she wanted to see Jack and meet more of his friends.

After she hung up she sat there for a moment before she realized she'd committed Emmanuel to drive her around some more. "I'm sorry, Emmanuel, do you mind driving me across?"

"No worries. You got problems with the man?"

Lydia loved how Emmanuel pronounced *man,* all drawn out and rounded like it was spelled *mon.* "I can't figure out what he wants. I mean, he knew I worked for PIs and was photographing prostitutes when we met."

Emmanuel chuckled softly. "Men just want their women to be safe."

"I suppose so." Lydia fished a comb and some lipstick out of the bottom of her bag. She would do her best to freshen up. At least her little black dress was fairly presentable and didn't scream funeral.

Lulu's was a bar that consciously strived to achieve its dive-bar status. The owners used dark stained wood in the construction, kept the lights low, and got all the furniture used and off the street. It was funky and dirty, and not at all the kind of place that financial guys should be attracted to. But that was also probably why the ties came in droves. It was considered cool to be somewhere completely different from their chrome-and-steel office buildings. Emmanuel dropped her right in front and scanned the front anxiously.

"Your man should take you someplace nicer."

"It's okay. We won't stay long."

Emmanuel drove away shaking his head. Lydia stifled a grin as she went in.

She scanned the bar and almost didn't see Jack among all the other white shirts and ties. It looked like a business convention from Iowa had taken a wrong turn from the Jacob Javitts Center. At last she spotted him. He was deep in conversation with two other guys dressed exactly like he was and a blond woman in a navy blue suit. Lydia made her way through the crowded tables and gently touched him on the shoulder.

"Hey," she said as softly as the bar would allow. Jack lunged from his chair and gave her a sloppy kiss on the lips that tasted like bourbon. She had to brace herself to keep from getting knocked over. He was definitely sloshed.

"Everyone, this is Lydia. Lydia this is Matt, Polly, and Drew." The threesome nodded at Lydia, not even pretending they weren't checking her out. On closer inspection, she could see that Drew's face was squarer and his coloring was more olive than Matt's. They went to the same barber, based on the identical haircuts, and bought their shirts and ties at the same menswear shop.

"Sorry I'm so late." The empty chair contained everyone's bags, and no one made a move to take them. Lydia looked at Jack and waited. When he finally realized that the stuff needed to be moved, he began shoveling the briefcases and suit jackets to the various people who owned them.

A harassed-looking waitress wearing tiny black shorts, a white tank top, and long blond braids rushed over. "What'll it be?"

After such an awful day, the only antidote was hard liquor. "A gin and tonic please." The others ordered more whiskeys and beer, and the waitress hurried back to the bar.

A silence fell over the table. Lydia was sure that the details of her day wouldn't encourage pleasant conversation, so she merely sat there smiling, doing her best nice-girlfriend imitation. Drew turned and stared at the TV over the bar showing a baseball game. Polly played with the straw in her drink, and Jack grabbed Lydia's leg under the table.

"Did you meet the new partner? He's from the DC office I think. I hear he loves scuba diving. If you want to get in good, talk about scuba diving," Matt said at very high volume. His accent was pure Long Island.

"I've never been scuba diving," Drew said, tearing his eyes away from the monitor. "I don't swim."

"Scuba diving is amazing. When my parents go to Club Med at Christmastime, we always go, too." Jack, Polly, and Matt began to discuss the merits of the Caribbean versus South America and the Great Barrier Reef. Drew tuned out and watched the game. Lydia knew nothing about scuba diving, and very little about baseball. When her drink came she grabbed it gratefully and drank it far too fast.

The conversation moved on to more people at their office that Lydia didn't know. The waitress was still rushed and didn't look as if she'd be swinging by again to offer refills. Lydia found it hard to stifle her yawns. Polly caught her on one of her jaw-breaking ones and looked momentarily sympathetic. "I need to go catch a cab. We've all got work tomorrow, remember?"

"Sure, sure." Matt seemed reluctant to leave the party, but Jack had already gotten unsteadily to his feet. They settled up the tab. Lydia always got sticker shock when she went out for drinks in Manhattan. She was glad she just owed ten bucks for her one g&t.

It wasn't difficult to score a cab on Delancey. The street was practically a sea of yellow. Lydia waved good-bye to all of Jack's work friends and stuffed him in a taxi heading back across the Williamsburg Bridge. By the time they got to the middle of the bridge, Jack was sound asleep and snoring like an old man with severe sinus problems. She directed the cab to her front door and then discovered she had no more cash. She had to search around in Jack's pocket to find his wallet and settle the tab.

"Okay, Jack, time to get inside," she said grimly, shaking him awake. He looked around blearily.

"I am so horny," he mumbled. "I missed you, babe." The taxi driver looked out the window, pretending not to hear.

"That's great, honey. But I need you to walk through the door."

Jack yawned and stumbled out of the car. She hooked his arm around her neck and managed to help him get inside without too much trouble. He wobbled backward one time going up the stairs, and she was afraid that he was going to knock them both over, but he recovered his balance just in time. She helped him over to her couch, praying that he wasn't going to puke everywhere. She would probably have upchucked herself in sympathy. She was bone-tired. Jack lay down and fell back asleep, still wearing his work clothes.

The cat waited in the kitchen until Jack was asleep and then came out tentatively, winding his tail around her ankle. "Hello, cat," she said, and petted him behind the ears. He purred encouragingly, and she felt more content than she'd felt all day. As earthshaking snores emerged from her couch, she had to admit that there were some benefits to cat ownership after all.

Chapter 22

When she arrived at the D'Angelos' the next morning, she had to search for the key in her bag to unlock the door. She was wearing a red wrap dress that made her feel beautiful without making her wish she were wearing pants.

Frankie wasn't in yet. He normally beat her to the office. He liked to read the paper first thing and give himself an excuse to leave early. But it wasn't just any morning, and at the coffee shop she'd caught sight of the daily paper Frankie preferred. The big headline read "Double Sex Murder in Williamsburg," and she knew the story was about Al's murder. She bought a copy. She imagined Frankie, Leo, and Mama were at their cousin's side. When anything happened in the D'Angelo family, they tended to huddle together and cook a lot of food.

She sat down at her desk with her coffee and opened the paper to the story. She cried out when she read the prostitute's name. Josefina Lopez. Lydia remembered her, the small, scared girl who had come aboard the bus. She needed more than just a pap smear, but she had refused their help, out of fear. Lydia thought that Gator was the one she was scared of, and she wondered if he had killed her. She had been so young, and Lydia had really wanted to help her. She put her head down on the desk and cried.

Crying wasn't going to solve the case, and it made her desk blotter extremely soggy. She tried drying the blotter with napkins and then went and splashed water on her face in the bathroom. She came back to her desk, took a deep breath, and read more about Josefina. There wasn't much information about her family, but the article said she'd died just seven blocks from where she had grown up. She was a local girl. She had been in and out of rehab and homeless shelters since she was fourteen. She'd had a sad life, and an even sadder death. She had not deserved to die.

There was a voice mail on her phone, and she wondered if Candi and the other women had heard the news.

"Send me those pictures now, or I'll come by and collect your camera." Lydia made a face at her phone as she listened to Romero's voice on her voice mail. Before she gave in to Romero's threats and nagging, she wanted to get a good look at the photographs she'd taken. She had been too sick and distracted to do much, but she had snapped a few of the car when they arrived, and the bodies in the car before the police had arrived. In the end, she only had five good shots to send Romero. She e-mailed them to him and hoped he would find them useful enough to lay off.

Ten minutes later her phone rang. Romero's name flashed on the caller ID.

"I got your pictures. I can't believe that was all you took."

Lydia frowned. "I was a little distracted by the blood and gore. I'm not as accustomed to it as you are."

"The photos don't show anything. I can't read a single license plate," Romero complained.

"Sorry. I told you we were parked far away." Lydia drummed her fingers on her desk, irritated. She had delivered photographs of the murder before the cops arrived, and this was the thanks she got.

"You're going to need to come in today." Romero sounded all business.

"Why? You interviewed me yesterday, and I told you all I know."

"We want to go over your story again." His voice sounded colder than the Arctic Circle. She shivered. She was in real trouble. He rarely insisted that she actually come to the station. She knew his department was under a lot of pressure from city officials to catch the killer. Before it had been prostitutes, but now that the johns were getting killed, she imagined all the politicians and big shots were getting nervous. They would want to see results before their constituents started picketing.

"How about five o'clock?" She knew she was stalling, but she couldn't face an interrogation right now. She felt too raw from hearing about Josefina's death. Besides, she'd missed a lot of work already this week.

"Sure, sure." Romero sounded like his mind was already on another case, or another suspect. Lydia wondered what he really wanted from her. Maybe just to tape the conversation as evidence.

Lydia turned back to her desk and began to file away a few of the cases that were officially closed. The task didn't take long. The D'Angelos had some open cases and pile of calls to return, but they didn't seem in a hurry to get busy. Leo had been dating, and Frankie had been his regular lazy self. If they let the business totally decline, she would have to look for another job. That would be too bad. For all her complaints about the D'Angelos, she had become rather used to them.

They had their quirks, and the job was certainly not nonstop excitement. The filing, billing, and expense reports sent her into a coma. But she'd found ways to do the minimum while getting credit for being highly efficient.

Around eleven o'clock, Lydia got up and stretched. She checked her phone and saw that she had missed a call. She wondered if it was Jack, and her heart skipped a beat. When she woke up that morning he had already been gone. Despite being drunk the night before, he had managed to drag himself out of bed at the usual time.

The message was from the vet's office. "We think we may have located a home for the cat. Please call us back as soon as you get this message."

Lydia should have been elated. She didn't want a cat, did she? She remembered the affectionate greeting she had received the night before. She wasn't going to get attached, but even she could see that the cat was special. After all, he had saved her life. The last thing she wanted was for him to go to a family that would hurt him. She would have to check them out before handing over the cat. She owed him that much.

Sitting lost in thought, she heard the phone in her hand ring. It was Princess.

"What's wrong with those pigs? They couldn't catch a killer if it bit them in the ass." Princess sounded pretty choked up, but she was also spitting mad. Lydia was glad she wasn't a cop. "Josefina was our sister. Is nobody safe?"

Lydia refrained from telling her that prostitution was a dangerous job, because it certainly wouldn't make her feel better. "I'm sorry for your loss. I met Josefina on the bus, and she seemed like a sweet kid."

Princess blew her nose into the phone. "She was. I knew her since she was a baby."

Lydia cleared her throat. "I was following the car she was in, and I think I arrived just after they were murdered."

"Not soon enough," Princess despaired.

No, it hadn't been soon enough to save their lives. She had once again come too late to be anything but a witness. She remembered pulling into the park when they'd spotted Al's car. A dark SUV had pulled out just as they'd arrived. She wasn't sure why it had slipped her mind. Gator owned one, and she hadn't seen the license plate to see if it was his vanity plate. He was violent and crazy, according to some reports, and maybe he had started killing the prostitutes who worked for him for some reason. He was worth checking out.

"Josefina worked for Gator, didn't she?"

Princess groaned.

Lydia took that as a yes. "Can you get me in to meet him?"

There was a long pause. Lydia could hear Princess breathing, considering. "You think he did it?"

"I don't know. I saw a car that looked like his at Grand right when she was killed."

"A lot of people drive SUVs," Princess said. Lydia remembered that Princess did, too.

"I don't have any other leads at this point, and I'd love to ask him some questions."

Princess let out a long sigh. "I'll talk to Cilla and see what she can do."

When Lydia hung up, Leo came into the office. He looked exhausted. He started shuffling through the mail and throwing out the junk.

"How is your cousin holding up?" she asked.

"She's as well as can be expected. My mother and Frankie are still with her." He tossed one piece of mail into the in-box, three into the trash can. Each made a satisfying thump when it hit the can.

"That's good. She'll need family at a time like this." Lydia fingered the file on her desk that had all the details of Al's infidelities. "What should I do with everything we collected on Al?"

"Pitch it. Patricia certainly doesn't need a divorce now she's a widow." Leo threw the last piece of mail away and went to sit down at his desk.

Al might have been a cheating bastard, but Leo's attitude seemed a little callous. She wondered if the D'Angelos were capable of getting rid of someone who had wronged their family. She wouldn't put it past them. And, because of their experience as PI's, they could probably figure out how not to get caught. But she doubted they would have killed the prostitutes, too. They had a protective attitude when it came to women, and the prostitutes had certainly done nothing to harm their family.

"In fact," Leo chuckled, "if you listen to Patricia now, she's convinced she was married to a martyred saint."

Lydia shook her head in disbelief. She supposed it was easier to delude yourself than face up to the truth about your marriage. "The cops asked for copies of my photos."

"Good. Help them with whatever they need to catch the guy that killed him. He was family." Al was back in the family's good graces now that he had been murdered. It was all very ironic. He certainly couldn't do anything further to disgrace them.

Chapter 23

After work, Lydia hopped on her bike and rode over to the police precinct. Going to talk to Romero was the last thing she wanted to do, but she had to do her best to give him all the information that she had. She wondered if the cops were more concerned with Al than with Josefina. The press was certainly making a much bigger stink about Al. Patricia had been shown on the news sobbing her heart out, and without bothering to do any digging, the reporters had bought her line about Al as her beloved husband. Lydia was aware that the police knew better, but she still felt a little unclean thinking about it.

Lydia announced herself to the police sergeant and sat down to wait. A few minutes later Romero came down to meet her.

"Thanks for coming in," Romero said. Lydia grimaced. He didn't even sound like himself. She followed him down the hall to a conference room, wondering what she was in for. The first night she had met Romero she had been interrogated in this room, and that hadn't gone well, either. She wished she knew what he was after.

Romero arranged the photographs she had taken on the table so each one was visible, and turned on the tape recorder with a click. "This conversation with Lydia McKenzie is being recorded." Romero recited the date and time and asked if she knew it was being recorded.

She rolled her eyes. "Yes."

"Do you confirm that you took these photographs?"

Lydia said that she had the night before, and recited the evening's activities.

"And your driver, Emmanuel Jordan, left the car at 5:30 and was gone for one half an hour?"

"Yes, I didn't walk by myself to look because I was afraid Al would recognize me. . . ."

"Were you able to see or hear Mr. Jordan during that time?"

"No, I didn't have a clear sight line. But he walked by the car and came back and told me about it." Lydia felt flustered. Emmanuel had been gone a long time, but she was positive he had just been checking out the car.

Romero made a note. "Has Mr. Jordan been with you at the scene of every other killing?"

"Not Glenda's death. I wasn't there, either. I just found her. But he was with me before Anna was killed. We left together."

"So you didn't see him after he took you home, and he could have returned to the scene."

When Lydia didn't answer right away, Romero looked up. He had on his poker face again, and Lydia felt like she didn't know who he was. She was appalled. "What are you implying? That Emmanuel is a killer?" Lydia shook her head. "He was only there because of me. Why would he want to kill prostitutes or Al? That's ridiculous."

"Please just answer the question."

Lydia felt sick to her stomach. If Emmanuel got roped into this because of her, she never would forgive herself. The criminal justice system was notorious in this country for chewing up black men and spitting them out in the middle of busy traffic. Emmanuel was a good guy with a hopeful future as a recent immigrant. He didn't deserve a murder rap.

"I hope you're not forgetting to question your high school buddies in your quest to pin this on an innocent guy," Lydia said scornfully. She knew she wasn't playing fair, but she didn't like the direction his investigation was taking.

Romero's nose pinched up, as if he had just gotten a whiff of a very bad stench. "We're following all leads."

"Great, you do that. Now, was there anything else you needed?"

"The rest of the photographs that you took," Romero said flatly.

Lydia folded her arms across her chest. "They were repetitious, I'm afraid. I threw them out when I downloaded these finished ones."

"Then I will have to confiscate your camera to make sure." Lydia stared at Romero in disbelief. She wished she could tell him to go screw himself and walk out, but she knew they could make her life miserable if they wanted to. With trembling hands she removed her camera from her bag and placed it on the table. She had scrimped and saved to buy that camera, and she knew it inside and out. She had rarely been apart from it, and she had no desire to become separated now.

"If you as much as scratch my camera, I want a completely new replacement from the NYPD." The slight tremor in her voice ruined its forcefulness.

Romero pushed across a paper for her to sign as a receipt, and she scrawled her name at the bottom. Her handwriting was so messy she could barely recognize it. Her hand was shaking too much.

"This interview is now concluded." Romero turned off the tape recorder and stood up like the marine he probably used to be. She almost expected him to apologize now that the interview was officially over, but she could see he had no intention of doing so.

Lydia didn't know when she'd been madder at him. If she didn't care about tracking down Glenda's killer, Lydia would have dared him to arrest her. She would have refused to give him her camera. And she definitely would refuse to answer his stupid questions about Emmanuel.

Lydia stood with as much dignity as she could. "Good luck, Detective. It looks like you're going to need it."

At her bike, her phone beeped that she had a text message. She opened it up, realizing that her hand was still trembling. Jack wrote that he was going to spend the night at his own place and catch up on his sleep. She realized she hadn't spoken to him all day. When they first started dating, they didn't go an hour without calling or texting each other. Reading between the lines, it sounded like he was about to say that they both needed more space. And everyone knows that asking for more space means you want to break up. Lydia wanted to call him, but his text message implied that he didn't want to hear from her. She needed a second opinion, and she needed to focus on something other than her camera and Romero.

Pacing around on Broadway in front of her locked bike, she dialed Georgia Rae's number. Georgia sounded overly chipper. But then she hadn't been stumbling across dead bodies all week or getting interrogated by the police. Lydia recounted the story of the text message, as well as the disastrous meet-the-work-friends drinkathon.

"Sounds like trouble in paradise, sugar."

"Do you think he's going to dump me?" Lydia chewed the side of her thumbnail. "I mean, I was pretty mad at him for being so bossy, but I don't want to get dumped."

"I don't know Jack that well . . . ," Georgia began. "But he looked really into you the other night."

Georgia was trying to helpful, but it was true that she had only met Jack once. Now that Jack was blowing her off, Lydia could only think of every amazing thing about him. He was handsome. He was smart. He was funny. He wasn't broke. His paintings were beautiful. They had so much in common. "What should I do?"

"Give him some space, of course. And then call him tomorrow and apologize for your horrible PMS at the drinkathon. Men believe that every time."

"Okay, thanks," Lydia said.

"Hey—did you read about all those hookers getting killed? What's your cop friend think is going on?"

"I'm not really sure," Lydia stalled. Georgia was an amazing best friend, but she had a hard time not gossiping. Lydia didn't feel right telling her about the gang, Al, and all the women in case Georgia blabbed it all over the neighborhood. She also didn't feel like telling her about her blowup with Romero. Georgia Rae might take his side, and then she would be mad at her, too.

"It's part of a case I'm working on for the D'Angelos. Romero and Jack are pretty mad at me for getting involved."

She hoped Georgia was right that absence made the heart grow fonder, and tomorrow would feel different. Jack was the most amazing guy she'd dated in years, and she let him slip away just because he was concerned for her and his work friends were boring. Every guy had a few duds for friends, and hopefully he would learn to trust her someday.

"What do you mean you're involved? Did you know them? Were you there?"

"It's kind of complicated," Lydia said, scanning around her for some sort of excuse. A large truck zoomed by and made talking difficult for a moment. "I can't really talk here."

"It reminds me of that play I was in last year." Georgia had starred in a musical about violence against women—the producers had hoped it would take Broadway by storm. It closed after a few weeks, much to her dismay. Apparently the world was not ready to be entertained with songs about battered women. "Prostitution is such a vulnerable profession. Women get killed all the time and the cops do nothing. Everyone just acts like they're asking for it, like they would be hookers if they had a choice."

Lydia tried to imagine what Glenda would have done if she could have been anything. With her talent for morphing into different personalities, she could have been an actress. Or with all her successful pitches for more money, a saleswoman. Anna's sweet personality and love of children would have made her a great teacher. And Josefina? Lydia didn't know anything about her, and she was still saddened by her death. None of them had the advantages of a good education, and none of them had seen any other choice. It was tragic.

Lydia and Georgia made a tentative plan to have dinner later in the week. She hated when they didn't have a chance to see each other for weeks. She missed talking to Georgia and hearing about her crazy life. She might have to go in and get some highlights at Georgia's salon just so they could hang out.

Lydia put her phone away and started biking slowly home. A few hookers were standing on a corner in tight dresses and too much makeup. Lydia wanted to stop and tell them to take a vacation this week and wait until the murderer was caught, but she doubted they would appreciate the warning. She was sure they desperately needed the money they would make tonight or they wouldn't be standing out there in the first place.

Lydia's phone began to ring a block later, and her heart skipped a beat at the thought that it was Jack calling to say he'd changed his mind. She pulled over to the curb and fished the phone out of her pocket. She didn't recognize the number, but she answered it anyway.

"It's Cilla. Princess said you wanted to see Gator?"

The train rumbled by on the elevated tracks over Broadway, and Lydia had to wait until it passed before she could hear the rest of the conversation. "Yes, I would. Do you think you could arrange it?"

"He's having a party at his pad tonight for clients. But you need to promise me that you won't make him mad, okay? He's still my cousin, and he does a lot for the family."

Lydia thought Gator might consider any questions offensive, but she couldn't miss the opportunity. She would just have to wish for the best. "Just let me know where and when and I'll be there."

Chapter 24

Lydia had surprisingly few options when it came to dressing super-sexy. She was afraid that any sort of modest clothing would make her stand out at a pimp party. She needed something seriously skimpy that would show a lot of cleavage and leg. She pulled out and discarded schoolmarmish blouses, skirts that went past her knee, and dresses that didn't fit. A figure-hugging purple dress with a flirty skirt went into the maybe pile, but looked a little too conservative. She dug out a sequined tank top with a scoop neck that she had forgotten about. It didn't get many points for cleavage, but it sure had flash. She also found a black miniskirt that barely covered her butt. When she tried it on, she remembered the reason it was at the bottom of her closet. The last time she had worn it, she'd had to fight guys off with a stick. It was absolutely perfect.

The search through her shoe collection was a little frustrating. The cat stopped washing his face for a minute to watch her progress. At last she found some silver pointed shoes that had three-inch heels. She held them up for the cat to see. "Ah-ha! Aren't these perfect?"

The cat just stared at her. He clearly didn't understand the finer points of human fashion. She was sure her feet were going to be killing her by the end of the night, but it would be worth it. She managed to dig up some stockings that were neither ripped nor too small and finished getting dressed. She kept her makeup subtle but put on a little red lipstick that looked great. She made a face at herself in the mirror. Her reflection reminded her of those lost girls on the corner waiting for customers. Would she be willing to sleep with strangers for money? Luckily she had never had to make such a choice and hopefully never would. She supposed that if she were hungry enough she would do anything to survive.

Her phone rang, and she lunged at it, expecting it to be Cilla. Instead it was her parents. "Hi, darling! You'll never guess where we are?"

Lydia grimaced. She loved her parents, and usually she was happy to hear from them. She hated to tell them she was in a hurry and risk hurting their feelings. She tried to remember where they had sent the postcard from last. It was difficult to keep up with their RV adventures since they had no fixed address.

"Idaho?" She guessed.

Her dad laughed, a funny guffaw that always made her smile. "That was last week. Did you get our card?"

"Yes—the one with the giant potato?" Lydia looked at her counter helplessly. It was covered with junk mail from the week.

"We put in a clue."

Lydia stood in her kitchen wearing her sexy outfit, glad her father couldn't see her. She couldn't figure out what her father was talking about. Before she could wonder too long, her mother seized the receiver. "Are you okay, honey?"

Lydia wished she could tell her the truth. Women she knew were being killed. She was going to a party in hopes of meeting a pimp and finding out if he was the killer. But she knew this would cause her parents a lot of angst. She didn't want to upset them. Chances are they would do something crazy like drive their RV to Brooklyn.

"I'm just on my way out. . . ."

"Oh, honey. We won't keep you then. We just wanted to call and give you our love from Des Moines."

It wasn't until Lydia hung up the phone that she figured out her dad's clue on the card. Scene of the birth referred to his birthplace. They had gone to Des Moines to visit the place where he had been born. She laughed to herself. She loved her father's quirky ways.

Now running late, she tottered into the hallway hoping not to run into any of her neighbors. They were suspicious enough as it was. She'd had Romero and other police officers visit her on numerous occasions, and she was convinced they all thought she was a drug dealer. She tucked her key next to her very small phone and a twenty-dollar bill in a small silver purse. She always carried cash for an emergency cab fare home. She wasn't sure how pleased Cilla was going to be with her once she'd questioned Gator, so she might have to find her own way home at the end of the night.

She was almost out the front door when she ran into Mrs. Zablonsky, an elderly Polish lady who had never learned to mind her own business. She took in Lydia's outfit with rounded eyes.

"Out for a night of fun?"

Lydia smiled sweetly, pretending that she hadn't heard. "Have a good evening!" She scooted out the door.

Lydia heard Cilla before she spotted her silver muscle car. The music coming from the speakers was so loud the bass line felt like it was shaking the stone steps of Lydia's apartment building. The car was built low so the muffler dragged on the street for maximum volume. Cilla peered out the window at Lydia as she approached. Lydia opened the door and climbed into the passenger seat, trying to resist the urge to cover her ears with her hands.

"You look really good!" Cilla sounded surprised. Maybe she thought Lydia would dress like a college professor and stand out like a sore thumb.

"You look good, too." Lydia had to shout to be heard over the music. In contrast to her earlier baggy jeans, Cilla had on a silver lamé dress that left little of her curvy form to the imagination. Her hair had been teased to stand six inches above her head, and her makeup was thick and plentiful.

"My cousin gets mad at me when I dress like this, but I'm not a nun, you know?" There are a lot of gradations in the sexual spectrum between a nun and a whore, but this wasn't the time to bring it up. Lydia watched as bystanders leaped out of the way of the silver car as it growled and zoomed down side streets. Cilla ignored the panicked pedestrians as she swerved around double-parked cars, roared through stop signs without stopping, and barely avoided colliding with an ice-cream truck. Lydia wondered whether she'd feel better if she closed her eyes, but then decided that she was too wound up to do so. She wondered why she never rode in the cars of good drivers.

"Gator throws the biggest and best parties," Cilla shouted over the music. The music abruptly changed from a rap song to an R & B ballad. It was strange to hear someone singing to their lover at an ear-piercing decibel. Cilla must have felt that way, too, because she reached over and turned it down slightly. It was still loud, but now at least Lydia didn't have to keep checking her ears to see if they were bleeding.

"Where does Gator live?" Lydia said loudly.

"He's got a place by the water. The penthouse. It was the second thing he bought, after a house for my aunt." He sounded like a saint taking such good care of his mommy. Too bad he could be a killer, too.

Lydia noticed they were driving the same way that Al had so many times by the water. She had been so eager to get pictures of him, never knowing that he would soon be dead. A few women were standing along the street tonight, waiting for customers. Apparently they hadn't made the invitation list. They were employees, and giving them the night off would probably cut too heavily into his profits.

Cilla screeched to a halt in front of a large glass building. Could only people in the sex trade afford the luxury condos in the neighborhood? Lydia was beginning to wonder. She stepped gingerly onto the sidewalk in her heels. She wasn't used to heels so high, and she had to remind herself to be careful. The music cut off abruptly with the sound of the engine, but the ballad still rang in Lydia's ears. The horn on the car honked as Cilla pressed a button to turn on the security system. Lydia pitied anyone who tried to steal her car. They probably wouldn't survive the initial blast of sound.

Cilla walked to the glass front door and hit a series of buttons on a silver console with the tips of her fake nails. They were painted with silver sparkles to match her dress. The intercom crackled slightly. "Yo."

"It's Cilla. Gator's cousin."

"Who you with?"

"My friend Lydia." Cilla sounded bored. Lydia felt strangely nervous. Conscious of being watched through the security camera, she tried not to look intimidating or suspicious. It must have worked because the door buzzed a few seconds later. She was in.

The inside lobby was stark and modern. There was nothing about it that was inviting or encouraging of visitors. She was sure it was intentional. The people living here paid for exclusivity, even in the middle of the industrial park. They didn't want anyone to feel like they could hang out there.

Cilla walked confidently up to the elevator and hit the up arrow. Watching her reflection in the metal doors, she fluffed her hair. Lydia averted her eyes from her own image. She didn't want to think about how much she looked like a hooker. She was here to find out if Gator was the killer, and to find out what he knew. She tried to think of what she could ask him without angering him.

The inside of the elevator was just as reflective. Lydia guessed there was a camera hidden behind the mirror, too. The place felt empty, but it also felt as protected as a bank vault. Clearly the residents wanted to protect their valuables. In Gator's line of business, there was undoubtedly a lot of cash around and the need to keep a veil of privacy.

The doors to the elevator opened on the penthouse floor, and a large intimidating man stood in front of the elevator, frowning. He was dressed in a sharp suit that in no way hid the size of his muscles, and he looked like a Latino linebacker. Lydia almost dived back in the elevator. Cilla charged over and gave him a hug and a kiss.

"Paco! Why are you frowning at me, Papi?"

"Gator isn't going to like that outfit. What would your mami say?"

Cilla pouted at him. "I think I look nice."

Paco jerked his chin in Lydia's direction. "Who's this?"

"My friend Lydia. Smile at her. Isn't she pretty?"

Paco did not smile. He wore an earpiece like a Secret Service man. He was probably paid to be overly careful. "You can stay until eleven, but then you've got to go."

Lydia wondered what happened at eleven. Music was pounding through the door, so the party had evidently started already. It was strange that Gator was so protective of his cousin, considering his line of work and considering the fact that a large number of her friends worked for him. Apparently Cilla had never entered the family business.

"You are so mean, Paco. I won't dance with you tonight, then." But Paco was already listening in his earpiece to further instructions. Cilla tossed her hair dramatically and pulled Lydia in behind her through the door.

Inside the loft, the walls and floor were painted bright white, and the furniture had been purchased to match. A disco ball spun, and strange lights pulsed from the corners. It took a moment for Lydia's eyes to adjust. The smell of incense mixed with alcohol and sweat was overwhelming. Topless women in bow ties circulated with trays, offering champagne and hors d'oeuvres. It was hard to know where to look, but it was difficult to look anywhere and not see naked breasts jiggling. Lydia was beginning to feel strangely overdressed.

Cilla snagged two champagne flutes from a passing waitress and handed one to Lydia. Cilla downed hers quickly, while Lydia sipped hers carefully. She reminded herself that she was working. She needed to keep a clear head, but the incense smoke was clearly masking the smoke of something stronger, and it was starting to make her feel a little fuzzy. Suddenly fearful, she wished she could walk back out. She took a deep breath and told herself to calm down. She had worked hard for the chance to meet with Gator, and she needed to follow through on the opportunity. It was doubtful she'd get another.

"I'm going to go get a real drink," Cilla said. "I'll be right back." Lydia almost followed her. All the guys looked as though they had just stopped by after work on Wall Street, and all the women, except for Cilla and Lydia, were half-naked waitresses. The guys in suits reminded her of Jack, and she checked her phone again. He hadn't called or texted her again since he told her he needed space. She wondered if she had completely screwed up the most incredible relationship she'd ever had. A guy like Jack was marriage material. The M word normally gave her the heebie-jeebies, but in the middle of all this excess—too much alcohol, nakedness, and drugs—marriage seemed more appealing than ever before.

When a waitress walked by with chicken satay skewers, Lydia lunged for the tray and snagged two. She knew it was impolite, but she had to get something in her stomach. The satay were cold but flavorful, and gone in just a few minutes. She wished she'd thought to grab more. But then another waitress walked by holding a tray of vegetarian sushi. Lydia took three and felt much better after she ate them. She was just wondering where she could throw away her dirty napkins when Cilla finally returned.

"I found Gator. He can talk for just a few minutes."

Lydia followed Cilla through the crowd, depositing the napkins on a passing waitress's tray. The party stretched on and on, and the loft seemed to contain an endless series of rooms. She saw one couple disappear hand in hand through a side door, and she wondered whether there was some sort of orgy happening in a back room.

Cilla nodded at a small man standing in a suit by a door. He nodded back and opened the door behind him. Cilla walked into the dark room and Lydia followed her. Here the pounding music, large crowd, and incense faded away. Gator sat in a La-Z-Boy chair in front of a large flat-screen TV. He was watching a baseball game with the sound off. One of his guards sat on the couch, and a beautiful woman hovered behind them.

"Did you see that? Did you *see* that? He was out." The guard was almost bouncing up and down like a little boy in his Armani suit. He had a round, happy face and an almost Santa Claus–like stomach.

"The umps are afraid of him, man. They won't call it." Gator had a shadow of a smile on his face as he stared at the TV. He wore all black, and tonight he was dripping with gold jewelry.

"They're all blind. Our man had him tagged."

Lydia didn't bother to watch. She had seen enough baseball to know the basic rules, but it wasn't an overwhelming love of hers. Professional sports players were becoming more and more oddly shaped as the years went on until, nearly grotesque in their extreme heights and weights, they no longer resembled the rest of the human race. Besides, she was more interested in observing Gator.

Cilla stood back, waiting. Lydia wondered if this was what it was like to visit a dictator or a king. It was difficult not to be intimidated by Gator's power, though. He could theoretically order any of the guards to kill them on a whim, and he could probably get away with it. But she didn't want to get too overawed. He was a pimp. Someday he would probably be disposed of by a jealous rival or die of an overdose or get nailed by the cops. His reign would not last forever.

Gator finally tore his eyes from the TV and fixed his gaze on Cilla. "Priscilla!" He addressed her softly in Spanish. His voice sounded gentle and loving, but Lydia felt Cilla stiffen next to her. It made Lydia uneasy, like she was witnessing a twisted family drama. Cilla spoke of Gator with both pride and fear, but Lydia was beginning to wonder about their relationship.

"I don't look like a whore, Gator. This is a nice dress." Gator shook his head. He was about to speak when Cilla interrupted. "This is my friend Lydia I told you about. She doesn't speak Spanish."

Gator looked her up and down, and Lydia tried not to blush. She wondered if he could tell that she had tried to dress like a hooker that night. "You're a friend of Danny's, huh? You work for the police?"

Lydia had to catch up for a moment. By "Danny," she realized he meant Daniel Romero. He had seen them together at Glenda's funeral. "I know Daniel Romero, but I don't work for the police. The Golden Horseshoe Gang asked me to look into the murder of the women on the waterfront."

Gator spat on the floor. It seemed very stagy, as though he was trying to remind her what a big bad street tough he was. "They were all my girls. I'll handle it."

Three of them had died while he was supposedly handling it, but she didn't think he would appreciate it if she brought up that fact. "Do you think it's someone who wants to put you out of business?"

"Like who? I own this neighborhood." Gator's knee began to jiggle. It appeared to be the only part of him that was not under his icy control.

"What about Sammy the Sauce?"

Gator sneered, revealing a gold tooth. "Sammy isn't a problem to nobody anymore."

Lydia was about to ask why not before she realized it was a stupid question. From his tone she could deduce that Sammy was no longer breathing, and either Gator or his guards had taken him down. So Gator was a cold-blooded killer. But had he killed the girls, too? Somehow sticking around and asking seemed too dangerous.

Gator had turned back to the TV. Their audience with the king was over. She and Cilla had been dismissed. Lydia was only too eager to leave. Her dress stank of the incense that permeated the party, and she felt unclean.

The guard on the couch got up and escorted them down a hall and out a door. They were back by the elevator with Paco again. "I want to go back to the party," Cilla whined.

"Gator wants you to go home and take off that dress," Paco told her. "The party is over." And he was clearly determined to make sure they left the premises.

Lydia took a deep breath of the night air, relieved to be out. The party had felt overpowering and dreamlike. While they walked to Cilla's car, Lydia couldn't stop herself from dialing Jack's number. She needed someone to hold her. Luckily, Jack answered right away.

"I miss you," she said quickly, letting all the longing enter her voice. She was done with playing games. She wanted him in her life, and she was ready to fight to keep him.

"Where are you?"

"I'm on my way home."

"I'm in the neighborhood. I can be there in ten minutes."

"Make it five," she said, getting into the car. Cilla didn't speak most of the way home but kept her music at a subdued level.

Lydia wondered what she was thinking about. "You're not scared of him, are you?"

"No, he is like my big brother. If I don't do as he says, he'll tell my mami and she'll scold me. He just wants his family to be respectable."

If Gator had such strong moral values when it came to his own family, then he certainly had an odd moral compass. "Thanks for taking me to speak to him. I hope he's not mad at you for bringing me."

"Do you think he did it?" Suddenly Cilla's voice sounded very small.

"I don't know," Lydia said. She didn't have the guts to tell Cilla what she really thought about Gator. Her cousin was a cold-blooded killer. He had thought nothing of murdering one of his rivals, so why wouldn't he do it to hookers who "belonged" to him?

At her door, she wished Cilla good night. Instead of walking in, she waited on her stoop for her lover to come. A few minutes later

Jack appeared around the corner, walking briskly toward her. He had a lope to his stride that gave her a pang in her heart. He looked like an artist when he walked, not an all-business banker. She felt like she was seeing his true soul. He stopped when he saw her and whistled with appreciation. She opened her arms and he walked into them. They embraced and kissed as if it had been years since they had seen each other.

A few minutes later they were upstairs ripping off their clothes. The scent of his skin was saturated with a smell that reminded her of the incense from Gator's party. But by then she couldn't tell if it was really the scent of her own skin as they lost track of where one of them began and the other ended.

Chapter 25

Lydia woke up alone in bed on Saturday morning. If the sheets weren't twisted and wrinkled, she would have thought she had dreamed that Jack had been there. He had left early to go to work. He warned her that he would, but it didn't make her feel any better. They were drifting apart. She had been so sure that he was the man for her. She decided she had to stop obsessing about their relationship, at least until after she had rustled up some coffee. The cat wound around her ankles as she washed her face. She filled his bowl with food and watched him eat a little delicately with his sharp teeth. She didn't enjoy scooping his litter box, but she had to admit he had been a pretty stress-free companion ever since he'd arrived. She knew she had to decide what to do with him soon.

Her local coffee shop was quiet on Saturday morning. Most of the residents hadn't woken up yet. Lydia's head still felt fuzzy from the night before. She sat on a stool and watched couples come in and out, some pushing baby strollers. Life appeared to be passing her by. Just a week ago she was a smug member of a happy couple, and now she felt like a kid locked out of a candy store. She could only stare longingly at the merchandise.

She felt restless and strange, so she decided to go to her darkroom. She needed to remind herself that she was an artist. She had to print more from her prostitute series and find out if she had something in her photographs that was worth working on. She had to refocus her energies on what she could control.

The darkroom was quiet, too. She lost herself in the smell of the chemicals and the deep darkness of the room. She was in her natural environment, and she pulled out her proofs, negatives, and box of paper without having to think. She felt purposeful and clearheaded again.

She examined her proofs from her shoot with Glenda. She had shot a lot and had a bunch of negatives that she hadn't considered because they hadn't fit the mood she was looking for. Here was Glenda close up, Glenda far away, and Glenda looking angry. She studied Glenda's eyes with a magnifying lens, as if they might hold the secret to her fate. But Glenda had been good at shuttering her expression and not revealing her thoughts.

Lydia turned with a sigh to a shot of Glenda making faces. At the time, Lydia had been annoyed. She had asked Glenda to look solemn and stand against a brick wall. She was trying to capture her dignity. Instead, Glenda had clowned around for a few minutes, and Lydia had caught some of it on camera, trying to stay patient. Now looking at Glenda fooling around made her feel wistful, as if she had missed some opportunity to reach out to her and make a difference.

She might not be able to figure out who killed Glenda, but she was determined to give her family a beautiful photograph. Near the bottom of the page, she found a perfect shot of Glenda laughing with her head thrown back. She looked strong and beautiful. In a few years, her kids might not remember her any longer. Susa would probably whitewash her memory for them, but they would find out about the darkness and tragedy of her death. Glenda had been careless with the love of all those around her. She had been an addict and, in the law's eyes, a criminal. But here on the page was another aspect of Glenda. Her vitality and her charisma. Candi was right. There was something special about her.

Before she knew it, the day was gone. She had missed lunch and was starving. She regretfully packed up her materials and reentered the sunlight of the real world. She picked up a falafel platter on the way home and ate it alone in her kitchen. She stayed up watching a stupid movie on television, telling herself she was not waiting for Jack to call, all while she listened for her phone. The last thing she was going to do was call him. But she did wonder what he was doing and who he was doing it with.

Chapter 26

Lydia picked up the phone innocently at the office, expecting it to be a routine inquiry about the business offered by the D'Angelos. Some callers were extremely concerned about discretion, and they needed careful handling. Others knew exactly what they wanted, and it was usually to talk to one of the D'Angelos right away. Instead, she found herself negotiating with the grieving widow.

Patricia Savarese sounded calm at first, but there was a strange hysterical edge to her voice that hinted she could blow at any moment. "I can't let pictures of my husband float around now that he's gone. I have to make sure he can rest in peace."

Lydia rolled her eyes. She was glad videoconferencing on phones had never caught on or she would be in big trouble. "Do you want me to send you our copies?"

"No! I want the negatives. And I want all the other copies destroyed." Patricia had to know that the cops had copies of everything

Lydia had taken, since she was there for her husband's blowup in the office. But maybe, with her selective memory about her husband's infidelities, she had forgotten this as well.

"So you want the originals," Lydia said. She thought for a moment about trying to explain digital photography to Patricia, but she remembered that she wasn't dealing with a rational mind.

"Bring them to me right away. I can't sleep or eat until they are all destroyed. It's not fair to my darling Al's memory." Patricia gave a little sob that sounded genuine and reminded Lydia that she had been through a lot. Lydia felt full of regrets about the part she played in Al's death, so it wasn't too hard to tug on her guilt.

Lydia found herself agreeing to bring the only copies of the photos in the world to Patricia right away. She was lying through her teeth, though. Not about coming up to Queens, but about giving her the only copies in existence. The photos still lived on her computer and still were at the police station. But she figured all Patricia needed was the illusion of letting Al rest in peace and then she would calm down.

After burning a CD of Al's drive-by sexual encounters, Lydia called Emmanuel. She figured she could charge the trip to the D'Angelos since it was their crazy cousin. Emmanuel didn't pick up his phone, which was unusual for him during business hours. She left a message, wondering where he was. He was usually so eager for work. She hoped he wasn't still getting hassled by the cops, and that Romero had turned his focus to finding the real killer. She waited a few minutes before calling a local car service company.

Lydia locked up the office and went out on the street to wait for the car. The eccentric lady next door was working in her garden. The yard was actually a patch of green Astroturf with white plastic angel statues holding down the corners, but the neighbor went out regularly to vacuum it clean. She always glared at Lydia when she saw her, so they had never spoken or learned each other's names. Lydia figured it was nothing personal. She probably didn't like having a detective agency next door and thought they were spying on her.

The car pulled up a few moments later. The driver was distracted by a conversation in Spanish on his cell phone headset, so Lydia sat back and enjoyed the ride. She knew the way very well since they had followed Al along the route. She allowed her mind to drift to the problem of why the killer, after killing just women, had suddenly lashed out at a customer. She wondered if it was a copycat crime. They always looked to the spouses at times like this, and Lydia thought about what she knew about Patricia. Patricia had wanted a divorce, according to her mother, Rose. Now she was a widow. It seemed pretty convenient. If Patricia wasn't such a doormat and clearly in love with Al, Lydia would have assumed that she had done it. But the pattern of prostitutes dying on the streets felt more like the work of a madman than a madwoman.

The car pulled up in front of Al's little house, and Lydia quickly handed over the money to the driver. She realized that she still thought of the house as Al's, and had to correct herself. The house belonged just to Patricia now.

The street was lined with cars, and Lydia was glad she didn't have to search for a parking space. She rang the doorbell, prepared to hand over her CD and run. But Patricia didn't answer the door: Mama D'Angelo did.

"Lydia! What are you doing here?"

"Patricia called me . . . ," Lydia began. She didn't get any further before Mama pulled her inside.

"How sweet of you to come by! Patricia needs friends and family at a time like this. She is devastated." Lydia was guided into a living room stuffed with family members. Most of them bore alarming re-semblances to the D'Angelos, and two of them were Frankie and Leo.

Lydia gave a weak wave, and Leo frowned at her. His girlfriend, Caroline, was sitting next to him, looking pale and sour. Lydia was beginning to wonder if this was her normal expression or if she just had a hard time dealing with the D'Angelos. They could certainly be overwhelming.

"Come eat! The buffet is over here. Patricia is powdering her nose and will be down again shortly."

The hour was dangerously close to lunchtime, and Lydia's stomach rumbled when she saw the table filled with food. She'd barely had any-thing to eat for breakfast, and the spread looked enticing. She picked up a plate and began to load it up with antipasto, pasta, and pizza. She found an empty chair away from the D'Angelo brothers and sat down to stuff her face.

Leo and Frankie whispered to each other, then Frankie sauntered over. "Is everything okay at the office?" Lydia knew this was his not so subtle hint that her job was minding the store while they were out.

"Everything is fine. Patricia called me and asked me to bring her the negatives of the photos we took of Al."

Frankie knit his brows. "Negatives? We didn't shoot film."

Lydia still loved the magic of film, and it was one of her sorrows that she had to shoot digital at work. She had to suppress a sigh. "Yeah, I know. So I burned her a CD and told her I'd erase our hard drive. I'm hoping it helps her let him go."

Frankie clapped Lydia on her back, almost causing her to drop her plate. "That's really nice of you."

"All in a day's work." Lydia began eating faster because she knew what was coming next.

"But as soon as you're done here, could you please hurry back to the office? We would hate for any of our clients to get the answering machine. It's not good for business if they think we're not taking good care of them."

Lydia didn't bother to tell him that hardly anyone ever called the office. If he wanted to believe that business was always booming, that was up to him. "Sure thing. As soon as Patricia comes down I'll give her the CD and go."

Frankie nodded and returned to Leo. Mama was in a corner with a woman who looked like her sister but must have been her cousin Rose. They both had the same beehive hairdo, too. The cousin was wiping her eyes on a big handkerchief. Lydia wasn't sure if she was sad for her daughter or sad about Al's death. Rose had certainly known about Al's infidelities when she asked the D'Angelos to follow him.

Lydia finished her plate of food and wondered if it would be piggish to help herself to more. She wasn't really hungry anymore, but everything tasted too good to waste. She was spared making the decision by the arrival of Patricia, freshly coiffed and made up. Lydia put down her plate and approached her.

"I don't know if you remember me. I'm Lydia. I work for your cousins."

Patricia turned and looked at her, but there was no recognition in her eyes. They looked so vague that Lydia wondered if she had taken a bunch of Valium when she was upstairs. She certainly couldn't blame her for wanting to check out and visit another planet.

Lydia handed her the CD. "Here are the photos we took of your husband. You asked us to give you the only copies, remember?"

Patricia nodded. "Yes. Thank you for coming."

"You're welcome." Lydia turned away with a shrug. The woman acted like a completely different person from the hysterical shrew who had called up demanding the negatives. Lydia hoped she didn't spend too long in la-la land, because giving up the drugs was going to be hard if she never dealt with the pain of grieving.

Patricia sat down next to her mother and started patting her hand. It looked as if Patricia was comforting her mother instead of the other way around. The whole scene was very strange. Lydia was ready to go.

Leo, looking cross, intercepted Lydia on the way to the door. "C'mon. I'll give you a ride back to the office."

The prospect of riding for twenty minutes in a car with Leo was a little daunting. She wondered if he knew how to make polite conversation. "It's okay. I can take a cab."

"I need to make some calls at the office," Leo said, guiding her toward the door. He reminded her of Mama D'Angelo. She was getting a little sick of being bossed around by the whole family.

"But what about Caroline?" Leo's mousy girlfriend was sitting still on the sofa, staring at the floor. Lydia would have been afraid to desert her without any support in the middle of such an insane family. Caroline acted so shy.

"She's going to stay with Mama a little longer and give her as much comfort and support as she can." Lydia wondered if he just wanted to save the cab fare from coming out of petty cash.

Mama hurried after them, clutching a little white cardboard box. Lydia instantly knew exactly what it was. Just like Pavlov's dog she began to salivate on cue. "Here are a few cannoli, just in case you get hungry later."

"Thanks, Mama." Leo sounded resigned.

"Thank you. I love your cannoli." Lydia took the box and smiled at Mama.

"That is because I make them full of love." Mama beamed at her. "Thank you again for helping Patricia."

"No problem," Lydia said. She could be easily bribed to forget a lot with a few good cannoli. But at least she admitted to being a total food slut.

As soon as they stepped into Leo's car, Lydia opened the box with anticipation. She took a huge bite of a chocolate-covered one and tried in vain not to drop crumbs all over Leo's car. Unfortunately, Leo decided to ask lots of questions now that her mouth was full. "I hope you're happy with us, Lydia. We think you're doing a great job."

"Thanks," she managed to say without spewing crumbs.

"I know that working in the office isn't as exciting as going out on stakeouts, so we hope you're not expecting too many other jobs to come up."

They wanted her to be just their secretary. That was okay for now, but it wouldn't satisfy her forever. "I think I've had about as much excitement as I can handle lately."

"We were all upset by Al's death. I hoped that following him and documenting his behavior would scare him straight, but he never got a chance to reform."

Lydia knew it wasn't considered polite to speak ill of the dead, but she didn't think Al could have changed his cheating ways any more than a bee could stop collecting pollen; at least not without some serious intervention or perhaps a lobotomy. If there really was such a thing as a sex addict, he fit the profile. "Patricia seems to be taking his death very hard."

"I think she was hoping to have a second chance with him, but it wasn't to be."

Leo was showing a lot of sensitivity for someone whom she had deemed emotionally challenged. Perhaps the mousy Caroline was changing him for the better. She could only hope.

Chapter 27

Not talking about a relationship could mean that everything is okay or that everything is about to fall apart. Lydia's problem was that she couldn't tell which situation was happening with Jack. Another day went by with no word from him, and she had no idea if he was mad at her or just busy. Lydia made an attempt to stay busy herself in order to forget about it, but it was difficult. The D'Angelos' temporary rush in cases appeared to have dried up. She made some follow-up calls with clients to remind them to pay their bills, and gave her desk a thorough cleaning.

Around four o'clock in the afternoon, her phone rang. Princess. She wanted an update, and Lydia had no idea what to tell her.

"We all got together at Anna's funeral and now we want to talk to you."

Lydia wondered what Anna's funeral had been like. She was sure it had been pretty different from Glenda's. She wondered if they had anything new to tell her about the women who had died. They just might because they hadn't contacted her since the initial meeting. "Where and when?"

"At the club at six o'clock, okay?" Lydia agreed and hung up the phone. She was ready for someone to start passing information to her instead of the other way around.

Earlier that day, a uniformed officer had dropped off a package with her name on it. It contained her camera with no note from Romero. She looked it over and was relieved that it looked fine. She was still a little mad at him, but she was willing to let it go. He had just been doing his job.

After work she walked slowly over to the club carrying her camera. The day was sunny and perfect for photography. She stopped and took photographs of everything that intrigued her. The shadows and light made familiar streets look moody and different. The plants pushing up through the sidewalk cracks and between the garbage in the empty lots looked both pathetic and hopeful. It was a long way from the gardens of Versailles, but it was also her home.

She didn't imagine any of the pictures she took would end up in a show—she just hoped they would help jump-start her creativity. She had been in a lull since Glenda's death, and afraid to continue the prostitute photos. She needed a new focus. She needed to play again. She stopped to snap pictures of a blowing plastic bag caught on a child's broken toy, graffiti painted on a crumbling wall, and the reflection of an old building in a puddle. It felt wonderful to take photographs again.

Princess was waiting on the street outside the clubhouse. She was smoking a cigarette and talking to two guys wearing leather vests with pictures of a dragon outlined in rhinestones on the back. Princess dropped her cigarette and stomped on it with gold glittery sneakers when she saw Lydia coming. She turned and headed back down the stairs. Lydia knew she was supposed to follow, so she did. The two guys watched her walk down, and she knew they were wondering what she was doing visiting the Golden Horseshoe Gang. She knew she didn't exactly look like a member.

The club was dark and dismal, and the air smelled stale and neglected. Like a bar, it looked less attractive and dirtier in the light of day. A few of the women were crying and were being comforted by friends. Anna had been much loved, both by her family and friends. She had been much more a sister to them than Glenda had, Lydia concluded. Lydia looked around but didn't see Cilla anywhere.

"People, people, look up here. Lydia is here with us," Princess announced. She sounded like a grade-school teacher, and Lydia had to hide her smile. The group settled down and turned their eyes to Lydia.

"I just wanted to say first that I am very sorry about your recent loss. I only met Anna once, but I could see she was a special person." Who just happened to be a hooker, Lydia didn't add. They all knew that already.

A few of the women nodded. One brave woman shouted from the back, "When will it end?"

"I wish I knew." Lydia decided not to tell them that she might very well have been thirty feet away when Josefina was killed. "I've been asking around, but I think the police have a much better chance of finding the killer. They can use stuff like fingerprinting, DNA, and all their resources to find this guy."

Princess nodded. "We heard they're about to arrest somebody."

"Who told you that?" Lydia felt an odd rush of disappointment, as if she had been banking on finding the killer herself. She should just be relieved it was over.

"We have a few police connections." Princess shrugged. "But they won't tell us who. We want to know if it's Gator."

"I honestly don't know. When I spoke to Gator at his party, he wasn't very enthusiastic about answering questions."

"He has no reason to kill them. They work for him."

Lydia wondered how a pimp had managed to create such loyalty in the neighborhood. She didn't think it was just from handing out gifts, but perhaps that was all it took.

"Do you think he's guilty or innocent?" Princess asked. Lydia wondered whether they had kept Cilla away deliberately for this conversation. Cilla would have felt obligated to defend her cousin, who had been so good to her family. But these women were determined to have the truth.

Lydia looked around the room helplessly. "I really don't know."

"This is messed up! We need a real private eye," Big Wanda complained loudly from the back of the room. "This girl doesn't know shit."

Lydia's cheeks burned. She hadn't wanted the job in the first place but had felt that she couldn't say no. But now that she was going to be fired, she felt upset. She knew it wasn't rational.

"No one cares that they're killing our sisters, here. Not the police, not the white community. No one. I'm tired of this!" Big Wanda stood up and spit on the ground.

Lydia wasn't sure if she should feel scared, being alone in the club without Jack or another ally. The hostility in the room was mounting, and she didn't blame them for being angry. But the killer was the one who deserved their wrath, not Lydia. The only problem was, no one knew who he was, and she was present and easy to blame.

"I'm not giving up," Lydia said forcefully. "Glenda was my friend, too. And I promise I'll do everything that I can to help." She waited a split second to see if Princess or any of the other women wanted to jump in and defend her, but they were quiet.

Upset and on the verge of tears, she stood up. "Call me if you find out anything, and I'll do the same for you."

The women were silent as they watched her walk out of the club-house. She felt like she had just let the team down, and it didn't feel good. But she couldn't promise something that was impossible. The police were doing their job, and that should be enough for everyone.

Back out on the street, Lydia took a deep breath and tried to pull herself together. She realized she was aimlessly wandering the neighborhood, with nothing to do and no one to do it with. Since she had started dating Jack, her nonworking hours had been filled with rushing about and trying to see him, but not anymore. She decided to walk over to Georgia's hair salon on the Northside.

Hair Today had successfully made the leap from an old-fashioned unisex barbershop to an upscale salon that catered to the artfully messy hair of hipsters, and it had adjusted its prices upward accordingly. It had kept everything that was artfully cool, the mustard yellow antique barber chairs and the barber pole. But Georgia had made it warmer, more welcoming, with interesting light fixtures and antique mirrors.

Georgia's face lit up when Lydia walked in. She was finishing a dye job on a woman who was adventurously going neon green.

"Lydia!" Georgia jumped up and gave her a big hug. "You want some highlights?"

Lydia was tempted, but she could see Georgia had already begun cleaning up the shop in order to close up. "It looks like it's quitting time."

Georgia shrugged. "My date canceled tonight. Let's order Thai and take care of your hair."

"You rock." Georgia, like a great best friend, didn't even mention Jack. She knew Lydia would talk about him when she was ready. And for now they would pretend that it was perfectly normal to not know where your boyfriend was or whether or not he was just about to dump you.

After the client left, satisfied with her fluorescent hair color, and they had put in an order for pad pak and pad thai, they settled down to the serious business of picking Lydia's highlights. Georgia had just got a new shipment of dyes, and she was anxious to try them out.

"Nothing too light," Lydia warned. "It always looks fake on me when I try to go."

"Of course," said Georgia, holding up various shades of red to Lydia's hair and squinting. There was every shade imaginable, but they quickly eliminated the ones that would make her look like Raggedy Ann or like she had just been exposed to too much radiation.

After agonizing over a few of the colors, Lydia's eyes began to cross. She finally told Georgia to choose for her since she trusted her to make her look good.

Georgia smiled and began to mix up her concoction. While Lydia was waiting, she decided to give herself a manicure and a pedicure. She knew it would improve her mood to be able to flash a little color.

"What's happening with the band these days? You were great at the rink."

"We're playing later tonight at the Spiral House. You should come."

"I'd love to." She wondered if Jack would come with her. It would feel strange to show up alone. Everyone would wonder where he was and ask her questions. Questions she wasn't ready to answer yet. Or they would assume she was single and that would feel even stranger.

"We've also been invited to contribute a song to a charity album. The money goes to Mexican kids who make their living picking through the trash." Georgia began to carefully separate out strands of Lydia's hair and apply the goop.

"They heard us at that concert and asked if we would like to participate. I read a story about those kids, and how they're trying to get them into school and give them health care and everything. I really wanted to help."

Lydia paused in the middle of applying Passionate Pink to her toenails. There were so many hungry, desperate people in the world, and here she was doing a beauty treatment. Glenda, Josefina, and Anna had also been defenseless and in need of help. She felt like she was ducking out on them. Another vulnerable woman could be walking the streets right now and be at the mercy of a cold-blooded killer. She blinked back tears as she stared at her toenails, half done.

"What's the matter? You don't like the shade?"

"Everything is so messed up. I don't know what to do."

The Thai delivery guy banged on the door, and Georgia fluttered off to pay him. Lydia felt relieved. She wasn't sure she was ready to talk about it. It all felt way too depressing. As they dug in to their food, Lydia sat with aluminum foil on her head and tissues between her toes, waiting to dry and dye. But Georgia didn't forget too easily.

"What's going on at work?"

Lydia sighed. Life with the D'Angelos had returned to normal. "Nothing."

"Then what's bothering you?"

"The Golden Horseshoe Gang wanted me to find out who was killing women on the waterfront, and I couldn't do it."

"Why would they expect you to do a better job than the police?"

"Most of them are prostitutes, and they don't trust the police. They think the police don't give the same kind of attention to the deaths of women of color that they do to the deaths of white yuppies."

"Are they right?"

Lydia shrugged. "The press certainly pays more attention to blond victims, but I can't imagine Romero having that kind of prejudice. He's Puerto Rican." For all her problems with him, she had to admit that Romero was taking the murders seriously and making every attempt to catch the killer. "Also, they just heard the cops are about to make an arrest."

Georgia speared a dumpling with her chopstick. "Ah ha! You're just sore because he isn't letting you in on the action."

Lydia had to admit she was sulking. She would like to know who was killing those women, especially since she was a witness and had known two of the victims. Her biggest gripe was over how little Romero trusted her. She was puzzled that it hurt so much. She had a boyfriend, a job, a calling in the arts, and lots of friends. So why did she care what a crabby detective thought about her? But somehow she did, and it made her uncomfortable.

She also had a hard time forgetting the female victims. "The gang is worried they might arrest the wrong person, just to grab someone, and then the real killer will keep on killing."

"What do you think?"

"I don't know." Lydia was getting tired of saying that. She liked to know things, which was how her curiosity got her into this mess. And she didn't have a clue who the murderer was. It was driving her crazy.

Lydia's phone rang. She hoped it was Jack. She lunged for it and examined the caller ID. It was a Brooklyn number, but not one she recognized. "Hello?"

"It is Emmanuel."

Lydia smiled. "Thanks for calling me back. I had to use one of your competitors to go to Queens. Are you off today?"

"No, no. I am not. I was hoping you could help me." Emmanuel sounded like he was in some place empty and echoing. He definitely wasn't in his car.

Lydia frowned. If something had happened to his car, he wouldn't be able to make any money. She knew his family relied on the cash he sent home. "Of course. What happened?"

"They think I'm a hot stepper." Emmanuel sounded nervous, and his Jamaican accent was in full force along with his slang.

"Some kind of what?"

"They've arrested me for the murders on the waterfront."

Chapter 28

Lydia was so angry she didn't even remember ripping the tissue from between her toes and rushing for the door. Luckily, Georgia had stopped her before she ran out onto the street with aluminum foil in her hair. She had to sit back down while Georgia finished the treatment as quickly as possible. But she refused to let her blow-dry or style it. She was in too much of a hurry.

On her way to the police station she tried to think of someone who would know a powerful trial lawyer. Emmanuel needed help. She was his one phone call, so it was all up to her. Most of her friends were underemployed artists who occasionally watched *Law & Order* reruns but didn't actually know any lawyers. At least not lawyers who weren't working pro bono for Greenpeace or something. She needed someone who rubbed shoulders with the rich and powerful on a regular basis. She decided in a flash of inspiration that she needed Candi. She dug for her phone in her bag.

Luckily, Candi's number was still in her phonebook from their recent photo date. Lydia called her up and got her voice mail. Candi never answered her phone. Lydia tried to collect her thoughts while she waited for the beep. "Emmanuel Jordan, a young man I know from Jamaica, has been arrested and taken to the Ninetieth Precinct for the murders of Glenda, Anna, Josefina, and Al Savarese. He's innocent, and as long as he is in jail, the cops will let the guilty guy roam free. He needs a lawyer fast. Can you give me the name of someone who could help?"

She hung up and rushed home to grab her bike. It would be the fastest way to get to the police station, even though she lost precious minutes going to get it. She jumped on the bike and headed for Broadway. Still worried about how she would get help for Emmanuel, she rode a little spacily. She almost didn't register the car service cutting her off, the hatchback that drove too close, or the truck that ran a red light. It was a miracle she wasn't killed on the way to the police station.

The clerk at the station didn't want to help her, but Lydia refused to leave until she saw Romero. She couldn't leave Emmanuel in there all by himself. She had involved Emmanuel in the case, and it was up to her to make sure he got out okay. To pass the time and to let Romero know she was dead serious, she called the detective's cell phone repeatedly. She knew he was going to lose his temper, but she didn't care. She wanted to make some waves, and she was angry, too.

She sat down on the bench, realizing that after going to all the trouble to get highlights, her hair probably looked limp and messy. She did her best to freshen up using her small mirror and whatever beauty products she could find in her bag.

Romero came down about thirty minutes later. He looked tired and fed up. Before he could yell, Lydia jumped up. "Emmanuel didn't do it. You have to let him go."

"You told us yourself he was gone for thirty minutes while you were waiting in the car and you couldn't see him. And that you don't know where he was before he came to get you, but that you knew he was following Al. How do you know he didn't do it?"

"He's not a violent guy. He was only there because I asked him to be there." Lydia stopped. Emmanuel had called her, picked her up, and taken her to the park. He was the one who led her there. She had asked him to follow Al, but he was the one who initiated it.

Romero sat down next to Lydia on the bench. "How well do you know Emmanuel?"

Lydia frowned. "What do you mean?"

"When did you meet him?"

"A week ago, I guess." That didn't sound long at all. "But you get to know people really quickly on a stakeout. He was really reliable and interested in being a private eye. He would never do something like this."

"Did you know he was arrested in Jamaica?"

"So he shoplifted or whatever. That doesn't mean anything. He probably just didn't pay off the right people or couldn't afford to. You know what the police are like down there."

"No, this is an assault charge." Lydia stared at Romero in horror. She had felt so sure she knew Emmanuel and he was a peaceful, kind person. But what if he wasn't? What if her instincts were wrong? What if Emmanuel was wanted for killing prostitutes in Jamaica, and she'd brought him in on a similar case and put temptation in his way?

Romero looked at her with some sympathy. "He could be a very violent man."

Lydia tried to imagine Emmanuel taking a gun and shooting someone, but she just couldn't picture it. She didn't know what to think. She would just have to wait and see what the evidence was. Meanwhile, it was up to her to make sure he got justice.

"Emmanuel is my friend. I think you've got the wrong guy, and as long as you're focusing on him, the real killer could be getting ready to strike again."

"Or maybe we've got the right guy based on evidence we've collected and you know nothing about, and we're making the streets safer for everyone. Why not give us the benefit of the doubt?"

"You know and I know that Gator stinks to high heaven. Why aren't you pursuing him?"

Romero jumped to his feet. "Are you saying I'm not doing my job?"

She had seen Romero angry before, but he looked mad enough to violate some of the basic tenets of the NYPD. Lydia stood her ground, her heart beating in her ears, and let her silence speak for itself. She thought it was Gator, and she didn't think the cops were doing their job.

The door to the precinct banged opened and a large man in his fifties strode in carrying a briefcase. He had on a sharp suit that probably cost the same as Lydia's monthly rent. He looked vaguely familiar, but Lydia couldn't place him. He certainly wasn't the type she'd seen hanging around the neighborhood. Lydia noticed with annoyance that the clerk didn't dillydally but came right to the window for this guy.

"How may I help you, sir?"

"William White to see Emmanuel Jordan. I'm his lawyer."

Romero turned to Lydia with a scowl. "This is your doing, isn't it?"

"I asked a friend if she could recommend someone. . . ." Lydia didn't want to go into details. Very likely this William White was one of Candi's customers, and she certainly didn't want to tell Romero that. If the guy liked transvestites, that was his own business.

"I didn't know you were acquainted with such a big shot," Romero muttered under his breath.

Lydia was confused, but before she could ask who the guy was, Romero had already stepped forward to speak to him.

"Mr. White, I'm the detective in charge of the case."

The lawyer checked his watch impatiently. "Then you'll understand why I'd like to see my client immediately, Detective."

"I'm not sure what a TV personality wants with an illegal car service driver." Romero and White were sizing each other up like bantam roosters before a cockfight. White was several inches taller and outweighed Romero, but they seemed like an equal match if it was simply a matter of testosterone levels.

"I believe in fighting against crime in all parts of the city. And I love to stand up for the little guy." The speech sounded canned. Lydia realized his face was one she'd seen on billboards. He was a commentator on one of the court shows. Candi had come through and managed to get a famous TV lawyer for Emmanuel. She couldn't stop the big grin that stretched across her face. She just hoped William White knew his stuff.

"I'm sure you've made most of your millions that way." Romero stepped back to take in the full effect of the suit, soft leather briefcase, and carefully coiffed hair.

The lawyer coolly checked his watch again. "Detective, if you're done trading insults, I'd like to see my client."

Romero shot Lydia a look that promised retribution at a later date, and led the lawyer away to see Emmanuel. Lydia just wished that she could have followed. She would have liked to ask Emmanuel about his arrest in Jamaica, and to make sure he was safe. But clearly to see anyone at the station you had to have a law degree.

Chapter 29

After waiting another hour for a glimpse of Emmanuel and the lawyer and seeing nothing, Lydia finally left. Emmanuel had asked for help, and she had provided the best she could. She called Candi and left a grateful message. Emmanuel wasn't alone and without allies now. William White wouldn't let the police force him into a false confession or anything. So for now Emmanuel was safe.

Lydia dialed Jack's number as she walked back to her bike. She was tired of waiting for him to call. Besides, she needed some sympathy. But Jack sounded brusque when he answered the phone. He was in total work mode.

She began to explain what had happened. "I'm worried that they'll deport Emmanuel."

"Who's Emmanuel?"

"The car service driver!" Lydia tried not to sound shrill, but she hated to be confronted by how out of touch Jack was with her life.

She knew she had told him about Emmanuel before, and she wondered whether he ever paid attention to what she said.

"Did he do it?"

"Jack!" Lydia protested. "Of course he didn't. He's a good guy." Lydia didn't want to fight with Jack. She wanted them to go on dates again, and be snuggly in love. She needed someone to hold her close and tell her everything would be all right. Why couldn't he go back to being the perfect boyfriend? Why did relationships have to be so hard?

Lydia took a deep breath and changed the subject. "Georgia Rae is playing at Spiral at eight. Do you want to meet me there?"

"I can't. I told you we have a big deadline coming up, and I'm not sure what time I can leave," Jack said. A woman was murmuring something in the background, and Lydia had a suspicion it was his co-worker Polly. When they'd met at Lulu's Lydia got the sense that Polly wouldn't have minded if Jack were available. The thought of them working late together made her jealous. "Gotta go. Bye."

Lydia stood on the street staring at her cell phone. What was happening to them? Suddenly they couldn't communicate or manage to agree on anything. She wasn't sure if he was deliberately blowing her off or if he was really having a work crisis. She thought reaching out to him would help clear the air, not make everything more confusing.

She rode home to get changed for the show. She decided not to think about Jack for the whole evening. Missing their date tonight was his loss. Besides, she had enough on her plate with Emmanuel and the murders. And she was determined to support Georgia and have some fun.

Going out alone was way more depressing than she remembered. Everyone else was paired up and cuddling in a corner. Lydia found herself drinking far more than she usually did. It gave her hands and mouth something to do, even though it didn't distract her brain very much. When Georgia's set was over, she sat down next to Lydia and looked her over.

"Uh-oh. Here's trouble. What's your poison?"

"Gin and tonic," Lydia said, slurring her words only a very little bit.

"How many have you had?"

Lydia gestured vaguely. "Two. I mean three. Not so many, right?"

Georgia shook her head. "Maybe not very many for some, but you're a lightweight."

"There's no danger of someone taking advantage of my state," Lydia said glumly.

"Where is handsome Jack? Moving money around?"

"I guess. I think he's still mad at me for investigating the murders."

"So what's going on?"

Lydia told Georgia more about Emmanuel's arrest, since she'd barely had time to tell her the gist when she had run out of the salon, but Georgia wasn't suitably outraged. "Romero is right. You don't know the guy that well. Could he have killed them?"

Lydia found it hard to explain how she knew that Emmanuel didn't do it after such a short acquaintance, but she was sure. "No way. I brought him into the case. He's just not that kind of person."

Georgia shook her head. "You need to be careful."

"I am, but I feel bad that I got Emmanuel in trouble. The only way to prove he's innocent is to find the real killer. I still think Gator could have done it, but the cops are scared of him."

"How could you prove it? Clearly the killer is not leaving any evidence behind."

"I have to catch him in the act." Lydia took another swig of her drink. A crazy plan began to form inside her head, one that no one was going to like but her.

"You've been just feet away before and haven't caught him. Why do you think next time would be any different?" Georgia said sensibly.

"It would be different if he were after me," Lydia said.

"After you?"

"Yeah. If he thought I was a prostitute."

Georgia snorted. "You? I can see mistaking you for a librarian, but a hooker . . ."

"Why not? With the right clothes, the right walk, and hanging out in the right place . . ." Lydia had dressed herself and her friends as prostitutes when she worked on her Lost Girls series, a series about women who had been murdered and never identified. She had photographed each of her models in a film noir style after researching the historic deaths of the original victims.

Georgia grinned. "You're more likely to get arrested, I'm afraid."

Romero would find it pretty funny to see Lydia get arrested for solicitation. But based on her experience on the waterfront, the cops tended to stay away from the whole mess. "It is helpful to look through the eyes of the victim, you know."

"Lydia McKenzie! Three women are dead already. Don't go looking for trouble."

"It would be much safer if I did it with a friend!" Lydia said, raising her eyebrows suggestively.

"You want me to be your bodyguard? I don't know if I still remember all those self-defense moves from class."

Lydia shook her head.

"No, no, no. You want me to dress up, too?"

"Why not? You're the one with all the acting experience."

"It's too dangerous," Georgia protested.

"Not if there are two of us." Lydia knew she was being annoying, but she couldn't help it. She really needed Georgia's help. "You wouldn't want me to go alone, right?"

"Don't be ridiculous. It would be like walking around the waterfront with target signs on our backs. Are you really that suicidal?"

Lydia frowned. She wasn't ready to give up. "I need to get down there again. I can't just sit here and do nothing."

"Why don't you go back on the bus, then? Those women seemed to keep the situation pretty safe."

Lydia considered the suggestion. On the bus Lydia would be in the middle of the action, and she would have an excuse for speaking to the prostitutes. And if all else failed, she could try to flush out the killer. "Can you come with me?"

"On the bus? You mean as a volunteer?"

"Sure. I'd like you to meet Iris and Sarah and the rest."

Georgia took a sip of her drink. "What would I do? Give free manicures?"

"Nah. You'd help fill out forms and stuff. It's not that hard."

"Not this weekend. I'm swamped with practice and the salon."

"Okay. Then how about Wednesday night? Would Wednesday night work?"

Georgia nodded reluctantly. "But the first sign of trouble and we are out of there, got it? We're not going to end up as another statistic if I can help it."

Lydia agreed. Her plan was coming together.

Chapter 30

Yes, yes, yes. You know what I like, baby. Please don't stop. Whatever you do don't stop, you burning naked hunk of love." Leo's girlfriend, Caroline, was whispering loudly into her cell phone, clearly thinking the phone somehow made her invisible and inaudible. Lydia was doing her best to keep her head down and not listen, because the situation was beyond embarrassing. But since Caroline was sitting just three feet away at Leo's desk, it was difficult not to hear her. Caroline had been on the phone ever since Leo had to run out and meet with a client, leaving Lydia and Caroline alone.

Lydia was more than a little grossed out thinking about Leo as a burning naked hunk of love. It was a little too much information. She wished they would confine their sex talk to outside the office and let her get her work done.

Lydia had always thought of Caroline as a meek, shy one-man woman, but when Lydia heard Caroline break off her call in midsentence and turn off her phone when Leo walked in, she knew the truth. Caroline's burning naked hunk had been someone else. She was cheating on Leo.

Lydia clenched her jaw in outrage. She personally couldn't understand why anyone might find Leo sexually attractive, but he was basically an okay guy. He worked hard, he loved his family, and he was pretty fair as bosses went. He didn't deserve to be cheated on. She knew that Leo was in love with Caroline, and she felt bad because she knew he was going to get his heart broken. If she stumbled in on Jack in a similar situation, she would be a wreck.

Lydia tried not to gag when Leo walked up to Caroline and kissed her. "I missed you, darling. Sorry you had to wait for me like that."

"That's fine. I got caught up on a few calls I had to make." Calls? More like a few affairs, Lydia thought bitterly.

"Great, great." Leo sounded hearty and happy. He didn't have a clue that his girlfriend was cheating on him. And Lydia didn't want to be the one to tell him. She hated to be the bearer of bad news. Even Mama D'Angelo really seemed to like Caroline, and she had high hopes that one of her sons was finally going to tie the knot.

"Are you ready to go now?"

"Sure," Leo said. "Lydia, we're going to run over and see a few apartments listed in the neighborhood and then have some lunch. Frankie should be in later so you can have a lunch break."

Lydia's smile was a little forced. They were planning to move in together? Maybe Leo knew about the other guys and didn't care, but she really doubted it. She had the feeling he believed in monogamy and didn't tolerate cheating. He was going to be devastated when he found out the truth.

Caroline got up and collected her handbag. Her bag matched her brown pants, brown loafers, and even her tan blouse. She looked so mousy and dull. If Lydia hadn't heard the steamy conversation with her own ears, she wouldn't have believed it, either. "Bye, Lydia. See you soon."

Lydia was amazed at her audacity. Didn't she know that Lydia had heard her on the phone? Caroline appeared to believe that her whispering had been too quiet for Lydia to hear. She watched as Leo gallantly held the door for Caroline, sweeping his arm as if he were paying his respect to the queen. Caroline sort of simpered at him as she walked out, and Leo beamed as if he'd won the lottery. She certainly didn't seem like an evil femme fatale, but she was clearly a very good actress. The whole relationship was a sham. But Lydia tried to tell herself it was no business of hers, and returned her attention to the papers on her desk.

Lydia had barely made a dent into her expense reports for the Patricia case when the phone rang.

"Lydia!" Mama D'Angelo boomed. "Come right away to the restaurant. I will feed you."

Lydia held the phone a few inches from her ear as her mouth watered in anticipation. She could only imagine the menu. "Leo asked me to stay here until Frankie came back."

"Bah! The office will survive. That's why they invented an answering machine. I want to speak to you about the boys."

Lydia wondered if Mama was curious about Caroline and wanted more information. She didn't want to be the one to tell Mama about the sex calls. She didn't like being a tattletale. But she couldn't ignore the siren song of Mama's cooking. She had become as weak as the D'Angelos in that respect. She turned on the answering machine and locked the door furtively. She knew the brothers would be mad about her defection, but she would be able to use their mother's call for an audience in her defense. Luckily, they were scared of their mother and did not like to cross her.

Mama's restaurant was not far. It was on the ground floor of a small building, and had been decorated with every bad cliché of Italy. There were cherubs, Mount Vesuvius, gondolas, olive trees, and old-fashioned maidens with kerchiefs on their heads—all painted on the front windows. Faux columns framed the doorway. Inside, pink and white ruled the décor. The white chairs were encased in plastic to stay clean, and the tables were all covered with pink vinyl tablecloths. A white or pink carnation in a small vase sat on each table. As soon as Lydia entered, Mama appeared out of the back wearing a purple velour sweat suit and purple rhinestone glasses. Her beehive looked higher than usual, and Lydia guessed she had just been to the beauty salon.

"Sit, sit. Tony will bring your dinner out in just a moment."

The time was not far past 10:30, but Lydia was not going to mention it. She could eat at any time, and her breakfast felt like a long time ago. Mama led her to a nearby table. She put her bag on the floor since the vinyl on the chair was too slippery to hold it.

"It was so kind of you to pay a call on Patricia. She is so sad about her husband."

Lydia winced. She had actually been there on business, and she hated to take credit for actually thinking about Patricia's grief and calling on her. "It was nothing."

"No, no, it was very important to her. She feels so alone now that her husband is gone. She has no children to keep her busy. She doesn't have many friends." Lydia smiled in sympathy. She thought Patricia was a little nuts, and it would probably help her if she got out of the house a little more.

"We've decided that she needs a job."

"A job?" Lydia thought the plan sounded a bit rushed. Al had been dead only a few days. She was sure that he had life insurance or something. If she had to, Patricia could probably sell one of the cars and live off the money for a while.

"Yes, yes. And we need your help." Lydia stared at Mama, mystified. She had no jobs to offer grieving widows. But Mama had helped her get the gig photographing Al for the D'Angelos, so she felt obligated to hear her out.

Tony exited the kitchen holding up a large silver platter. He was a waiter in his fifties who had once been extremely handsome and now looked like an aging lothario with his comb-over and tight uniform. He set the platter of bruschetta in front of Lydia with great flair and gave her a flirtatious grin. "Your bruschetta, Madame."

Mama frowned at Tony and waved him away impatiently. He disappeared back into the kitchen, and Lydia dug into the appetizer. Tomato, onion, garlic, and basil oozed over the edge of thick toasted bread. The taste was tangy and flavorful, and Lydia had to remind herself not to eat too fast.

"My sons love the work you are doing, and they don't want to lose you. You've shown much more creativity and interest than any of their former helpers." Lydia froze midbite and a piece of tomato slid down her chin. Although it was certainly nice to receive compliments, this one was beginning to sound like a brush-off. Could they have given the job of firing her to their mother? Could they be that lazy? Lydia stopped herself from asking that question. Of course they were.

Mama continued without paying any attention to the errant tomato. "Patricia cannot get a job unless she gets some experience in an office environment. So they were hoping that you would be willing to train her and teach her how you do your job."

Lydia chewed carefully and swallowed. They wanted her to train her replacement. She had told herself for months that she would love to get rid of her job. The D'Angelos were cantankerous, most of the work was extremely boring, and she hated that she didn't get to work on her own photography as much as she would have liked. Maybe training her replacement, Patricia, would be a good opportunity for her to refocus and figure out what she should be doing, rather than running around trying out the job of private eye.

"Certainly," Lydia said, carefully wiping her hands on a giant pink linen napkin. "I would be happy to help out."

Mama looked relieved. "We really must find a way to keep her busy." Perhaps Mama was thinking of her own widowhood. Burying herself in the daily workings of her restaurant had undoubtedly been a good distraction from her own grief. Lydia wondered what Papa D'Angelo had been like, and imagined he was just as enthralled with Mama as her sons were. Patricia's own marriage had not appeared to be particularly loving, so Lydia was still skeptical about how much Patricia herself was grieving. But she didn't dispute that she needed a vocation.

Lydia allowed herself to take another nibble of the bruschetta. It practically melted in her mouth. She was relieved that her bribe at least was something delicious and amazing. It would somehow cheapen the whole encounter to eat something just so-so.

Mama leaned forward with her elbows on the table. "Now, what do you think of this Caroline? A nice girl, huh?"

"She's pretty quiet," Lydia said, neglecting to mention that Caroline seemed to have plenty to say on the phone to some guy other than Leo. She had told herself it was none of her business.

"Yes, yes," Mama said. "But there is something . . ."

Lydia wondered if Mama had discovered Caroline's secret. "Yes?"

Mama tapped the surface of the tabletop with her nails. They were cut short and square, probably for practical reasons. "There is something that feels odd."

"You'll have a chance to observe them again when they come for lunch today."

"What? They're coming today?" Mama's black beehive quivered in outrage. She didn't like to be behind the curve on anything. "I heard nothing."

"I just assumed . . ." Lydia wondered if she had put her foot in it. "Leo told me he and Caroline were going out for lunch and I couldn't imagine where else they would go. Unless they had a sudden hankering for sushi."

"Sushi! What does a nice Italian boy need with sushi?" Mama slapped the palm of her hand down on the table. The glasses shook. "I will call him on his cell phone and demand that he bring Caroline over here."

Mama got up and sailed back into the kitchen. Lydia wondered if Leo had told Mama about his plans to move in with Caroline, and was glad she at least hadn't spilled the beans on that piece of news. Her stomach rumbled as she got up, figuring that was the end of her snacks. But Tony reemerged from the kitchen with a takeout container. "Here's the stuffed shells special. Mama thought you might need to get back to the office."

Lydia did. She took the takeout container and scrammed. She just hoped Leo wasn't too mad at her. And she hoped that Patricia was a fast learner. The whole family was driving her nuts.

Chapter 31

Filing? But I could break a nail!" Patricia whined.

Lydia took a deep breath and reminded herself to be patient. Patricia was, after all, recently widowed. But if she was ever going to get a job and work for a living, she was going to need a serious attitude adjustment. She had arrived an hour late for work in a car service and demanded money from petty cash to pay for her ride. The D'Angelos didn't like it, but they didn't object, either. Mama had them convinced a job was what Patricia needed, and had played on their guilt about being failures in the husband surveillance department.

She quickly figured out that they wanted nothing to do with Patricia's training. After "settling her in," which really consisted of the brothers saying awkward hellos to Patricia, Leo and Frankie told Lydia to start showing her the ropes and disappeared in the direction of Mama's. Now Lydia understood why.

"Would you like to start with putting in the numbers for the latest expense reports instead?"

Patricia frowned and twirled her very expensive gold watch. "I really don't type very well."

"Take as much time as you need," Lydia said heartily. She led her over to Frankie's desk, opened the file, put the receipts in front of her, and walked back to her own desk. Lydia was sure that whatever she gave Patricia to do, she would have to do over. Patricia was no help at all. But Lydia had her own work to do and couldn't keep babysitting her all day long.

When Frankie and Leo came back a few hours later, Patricia excused herself. "Mama asked me to come over for lunch. I'll be back in a few." By a few, Lydia guessed Patricia didn't mean a few minutes. Lydia breathed a sigh of relief. Patricia took up way too much of the available oxygen in the room.

"How is Patricia doing?" Frankie asked heartily, slurping on a cup of coffee. "She settling in okay?"

Lydia shook her head. Annoyed by the whole family, she had no desire to cover for her. "She can't type, she says filing breaks her nails, and she drained my petty cash fund with that car service."

"She's just lost her husband, and her car is in the shop. We have to make allowances, you know." Leo looked so sour that Lydia could tell the allowances were a real hit below the belt. Leo didn't like to see the petty cash fund drained for nonbillable expenses, and he didn't like to see anyone but himself and his brother slack off.

"All right, but don't be surprised if nothing gets done when I have to spend every day explaining how to add rows in Excel and showing her how to adjust the brightness on her screen. She's pretty clueless." Lydia hated to whine, but the mess Patricia had made was the last straw. After spending most of the morning shopping for clothes on the Internet, Patricia had left her dirty coffee cup for Lydia to clean, and then had disappeared for a long lunch. Lydia was going to be eating a lowly peanut butter and jelly sandwich at her desk while Patricia dined in splendor with Mama. She was feeling like Cinderella.

"Don't worry. She'll figure everything out soon. She always was a bright girl." But Frankie was too much of an optimist. Patricia was even more useless when she returned from lunch. She spent the afternoon making a hair appointment, talking to her personal shopper at Macy's, and yelling at a travel agent for not letting her return nonrefundable tickets.

"I'm bereaved here! Can't you show a little respect?" Patricia bellowed into the receiver. "What do you need? A death certificate?"

Lydia dug up her pack of Life Savers and a Tylenol. She couldn't stop herself from leaving another pathetic little message for Jack, asking what was going on. When he didn't call back, she forced herself to believe that he had to work again that night.

Patricia slammed the phone down and sat back, breathing hard. It was as if she'd run ten miles instead of just balled out a travel agent.

Lydia forced herself to smile sympathetically. "You sound really upset." She was shocked when Patricia burst into tears and put her head down on the desk. Maybe Patricia was a lot more in love with Al than she had given her credit for. Rose was, after all, the one who had hired them.

Lydia found a big box of tissues kept at the ready for weepy clients and brought it over. She patted Patricia's bony shoulder tentatively. "There, there," she said.

Patricia sat up and grabbed a whole bunch of tissues. She blew her nose loudly and gave a pathetic sigh followed by a hiccup. "I fell in love with Al when I was just nineteen. I thought he was the smartest, funniest guy in the world. And I never stopped being in love with him, no matter how many times he cheated on me."

Lydia thought of her own pain with Jack. Would their relationship survive infidelity? Probably not. But they hadn't been together for years and years. They hadn't even been together one year.

"He wasn't around much, but he took care of things for me. I feel so helpless with all these bills and details." Patricia gestured helplessly at the pile of paperwork on her desk. "I just want him back."

"I'm so sorry." Lydia was even more sorry that she couldn't think of anything good to say. Al was a low-life, and no amount of glossing on Lydia's part was going to erase the tarnish on his image. At least Patricia admitted that he was cheating on her, and was no longer acting like he was a martyr.

"And I want that murderer caught!" Patricia slammed her tissue down on the table. It bounced quietly onto the floor.

"I know. We all do." Lydia got up and made coffee for Patricia and herself. They took a companionable coffee break together and talked about some of Al and Patricia's good times. They talked about the trip Patricia and Al had planned to take to Las Vegas, and how they had been saving for a beach house out on Long Island. Lydia told her about her trip out to the beach, and Patricia asked if she'd tried a famous seafood place out there. It was kind of a nice change to have a coworker who wasn't your boss, Lydia mused.

Later, after Lydia got back to work and Patricia went back on the Internet, Lydia wondered again what answers she might find on the waterfront. It had to be the perfect night to go back down and see if anyone could remember anything else about the nights the murders had occurred.

She dialed Georgia's number. "So, are we on for tonight?"

Georgia still sounded uncertain. "Are you sure this is a good idea?"

"Why not? You're not afraid, are you?"

"No, that's not it. I'm curious about the bus."

"Let's go down there for just a few hours. And if we don't find out anything, I'll give up on it. Okay?"

Georgia sighed. "Okay."

"You're the best. Meet me at my house and we'll go over to Kent together." Lydia smiled as she hung up. She swiveled in her office chair and found Patricia watching her strangely.

"What are you up to tonight?"

"Nothing," Lydia said quickly. She felt uncomfortable discussing her plans with Patricia. She didn't want to get Patricia's hopes up that she might help find Al's killer and bring him to justice. Patricia should be relying on the police to do that.

"Is your boyfriend going?" Patricia said, arching her eyebrows. Patricia might have just confided in Lydia about her finances and her marriage, but Lydia had to remember that Patricia could rat her out to the D'Angelos and steal her job.

"No, it's strictly girls only." That was true, at least until the murderer showed up.

Chapter 32

Georgia Rae and Lydia waited for fifteen minutes on the corner of Kent and Grand Streets for the rainbow bus to arrive. Instead of feeling excited, Lydia couldn't stop thinking about Jack. She wondered how he could be so busy at work that he couldn't take one minute to call her back. When they first started dating, he had never worked late or gave her any excuses for why they couldn't get together. He called her several times a day just to say he was thinking of her. It seemed like they were either together every free minute or they were cooing at each other on the phone like teenagers. Either he'd been going through a slow spell at work in those early days or he was totally over her now.

She knew he had begun to cool when she had become involved in the murders. She told herself that if she wanted to keep him, she could just give up and let the police do their job without her help. But she didn't want to. Women had been killed with no one to defend them. And there were still women out on the streets who could be attacked again at any time. If she didn't try to stop the killer, she would be disappointed with herself.

"Stop me if I try to leave Jack any more messages," Lydia said grimly.

"Uh-oh, that sounds bad, sugar."

"You don't know half of it." Lydia tried to explain the last couple of days, but she stopped because she sounded so whiny. She hated whiny people.

"Sounds like you just left the honeymoon stage," Georgia said philosophically. As a hairdresser, she probably heard as many confessions as a bartender and a priest put together. "Some people can't stand to leave that stage, and they keep dating new people just so they can have the first glow back again."

Georgia ignored a car that honked at them as it drove by. "I think that stage is overrated, though. Anyone can feel great when it's exciting and new, but it's the long haul that tells you if he's really the one for you. And I never really relax until I know a guy really well."

Lydia and Jack hadn't been dating very long, really. They had rushed into the intimate stage with alarming speed, and now they were hovering at the stage just before deciding whether to take it deeper and move in together or something. Instead, they had both pulled back. "I just want to know if he's really busy or if he's just avoiding me. I mean, I'm out at night on the waterfront, and he doesn't know where I am since he doesn't bother to call!"

"True enough. Sometimes absence makes the heart grow fonder, though."

Lydia fingered her cell phone in the pocket of her light jacket. She had twenty dollars for a car service, her keys, and her phone. She had wanted to travel light tonight.

"Here's something for you," Georgia said, handing Lydia a small orange canister. "Just in case."

"What is it?" It looked like a strange lipstick, and not at all her shade.

"Mace."

Lydia slipped it into her pocket, feeling even more apprehensive. The waterfront looked a lot more sinister at night. "Do you think we'll really need it?"

Georgia shrugged. "Better safe than sorry, my mama always used to say."

The sun had just gone down, but already they were under observation by the passing cars. Some of the cars actually slowed down to check them out, and Lydia wondered nervously when the bus would arrive.

Lydia admitted she hadn't thought out the whole exercise very well. She hoped that they would see something that would help them figure out who the murderer was right away, and avoid any unpleasantness. Emmanuel was wanted for murder, and she wanted to prove that he hadn't done it. As long as the police believed it was Emmanuel, they wouldn't look for anyone else.

At last the rainbow-colored bus lumbered up to the park. Lydia grinned when she saw Georgia's astonished face. Iris opened the door for them. "Good evening, ladies. Sorry we were running late. I had to track down a box of syringes."

They climbed aboard and Candi came up to greet them, dressed in a beautiful green silk suit that looked more appropriate for the boardroom than the streets. Georgia and Candi exchanged cheek kisses and compliments, then Candi introduced Georgia to everyone on the bus. Georgia wanted to see everything, even the examination room, and Lydia could tell she impressed everyone with her enthusiasm.

Sarah, Candi, and Lakisha were all on board, already hard at work. Lydia felt like a bus regular as she grabbed a clipboard stuffed with forms and made her way past the coffee and doughnuts to find a seat.

"I'm not sure how much business we'll get tonight, girls. I think everyone is staying off the streets until they're sure the murderer is caught," Candi said as she walked the bus, checking on everyone's progress.

"I don't think we'll have to worry about that much longer," Sarah piped up. "I heard they've already arrested someone."

Candi and Lydia exchanged a look but said nothing. Lydia planned to thank Candi again privately for sending Emmanuel a lawyer. She didn't want to bring it up in front of the gang, though. Candi might want to keep her generosity quiet, and she might not want to let it get out that she was helping to provide a lawyer to the accused killer.

Business was indeed slow that night, and soon everyone was yawning, eating way too many doughnuts and drinking too much coffee. Georgia and Candi gave each other manicures and talked hair. Lakisha curled up with a book about urban planning. Iris played solitaire and chatted with Sarah about some of their more dramatic nights on the streets. Lydia looked out the window, trying to get a glimpse of anything or anyone that might tell her what was going on. A killer was out there, and until he was caught, the women were vulnerable.

Every once in a while a car would drive slowly down Kent Avenue looking for women. But no one was out tonight. She didn't have any sympathy for the johns, but she knew the women didn't have large savings accounts to fall back on. Too many nights of unemployment could be disastrous for them. She thought about Gator's opulent apartment and wondered how his finances were faring. If the killer wasn't Gator but someone trying to hurt him, he had managed to do it right in the pocketbook. There would be no big parties or wider wide-screen TVs until the women were working again. Gator had arrogantly assumed that he had successfully fought off all his rivals, but maybe he was wrong.

Lydia stifled a yawn and checked her phone again. Only five minutes later than the last time she'd checked. She still had no messages from Jack. She tucked the phone back into the pocket of her jacket that was lying on the seat. She caught Candi watching her and smiled sheepishly.

"I think it's going to be a quiet night, girls," Candi said. "Why don't you two call it a night?"

Georgia didn't hesitate, just grabbed her bag and got up. "Good night all. It was a pleasure."

Lydia said good night and had to hurry to catch up to Georgia. The air outside was still warm, but there was a breeze from the river. She could smell the scent of organic matter in the water. It was an earthy smell that reminded her nature still existed even in the city. It was late and the street was deserted. They walked several blocks in silence, and Lydia felt the need to keep looking over her shoulder.

It was one thing to know that prostitutes were vulnerable, and it was another thing altogether to experience the feeling for herself. As the lights of the cars swept by, Lydia could sense the hunger in the darkness of the car windows and she shivered. The waterfront felt deserted, empty, and dangerous. The shadows concealed rats and other scary things. She shivered as the breeze caressed her bare arms. She wanted to run in the other direction as fast as she could.

"Maybe we should call a car service," Lydia said to Georgia, trying to keep her voice low and quiver-free.

"No way. This reminds me of when I used to try to scare myself as a kid by going to the cemetery." It was just like that. Except this time it wasn't a child's game. If she was right and Emmanuel was not the killer, then there was still a killer running around who was targeting prostitutes.

Lydia shivered again and realized she'd left her jacket on the bus. "Oh, God! I don't have my phone or my car service money." Or the Mace.

They stopped in the middle of the sidewalk. "Do you want to go back and get it?"

Lydia thought about how much she didn't want to retrace their steps in the darkness versus how much she would miss her phone. The bus was probably already gone anyway. And Candi would notice the jacket when she cleaned up and would probably take it home with her. Lydia could pick it up from her tomorow. Luckily, she had stuck her keys in the pocket of her pants, so she could at least get into her apartment tonight.

A giant black SUV pulled up next to them with a screech. Georgia and Lydia froze. It looked exactly like the one that had nearly run her over. The tinted window slid down, and Gator's bodyguard popped his head out the window. "Who you working for, chicas?"

Lydia swallowed, wondering if Gator was in the car, too. He would recognize her if she spoke. She somehow didn't think that would be a good thing. She had been asking Gator uncomfortable questions. She hoped that if they kept walking he would see they weren't hookers and leave them alone.

But Georgia had already turned toward the car, sliding into her southern accent. "Just ourselves, cowboy." Lydia nearly moaned out loud. Georgia probably thought this was some kind of perfect place to work on her acting skills.

The bodyguard frowned, tapping his edge of the door. "Don't you know there's a killer out here? You girls need some protection."

Lydia decided that Georgia Rae was standing too close to the guy, and something had to be done. She didn't want her to get hurt just because Lydia had dragged her down here. Lydia stepped in front of Georgia to deflect attention away from her, but still tried to keep her face averted. "Didn't do those other girls any good, did it? We prefer to be solo."

The bodyguard grabbed Lydia's wrist and yanked her toward the car. She could smell the mint on his breath mixed with something pungent and unpleasant. "You tell whoever you're working for that this is our territory, and bad things happen to girls who don't listen." The bodyguard whipped out a switchblade with his other hand and flipped it open.

Lydia, suddenly remembering a move from the self-defense classes she had taken months ago, twisted her arm toward his thumb and popped her wrist free from his grip. She pushed off from the SUV with her other hand as hard as she could and stumbled toward Georgia.

"Run!" Lydia yelled. Luckily, Georgia appeared to have seen the knife and didn't argue. Together they sprinted down the street toward the Northside and, she hoped, to safety.

"Who was that?" Georgia shrieked.

"Gator's bodyguard. Unfortunately, he's one of my suspects." Lydia tried to pretend she was wearing running shoes, but it wasn't working. Her shoes didn't have heels, but they were definitely not made for running.

Georgia took large gulping breaths as she ran. She wasn't exactly a regular at the gym, either. Her idea of exercise was jumping into a mosh pit. "What should we do?"

A quick glance back confirmed that the SUV was in pursuit. "I don't know!" The SUV pulled ahead of them and drove up onto the sidewalk. The bodyguard opened his door and started to get out.

"Split up," Lydia gasped. "Run toward Bedford and get help!" Georgia obediently charged across Kent and down North First. Lydia hoped Georgia would be okay as she kicked off her shoes, turned, and ran back the way they had come. The bodyguard chased after her. He was a big guy, and she was worried he might be able to outrun her. But he must have spent his time at the gym lifting weights rather than doing cardio, because he was huffing and puffing after just one block.

She sped up as she ran back past Grand Street Park, adrenaline and sheer terror on her side. She had no desire to be caught in the darkness alone and vulnerable. She hoped she would see a cop soon so she could flag down the squad car, but she saw no one. She couldn't stop to call the cops because the bodyguard would catch up with her.

The next thing she knew, a dark-colored SUV pulled up next to her on the sidewalk. Lydia panicked, turning to run back in the other direction. Then Patricia Savarese stuck her head out of the SUV window. "Get in! Get in! He's gaining on you!"

Lydia was never so relieved to see anyone in her life. She jumped into the backseat of the dark green SUV and slammed the door behind her. As Patricia peeled away, Lydia watched out the back as they left the running bodyguard and she found Gator's giant SUV in the dust. Lydia took deep gulping breaths and tried to settle her heart rate. "Thanks for rescuing me. We need to find my friend Georgia and call the cops."

"I think they might be a bit suspicious when they hear you're down here. What were you trying to do?"

Lydia thought about explaining that they had come down to bait a killer and it had worked out exactly as planned, but then she decided that Patricia probably wouldn't understand. She slowly got her breath back. Patricia was a terrible driver; she went around corners with a squeal of tires. They crossed Bedford Avenue and kept going. Lydia wondered belatedly what Patricia had been doing on the waterfront, and where she was taking her.

Chapter 33

Y ou can drop me off anywhere," Lydia began, bracing herself against the door as they screeched around a corner. She wiggled to the middle of the backseat so Patricia could hear her better and fastened her seat belt so she wouldn't keep sliding.

Patricia met Lydia's eyes in the rearview mirror. "What the hell did you think you were doing out there? Don't you know it's dangerous?"

Lydia wasn't sure if her heart would ever beat again at a normal speed. She took a deep gulp of air and told herself she was safe now. She felt stupid for putting herself in such a vulnerable position, but she found it strange that Patricia was suddenly taking her to task for it.

"I really appreciate you helping me get away from Gator," Lydia began.

Patricia pulled out and passed a double-parked car. Lydia shut her eyes briefly, wondering how she could get her to slow down and drive her home. "But I have to warn you, I have a tendency to get carsick."

Patricia ignored her and stepped harder on the gas. Lydia's head slammed back against the seat.

Lydia had a sinking feeling in the pit of her stomach, and she didn't think it was the remains of her dinner. Something wasn't right. Patricia had acted erratically before, and at times she seemed to have a split personality. But now she was acting really bizarre. Not at all who Lydia wanted behind the wheel of a car when she was a passenger.

She wished she had her phone more than anything in the world. Leaving her jacket on the bus had definitely been one of her more boneheaded moves. That and thinking that she could solve the murders of prostitutes by going back to the waterfront.

Lydia cleared her throat. "Could you please drop me at the subway? Or a bodega with a pay phone? I need to make sure my friend is okay."

"Your friend? Who? Where is she?" Patricia's rapid-fire questions assured Lydia that she was not taking Valium today. But Lydia was worried she might be on some other substance.

There was no way Lydia would let Georgia get in the car with Patricia while she was driving like this. She felt pretty confident that Georgia had managed to get away since both the bodyguard and SUV had followed Lydia. "She's probably home by now, but I'd like to make sure."

Patricia zoomed around a corner at top speed, the tires squealing on the pavement. Lydia closed her eyes again briefly. She had suspected that Patricia had some kind of personality disorder, but she had thought it was because of the situation she found herself in. Patricia must have been down on the waterfront remembering Al. Becoming a widow, despite her horrible marriage, had been earth-shattering for her.

But none of it really explained her out-of-control behavior.

Patricia swerved around a pothole and Lydia's stomach lurched again. "I think a ginger ale would make me feel better. If you'd just pull over to a bodega, I could run in."

"No way. Not while that pimp is still following us."

Lydia scanned the road behind them but could see nothing that looked like Gator's SUV. She suspected that they had lost him almost immediately. He didn't want two women walking the streets in his area, and he had made his point and driven them out.

"He's gone. Don't worry about it. I can get out here and walk home."

Patricia began to mutter under her breath, and Lydia couldn't understand what she was saying. She wished she knew what was going on in Patricia's head. Another quick turn and they nearly ran over a pedestrian, who leaped out of the way. Lydia clutched the seat, relieved not to hear a bump against the car. She wondered why she had never noticed that Patricia drove a dark SUV, not unlike the one that had tried to run her over.

"Everyone underestimates me. Everyone. My family thinks I'm weak and stupid. You think I can't do anything. Ha! I'll show all of you."

Lydia had no desire to be shown anything. But she had to ask herself if Patricia could have killed Glenda, Anna, Josefina, and Al. Just yesterday, she would have laughed at the possibility that the alternately spacey and spoiled woman could have strangled or shot anyone. But Patricia's anger and bizarre behavior tonight made her a much more likely suspect. Perhaps she'd killed the other women just to distract people from her actual target—Al. He hadn't been the most satisfactory husband, and it wouldn't have been a big surprise if

Patricia had wanted to get rid of him. The grieving widow act had felt phony from the get-go, but Lydia had never suspected her of knocking her husband off.

More than getting an answer, Lydia wanted to be out of the car and away from Patricia. She had no desire to jump out of a speeding car, since she knew from experience that it really hurt, but she wasn't sure what her other options really were. She tried her door handle and was alarmed to find it was locked. Patricia had activated all the locks. She would have to figure out another way to get away.

Lydia made her voice calm and gentle. "Everyone is so sorry about your loss. And we're sure that you'll do great in the office once you get comfortable there. Why don't you let me out at Mama's restaurant and I'll see you at work tomorrow?"

Patricia laughed. It was an unpleasant, grating laugh. She didn't slow down or pull over. Placating her wasn't working at all, and Lydia wondered where they were going. She thought about the other women who had possibly died at Patricia's hands, and knew that she was in danger of dying, too, if she didn't find a way to get out of the car.

Lydia turned around and gave a shriek. "Oh my god! It's Gator's car. He's after you. I gave him the evidence. He knows what you did, and he's going to kill you."

Patricia turned back to look at Lydia and the SUV swerved wildly. Lydia clutched the door handle, not sure if her plan was such a great idea after all. If Patricia crashed the car they could both be killed. But Patricia turned back around just in time to jerk the wheel to the right and stop them from hitting a parked car. "What are you talking about?"

"I've got pictures, remember?" Lydia hoped that somewhere in the pictures she took was some sort of evidence that would prove Patricia's guilt, but right now she was just bluffing.

"You gave me the pictures. You told me you destroyed the negatives."

"I guess you don't really understand digital photographs." Lydia peeked out the window. At some point, Patricia was going to have to stop. She couldn't keep gunning it and driving through stop signs without consequences. And then Lydia was going to have to make her move. "I gave you copies, but the originals are still on the hard drive of my computer."

"You lied to me!" Patricia shrieked, thumping the steering wheel with her hand. "You're a liar, just like Al. He swore he would love me and take care of me, and all the while he was sleeping with those dirty whores."

Lydia hoped that Patricia would keep ranting while she figured out a way to disable the door lock and get out of the car. She was willing to acquire any number of scrapes and bruises in order to stay alive.

"They thought he was so easy. They thought they could just spread their legs for him and collect the cash. But I wouldn't stand for it. I taught them all a lesson."

Lydia could imagine Patricia killing the women, and her heart went out to them. Glenda, Anna, and Josefina had not deserved her wrath. Those women had done nothing but try to make a lousy living in a harsh and dangerous world. And Al had been a scumbag, but he hadn't deserved to die. Patricia made it sound like killing them all was completely justified. She was insane, and capable of anything.

Lydia's heart beat loudly as she tried to think of something to say to keep the conversation going. "I thought your original plan of a divorce was a good one. A few pictures, and you'd have any jury in the world awarding you the house and car and an allowance."

Patricia pounded the steering wheel again, swerving wildly down the street. "Ha! My church does not believe in divorce."

The last time Lydia had checked, the church didn't believe in murder, either, but she supposed there was forgiveness in there somewhere for those who sinned. She realized that Rose must have called the D'Angelos without her daughter's consent. Patricia had had no desire to have witnesses when she killed Al and the prostitutes, and then she'd had to move fast to get rid of the evidence.

"You could have held the pictures over his head and got the marriage annulled. Murder is so . . . messy."

"Murder is easy," Patricia said, and laughed. The high, grating sound of her laugh made Lydia's stomach tie in a knot. She could feel the contents of her stomach threaten to come back up. "I made Al beg and then I shot him anyway. He never saw it coming."

Lydia saw Crest Hardware go by again and guessed that they were driving around in circles. She wasn't sure if Patricia was lost, confused, or trying to throw someone off their scent. The other strong possibility was that she was completely bonkers and Lydia was in terrible danger. That last theory became more likely with every passing second.

Patricia turned back again to stare at Lydia with a crazy look in her eye. "No one suspects me. No one. They all think, 'Poor Patricia. She couldn't keep her man. And then she became a widow.'"

Lydia couldn't tell whether being thought innocent was galling for Patricia, or not. She seemed to revel in her power, but at the same time didn't want to get caught. And Lydia wasn't sure what Patricia intended to do to her now that she had confessed. If Patricia didn't want to get caught, then she had to get rid of her witness. And Lydia wanted to live with an overwhelming passion. She would not become the next victim. She fervently wished she had Georgia's Mace but wasn't sure if spraying it at a speeding driver was such a great idea. Having her cell phone would have been even handier, but both were on the bus.

Out of nowhere a garbage truck appeared, backing up to the curb in the middle of a side street. Patricia slammed on the brakes but couldn't stop in time. She hit the truck going about twenty-five miles per hour. Luckily, Lydia's seat belt kept her from flying through the window. She jerked against it and fell back against the seat. The air bags in the front deployed, trapping Patricia against the front seat.

As soon as Lydia got her breath back she unfastened her seat belt and felt along the door next to Patricia. Patricia was squirming and cursing. Lydia knew this was her one chance to escape. Patricia could still have a gun or something in the front seat and try to take her out. She found the unlock button near Patricia for all four doors and pressed it. And then she bailed out of the backseat.

The garbagemen had come around to see who had hit their truck. They were big guys dressed in green, and they had on work gloves. They were not happy as they surveyed the damage. "Hey, lady! Didn't you see us backing up?"

Patricia was still trapped behind the air bag. Lydia didn't have time to stay and chat. Patricia could get free at any moment "I think the driver is hurt. I'll go find help."

"Hey, lady . . . ," one of the men protested, but she darted away. He couldn't make her stay. She wasn't the driver of the car, and her safety depended on getting away fast. Lydia trotted quickly to the main road, wincing as her shredded stocking feet hit the pavement. The road had not been good to them earlier, but her shoes were long gone. When she arrived at Metropolitan Avenue, she was relieved to see people and cars going by. She flagged down the first car service car she saw and jumped in.

She gave him her address. "Please hurry," she said.

As she settled back against the seat, taking deep breaths, she tried to process everything that she had learned. All she knew was that she'd found the killer, nearly gotten herself killed, and she didn't have the faintest idea what to do next.

Chapter 34

Lydia's first concern, after locating an emergency twenty-dollar bill in her apartment to pay the car service, was to get in touch with Georgia Rae and make sure she was all right. She borrowed her neighbor's cordless phone, which miraculously worked in her own apartment. She was relieved to find she had about seven voice mail messages from Georgia, all telling her to call immediately. She did.

"What happened to you? Did Gator chase you?" Georgia's southern accent came out in spades when she was upset. "I was worried sick."

"I got picked up by Patricia, the D'Angelos' cousin. She took me away from the waterfront."

"What on earth was she doing there?"

Lydia took a deep breath. "She was there because she overheard that we were going to the waterfront, and she wanted to stop us from finding the killer."

"Wait—isn't she the wife of the guy who died?"

"Yes. Apparently the church doesn't look favorably on divorce, so she decided to take matters into her own hands." The cat jumped up onto Lydia's lap and began purring. Lydia sank her fingers into his fur gratefully. He was warm and soft, and she still felt chilled all the way through.

Georgia whistled. "So it was a woman scorned. Why was the pimp chasing us?"

"I guess because Gator thought we were a threat to his domination over business on the waterfront. Or maybe he suspected that we were looking for proof that he was the murderer."

"Did you call Romero yet?"

Lydia had to admit that she had been too frantic and confused to call the police. She didn't have any evidence that Patricia had killed the women, just the ravings of a madwoman possibly pumped up on drugs. But she owed it to Emmanuel and all the others to call the police and make sure Patricia was brought in for questioning.

She called Romero's cell phone and left a voice-mail message for him to call her on her neighbor's number. She said it was urgent and she had a lead on the real killer. Lydia wasn't surprised when he called her back in under a half an hour. She had piqued his curiosity bigtime.

"What have you got, McKenzie?"

"Patricia Savarese, Al's wife, picked me up and confessed to killing all the women and her husband out of revenge."

"The widow?" Romero didn't sound completely incredulous, so she plunged ahead.

"She's completely insane. She picked me up in her car and then told me all the gory details."

"Huh. Sometimes people make stuff up to get attention."

"I don't think so." Lydia thought about Patricia's recital of her crimes and shuddered. The woman had ended four lives and felt no remorse. In fact, Patricia had been downright gleeful about it.

"We'll check it out."

"She had an unfortunate run-in with a garbage truck on Frost Street. I bailed and ran home."

"That's the first sensible thing I've heard you do."

"Thanks, Romero." Lydia was too tired to argue with him. She had done all she could. But she wondered if the cops would find any evidence to convict Patricia. Patricia would probably deny everything. Lydia paced around her apartment, still unable to calm down. She checked all the locks three times before she remembered her promise to the Golden Horseshoe Gang. She called up Princess and told her the news.

"She killed them all for her husband?" Princess sounded skeptical. Maybe no man was worth it for her.

"She didn't like him much, either. She killed him last."

"What was her name again?"

Lydia told Princess Patricia's name again and about the accident on Frost Street. "The cops will arrest her soon. Don't worry. It's over."

Princess snorted. Lydia took that to mean that she didn't really believe her. Maybe Lydia *was* naïve. The justice system was broken, and maybe Patricia would get off with no more than a slap on her wrist. "Thanks for your help. We'll drop the dough off soon."

Lydia was about to protest that they didn't have to pay her. She felt dirty accepting the money. She'd made a hash of the case while women continued to lose their lives. It didn't seem fair that she should get rewarded for it. But she realized she would be talking to a dial tone, so she hung up.

Still restless, she realized she desperately wanted company. She called Jack. Surprisingly enough, he picked up immediately.

"Where are you calling from?"

She realized that he didn't recognize her neighbor's number. She didn't want to explain everything. "I misplaced my phone and had to borrow my neighbor's. Are you busy tonight?"

"I was just about to watch a video," he said.

"Why don't you bring it over here?" she asked. Her TV wasn't the greatest, but they could snuggle and watch from her bed. She really didn't want to be alone, and she was ready for them to put their misunderstandings in the past.

He agreed, but didn't sound very excited. She still had a lot of work to do. She moved the purring cat off her lap and went to the bathroom. She caught a glimpse of herself in the mirror and gasped. She was a mess. She quickly scrubbed her face and changed into a comfortable sundress with a little cleavage.

Once she looked more presentable, she went to the kitchen to pop some popcorn. She liked to do it the old fashioned way in a big pot on the stove. It was about the only thing she ever used her stove for, besides soup and tea. The popping sounded cheery and satisfying, and she loved the way the smell of the popcorn filled the apartment. She poured the popcorn into a big bowl and carefully dripped melted butter on top.

When Jack arrived, Lydia gave him an enthusiastic hug and kiss. He returned them both a little less enthusiastically, as though he wasn't sure where they stood. Lydia wondered how much work it would be to get their relationship on track again. She wasn't sure exactly what had happened to them.

"What have you been up to?" she asked brightly, hoping he wouldn't ask about her day and evening. It was too hard to explain.

"Working." Jack took off his messenger bag and dumped it on a chair. She wished he would hang it up somewhere, but she stopped herself from saying anything. She didn't want to nag. "The popcorn smells good."

"Do you want to open a bottle of wine? Or have a beer?"

"A beer is fine." Beer was less romantic, but she wanted him to feel comfortable. She dug around in the bottom of the fridge until she unearthed two pale ales made by the Brooklyn Brewery.

They stood in the kitchen sipping their beers and not talking. It all felt terribly awkward, like they were on a blind date or something. Lydia suddenly realized how much she was holding back with him, and censoring her own life. She wasn't sure how she felt about it or what she should do to fix it. Jack had shut her out, too, and their relationship had turned cold. The cat jumped up on the table and sniffed the bowl of popcorn.

Lydia gently shooed him down.

He said, "I see the cat is still here."

"Yeah. The shelter called the other day, though. They think they have someone who wants to adopt him."

"Are you going to do it?"

"I don't know. I've kind of gotten used to having him around." She didn't want to think about it yet. She had no desire to be alone. She picked up the bowl of popcorn. "Should we watch the movie?"

"I'm not sure you're going to like it." Jack seemed nervous, and Lydia wondered why.

"What is it?"

"You'll see."

Lydia settled on the bed with the popcorn, cradling her beer on her chest. She hoped it wasn't some ultraviolent film. After tonight, her stomach still wasn't up for huge car chases or shoot-outs. It seemed too close to home.

Jack sat next to her on the bed, moving the bowl of popcorn so it sat between them. When the film started, it took only about ten seconds of images for Lydia to register that the movie he'd brought over was pornography. They sat side by side watching as a party by a pool turned into an occasion where everyone stripped off their clothes. There were threesomes and foursomes around and in the pool, and the film made sure to show everything.

Lydia didn't consider herself a prude, but she hadn't watched much porn before. And she hadn't seen any since she had started her project photographing prostitutes. Now she recognized in the women on the screen the same vacant stare, the clear desire to be anywhere else, and the feigned enthusiasm that she'd seen with the hookers. She wondered how could Jack possibly find any of it sexy. It felt staged and emotionless and cheap.

The sex went on and on, growing more and more mechanical and feigned. Lydia just tried to eat her popcorn and ignore the film. But she could tell Jack was excited by the sex on the screen. He probably wanted her to copy all the moves from the women in the movie. But she couldn't. She wouldn't. She identified too much with them. She had walked in their shoes tonight and had nearly been murdered just like Glenda, Anna, and Josefina. It didn't feel fair to witness the women's humiliation, too.

She got out of bed and abruptly turned off the VCR. A local news station came on the TV as soon as she did, and the weatherman reported more rain in the forecast.

"What's the matter?" Jack asked.

"I don't like it," she said.

"You're uptight," he complained. "You need to relax."

"Maybe. But it makes me uncomfortable. Those women are victims."

"Come off it. They're getting paid," Jack said. He looked disappointed that she was ruining all his fun. "They're no more a victim than I am at my job." Lydia had never heard of anyone equating trading stocks with hooking, but she supposed there were some similarities there somewhere.

The memory of the scent of Jack's skin when she returned from Gator's party came back to her in a sickening wave. If he was attracted to porn, could he have stooped to visiting hookers and attending Gator's orgy? She had no desire to be with a man who cheated on her. She was no victim. And she could see that she had passed the point of trust with Jack if she could easily imagine him cheating on her.

The weather ended, and a reporter on the street appeared with her name and WILLIAMSBURG, BROOKLYN spelled out on the bottom of the screen. A picture of a familiar black SUV with one door hanging open flashed up on the screen. "Is it a mob killing? That's what the police want to know. Just a week after she became a widow, Patricia Savarese was in a car accident on her way home to Queens. Waiting for the cops at the scene, she was shot in cold blood in a drive-by shooting. Witnesses at the scene said it happened too quickly for them to identify the assailants."

"Oh my God." Lydia sat down with one hand over her heart, hardly hearing what the newscaster said afterward. She knew the information she had passed on to the girl gang had caused Patricia's death. She had hoped that they would wait for justice to prevail, but she should have known better. They had told her time and time again that they did not trust the police. So they had taken matters into their own hands. She had told them Patricia's name, and signed the widow's death warrant.

Chapter 35

The next day at the D'Angelos, Lydia was alone. She wasn't surprised. The D'Angelos gathered together in their clan when tragedy hit, and she envied their closeness once again. She would have loved to have someone to lean on today. She was officially single once again. Jack had left last night disgusted with her reaction to the porn and grossed out by the murders that she had become involved in. Suddenly the two of them had nothing in common. Lydia's heart ached, but she felt that she had also dodged a bullet. She had been ready to commit herself to a man who would have made her life miserable. Breaking up now was much better. But it would have been nice if it didn't hurt so much.

She had run out first thing in the morning to pick up her jacket and cell phone. Candi had gone to work and left it for her at a local bodega. Lydia gave the guys there a couple of bucks and bought a cup of weak coffee from them.

A messenger in a sleek black warm-up suit arrived at the office just before lunch, and she was relieved to see and talk to another human being. "A detective agency," he said, looking around the office. "Cool."

"Some days it is," Lydia said grimly as she signed for the package. She was surprised to see it was addressed to her. After the messenger left, she opened up the padded envelope. A pile of one-hundred-dollar bills slid out. Her stomach lurched. The Golden Horseshoe Gang had just paid her for services rendered. She had told them the name of the enemy, and they had killed Patricia. Lydia's guilt gnawed at her insides. She quickly stuffed the cash back into the envelope and stared at it miserably.

Her cell phone rang. It was Romero. Even though he couldn't see her or the cash, she had to stuff the package into the depths of her desk drawer before she answered her phone.

"We found the weapon in her car," he said, without bothering to say hello. "She was also a budding photographer. She took some pictures of her victims before she left the crime scenes."

Lydia groaned. She didn't know what to say.

"We're still not sure why she strangled the first two women and then shot Al and Josefina. Maybe she was just trying to throw us off her trail."

It was unusual for women to commit those kind of crimes. Most women would just poison their husbands at home, but Patricia had clearly had a flair for violence.

"It's too bad we won't have a chance to prosecute her. Do you know who killed her?" Romero asked.

Lydia was silent. She didn't want the Golden Horseshoe Gang to get in trouble. She didn't approve of what they had done, and she wished they had just let Romero take care of Patricia, as Lydia had requested. But they didn't really believe in justice, and Lydia couldn't blame them. She would say nothing and hope the cops would figure it out on their own eventually.

"Are you going to let Emmanuel go now?"

"He's already out," Romero told her. "We couldn't keep him after we collected all the evidence against Patricia. And that assault charge in Jamaica turns out to have been a bar fight."

Lydia almost smiled. It wasn't hard to imagine Emmanuel defending someone's honor or fighting an injustice. She was glad he was out, but there was too much tragedy involved to celebrate.

She still had so many questions about the murders, but she could see a great deal would remain a mystery. She remembered that the first time she had followed Al, a VW bug had shadowed them. Maybe Patricia had owned more than one car, or maybe it had been all in her imagination.

"Tell the D'Angelos that I'm sorry for their loss. I have a kid of my own, and I would hate for anything to happen to him."

A sudden disturbing image of Romero with a wife and kid popped into Lydia's head. "You're married?" She was embarrassed that she had blurted it out.

Romero sounded amused. "Divorced."

She had never imagined Romero as a husband or a dad. "How old is your son?"

"Seven."

He was probably adorable. A picture of a cute boy with Romero's brown eyes and rarely seen grin popped into her head.

"So are you headed to the altar soon with that guy—Jack, was it?" he asked her.

"Oh, no. That's over," Lydia said. She felt sadder about her disillusionment than the end of the relationship. Why was it so hard to find a good man in this town?

"He seemed like a cold fish. You can do better."

Lydia almost smiled when she heard his words. It was nice to know he had a good opinion of her, despite all the abuse he'd handed out over the last few weeks. She wished they could be friends. He was an attractive man, and she imagined what it would be like to kiss him.

Her face went red, and she was glad he couldn't see her. She heard talking on Romero's end of the phone, and he held the receiver away from his mouth to yell, "I'm coming, I'm coming." He came back on the line. "I gotta go. There's stuff I need to take care of."

"Okay. Thanks for calling."

"Take care of yourself, Lydia. I'll see you soon."

She said good-bye, wondering if the vow was a promise or a threat. She felt a little melancholy. She had just a small glimpse into his life during this case, and she strangely wanted to know more. But there was no way her life was going to intersect with Romero's again unless she got involved with another murder. And she certainly didn't want that to happen.

She pushed papers around her desk for an hour, not able to concentrate or achieve anything. About lunchtime, Leo, Frankie, and Mama D'Angelo all came into the office. Mama was crying into a handkerchief. Leo and Frankie looked annoyed.

"You tell them, Lydia, that they have to find out who murdered our little Patricia. So young! So beautiful! My cousin had to be sedated, she was so grief-stricken."

Leo flopped into his office chair. "We don't work on murders, Mama. You know that. We'd lose our license for interfering with police business. You tell her, Lydia."

The D'Angelos had a tendency to involve her in all their disputes, and she didn't want to touch this one, even with a fifty-foot pole. Patricia had been a deranged killer, and Lydia had a pretty good idea who had killed her. But the killing had to stop. And the revenge had to stop somewhere. Eventually everyone had to calm down and return to the mundane tasks of the living.

"I just got off the phone with Detective Romero in Homicide, and he says they're working hard to solve the case," Lydia told them.

Mama sniffed indignantly, as if to voice her opinion of the police. But Leo seized on Lydia's story. "See, Mama? The police are working hard, and we need to let them do their job. There's nothing we can do. We have no contacts in the gang community."

"Can we really put Patricia into the cold, hard ground next to her poor husband without giving either of them justice?" Mama blew her nose loudly in her handkerchief. Her sons looked guilty, but Lydia knew that they weren't going to do anything.

If there was a just God somewhere, Lydia thought that perhaps the best punishment for both husband and wife was to have to lie in eternity side by side. None of this mess would have happened if they had just been willing to let go and move on. So many other lives would have been spared. It was an excellent argument for no-fault divorce.

Mama put her hand on the desk with an authoritative thud. "I want the whole family to be at that funeral. Patricia is not going to be humiliated by having just a few mourners. Bring that girlfriend of yours, Leo. Okay?"

Leo turned strangely pale. He had been so eager in the past to drag out his girlfriend for display that Lydia couldn't help but wonder what had changed. Perhaps he had finally figured out that she was cheating on him. It seemed that none of them was destined to be lucky in the love department.

Mama swept out of the office a few minutes later, declaring she had to get back to the restaurant for the lunchtime rush. The brothers both visibly relaxed once she had left. Having a mother who constantly dominated them was hard work.

"Why isn't Caroline coming to the funeral?" Frankie was as curious as Lydia about the fate of the saintly girlfriend.

"She's just not." Leo buried his head in some paperwork.

"Why?" Frankie persisted. He never knew when to quit.

"We broke up. And I'm sorry that I ever introduced her to any of you. I apologize."

Frankie looked shocked. No matter how many times his heart was broken, Frankie persisted in believing that women were perfect. "She seemed like such a nice lady. What happened?"

Leo stood up, pushing back on his office chair. The wheeled chair crashed into the wall behind him. "She lied to me. She was secretly working as a sex phone operator."

Lydia's mouth fell open, and she had to swallow a giggle. She had assumed it was a boyfriend on the phone, but the idea that Caroline made those calls for a living was surprising. Leo must have been horrified when he found out.

Frankie turned a strange shade of purple. "That's terrible," he spluttered. "Don't let Mama find out."

Lydia smiled to herself. Somehow life with the D'Angelos always came down to protecting each other from hurt and pain. She couldn't help but admire their love for each other, even though they still drove her crazy.

On her way home, she felt the weight of the money the gang had given her at the bottom of her bag. There was no way that she could keep it. The money might as well be dripping with Patricia's blood. It made her feel like a murderer to have it. She had to get rid of it. She imagined tossing it off the Williamsburg Bridge and watching it float down into the water. She imagined putting it into a musician's guitar in the subway or stuffing it into a homeless man's hat. Any of those actions would get the money out of her hands, but none would get it off her conscience.

She decided that she needed to compensate the victims for their loss. The right thing to do was to give a third of it to Glenda's kids, a third to Anna's family, and the last third as a donation to Candi's bus. The murders had deprived children of their mothers, and they needed money in order to have some kind of future and break the cycle of poverty. And the bus was doing a great job protecting women on the street and helping them get the services they needed. She would distribute the cash anonymously tomorrow.

At home, the cat wound around her ankles and purred a greeting. She was glad to see him, the apartment would have felt too quiet otherwise. There was no possibility that Jack was ever coming back. She went through her mail—a pile of bills—and thought about calling her parents. In a few months she would try to get some time off and meet them. Family was too important for her to let too much time go by without seeing them.

She dropped her bag and sank into a chair. The cat jumped up on her lap, as if to comfort her. She petted him, relieved that she was not in the apartment all by herself. She scratched his ears, noticing how he'd filled out in the past week since he'd been getting regular meals. There was no way she could give this cat up. She would call the vet tomorrow and tell them.

"The first thing we need to do is give you a name." The cat purred and butted her hand. "How about Fred? Are you a Fred?" She assumed the purring meant that he didn't object. Fred he would be. A nice simple name.

She sat on the couch for a long time, watching the light disappear from the sky. Just a woman sitting alone with her cat.

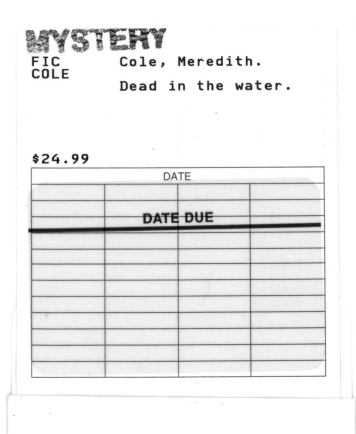

MYSTERY

FIC
COLE

Cole, Meredith.

Dead in the water.

$24.99

DATE			
DATE DUE			

JUN 0 1 2010

BAKER & TAYLOR